Drowse

Derek Langley

This is a work of fiction. Although many of the place names are real, other names, characters and incidents are the product of the author's imagination or are used fictitiously, and no other identification with actual persons (living or deceased), places, buildings, and products is intended or should be inferred.

Front cover artwork design by Derek Langley using WOMBO Dream AI "Mystical" art style seeded with "A youth's hands holding a massive loop of light".
All glyph designs by Derek Langley.

ISBN-13: 9798791275356
Independently published. First edition 2023

For Carol.

I don't know if any of our cat's cradle patterns have names, but they have all been complicated and fabulous.

Preface

Having had the "big idea" sometime in 2015, I started writing Drowse while on various short holidays in Wales, Norfolk and Oxford, and over numerous weekends and evenings until around October 2019. I wrote whenever I could manage time away and get my head out of my job and I'm delighted to report that much of it was done well into the small hours with a hefty tumbler of decent whisky in hand. I do love a cliché ... Having tried unsuccessfully to land a literary agent, I put Drowse away for a couple of years, a bit dispirited, to be honest with you.

You will, of course, notice that this writing phase predates the COVID pandemic. I was fortunate enough to lose nobody to COVID – Carol and I caught it ourselves only towards the end of 2022 having been fully vaccinated and boosted and I feel immensely lucky to have escaped the worst of its effects. So if the idea of a book centred around a worldwide disease seems like a cheap shot from our current perspective, please rest assured that it was all done and dusted well before that terrible event got started. I had to go back in and at least make mention of it, of course, but it doesn't figure in the story. My heart goes out to those very many people who have suffered long-term side effects or bereavement. What a dreadful time it was.

I finally picked Drowse up again in late 2022 and decided to go ahead and self-publish on Amazon – I harbour no illusion of buying speedboats on the proceeds but, if I could have my way, Drowse would be read by a good few and hated by only a handful.

So I wrote some MS Word macros to help me focus on some writing details like adverbs and evidence of being too expository (more show, less tell – feedback from one of the literary agents) and spent many months rereading and rewriting until I essentially ran out of excuses as to why I wasn't publishing. I managed to delay things still further by setting up the author's website and the mailing list but here we are now, freshly printed, whether real or virtual, and poised for what I hope you will judge to be a decent read.

Please enjoy, and thanks for dedicating your time.

Derek

Drowse

Derek Langley

Imagination is the
only weapon in the
war against reality

Lewis Carroll

Prologue

Index

STEVEN CRESSWOLD PARKED THE car and slowly crunched through the gravel to the front door. He 'printed the touch-latch and shuffled into the hallway, nudging off his shoes and draping his jacket over the already-laden chair. He could hear Celia in the kitchen.

'Ceel, I'm home,' he shouted. 'Don't think I'm up for Charlie and Sonia's tonight though, I'm bloody flaked.'

Celia called through, 'But they're expecting us in an hour.' She stepped into the hallway. 'Oh, but you look washed out though. Must be coming down with something. Are you hot or achy?'

'Nah, just knackered. I was fine this morning but just now I could hardly get out of the car, really weak. I'm going to have to lie down, I think. Sorry about this, I'm hopeless.'

'Don't worry, love, I'll give them a comm and cancel. They'll understand. Want any tea?'

'No thanks, I'll just crash.'

And that was the start of it. Two days later, Steven Cresswold was completely bedridden and unable to feed himself or move under his own steam. Celia hand-fed him water and soup for a day until their GP called at the house and diagnosed chronic fatigue syndrome. The following day her husband was unable to even lift his head and he slept constantly. Somehow, Celia bundled him into the car and drove to the hospital.

'The decline is too fast for CFS,' the consultant at Emergency Admissions told Celia, a careful distance away from Steven's bedside. 'It's probably viral but I'm going to admit him for observation.'

That evening a crash team moved Cresswold into intensive care.

Celia paced the corridors outside the ward, the drinks machine a blur through her teared eyes. Steven was a pretty-fit bloke: weekly five-a-side with the guys from work, she and he regularly swam together, and they had often chosen hillwalking over more sedentary holidays. To witness him felled like this was not right, not possible.

'The results suggest no reason for concern over your husband's life, let me reassure you Mrs Cresswold. But he will be needing 24-hour care until we see an improvement. And we will keep testing, of course.'

Celia did not hear much else, although the consultant continued to talk. Finally, he touched her arm as if to make sure she knew he had stopped, then added, 'Try not to worry.' Then she was alone in the corridor, slumped in a chair as nurses and doctors rushed past her, going about their normal duties.

Celia visited Steven in ICU every day for the next six weeks. He was stable but showed no signs of any improvement.

Ronine Weston, Celia's long-time school friend who lived on the next street, quickly became Celia's rock. She lived alone and was always there when Celia needed a shoulder to cry on, or sometimes a room to scream in. Some nights the two of them fell asleep in Ronine's flat, Celia embryonic against Ronine's side, Ronine just happy to be able to help her friend through this unthinkable crisis.

One night at Celia's, Ronine puffed her cheeks and said, 'I reckon I'm in for an early one tonight, Ceel. I'm feeling pretty knackered from work. I'll be OK once I've had a doze.'

'Lightweight. It's only six o'clock,' Celia teased but put her arm around Ronine's shoulder. 'You feeling OK?'

But Ronine was already asleep in her arms. The next morning she was unable to stand up without Celia's help. She was admitted to the same hospital as Steven and transferred to ICU the same evening.

'Mrs Cresswold, we'd like you to stay overnight while we run a few tests.' A different consultant; older, but Celia noticed he was less grey-haired than the previous one.

'But I'm fine.'

'Please, Mrs Cresswold. This way.' The consultant was joined by two nurses and another couple of men, all wearing masks. 'It's just a precaution, nothing to be concerned about.'

'Do you think I've caused this somehow? Steven and Ronine? Like some fucking Typhoid Mary? Oh my God!'

'No, no, Mrs Cresswold. It's just standard procedure for anything like this. Until we know more about it.'

Celia took nothing in as she was escorted to a temporary prefab building out in the rear car park of the hospital. She was vaguely aware of the rattle of plastic sheeting being unzipped and rezipped. Through the foggy transparent barrier, a man from Public Health England in a shiny-elbowed suit ran through a set of questions about holidays, substance abuse, promiscuity, etc. She surrendered samples of her saliva, blood, urine and faeces, and four or five nurses enclosed in hooded plastic outfits with pipes emerging from their backs carefully placed test tubes in sterile boxes and took them away.

'But what is this? What's wrong with Steven and Roni? I don't feel ill, there's nothing wrong with me!'

'Try to keep calm, Mrs Cresswold. You will be kept informed of any developments. If there is anything you need, please ask one of the nurses and we will endeavour to help.'

Then he was gone. The astronaut nurses in their too-bright white spacesuits and clean air feeds were all very nice, trying to keep Celia as comfortable as possible, but the whole situation was just insane. She tried watching some banal TV series from the Yesteryear archive as a distraction but couldn't focus. As a last resort, she gestured the stream over to the news feed.

More new cases of the mystery sleeping sickness have been reported across the UK today, bringing the total number of admissions to just over fifty. The Department for Health Chief Medical Officer today issued this statement:

'The situation is under control and the public has no cause for concern. No firm diagnoses have been made so any speculation is completely inappropriate and, frankly, misleading at this time. There is no confirmed evidence of any epidemic pattern and the public may be assured that standard healthcare procedures are all that is necessary, and that is precisely what we are doing. The situation is, of course, constantly under review and we will continue to do the right thing.'

Jenny Tollgate from Chichester has been visiting her son in hospital.

'He started out by just saying he was a bit tired and he went off to bed dead early for him. Usually, he's up late

playing on his games. Then, next thing I know, he can't get up in the morning and the doctors don't know what's wrong. He can't even feed himself now and they've got him all wired up with tubes and wires and he doesn't even really wake up properly when I'm there so he ... when I ... just last week he was fine ... sorry, I'm sorry, I can't ...'

Celia's breath released with a loud gasp. Steven and Ronine. And now all those others. Why didn't the woman on TV catch it when her son did? And why not Celia herself? Why was she special?

Tokamak

It required the construction of a vast device to continue mankind's great hope for energy. Fusion on an industrial scale: that dream of science and men that had persisted since the stellar processes began to reveal themselves in the early twentieth century.

Unimaginable funds of billions upon billions from 35 countries were consumed in this endeavour: in the end, the sums became so large that any scaling owing to currency differences was almost academic. Many attempts floundered and fell away in the pursuit of this prize until, finally, the Hornbill Tokamak towered fully three hundred feet above the ruins of a long-abandoned airstrip.

The huge magnetic coils of the tokamak enclosed an enormous toroidal chamber, into which unfathomable quantities of energy were to be poured. Just as the word itself was inserted into the English language from the Russian, the giant machine imposed its silhouette upon the Oxfordshire countryside, as alien to the eye as the word in the mouth.

Shrouded in security and secrecy by its holding company, Perpetua, the project outgrew its eight-year schedule by forty-three months, forging scientific careers and leaving wrecked political ones in its wake, until the machine finally sucked energy into its core. Suspended within enormous magnetic fields, a devastating plasma of hydrogen isotopes was energised by a complex combination of vastly powerful excitations to 200 million degrees, the ensuing neutron harvest surrendering its energy to the gigantic lithium blanket modules of the tokamak, and thence on to colossal heat exchangers and turbines. A terawatt of sunshine from our very own earthborn mini star.

Final Phase commenced at the end of the first year, with bursts of 50/50 on/off operation stable and everything green. It self-powered on midsummer's day at eleven minutes past three in the afternoon, the energy to fire each subsequent surge being drawn from the inertia of its own flywheels.

External power was removed at thirteen months and, when total synchronisation with The Grid finally occurred, the world rippled with possibilities as, every nanosecond, trillions upon trillions of neutrons spun up the flywheels of mankind's ultimate dream.

Perpetua shares began to take off. Power generation indeed.

Month fourteen.

Something odd.

Sixty reassuring days of rock-solid and full-scale operation and then one small glitch. No, not even that. A wobble. A tiny bulge in the plasma, which circumnavigated the toroid in less than a microsecond and was gone. Only the most sensitive Thomson detector spotted it but there it was, nevertheless. The surge continued otherwise uninterrupted until the hour was up. Neutral beam and HF boosters were powered down as usual and the tokamak's electromagnetic field de-energised, allowing the plasma to deform and dissipate as it had done a thousand times before.

Except this time it remained. The plasma persisted.

Persistence.

Still forming a stable ring, still incredibly hot and still circulating. Also, still radiating, but no longer neutrons. In their place flowed only infrared radiation, enormous quantities of it, flat right across the 0.7 to 1,000-micron range. The radiation struck and heated the lithium blankets just as the neutrons had done and the heat exchangers converted this heat into steam to power the turbines, spinning the wheel, as though nothing had changed. And indeed, nothing was changing now. In the absence of neutron bombardment, no lithium-tritium conversion occurred in the blankets and they remained stable without the need for replenishment or replacement. A perfect toroid of what became known as hyperplasma suspended itself symmetrically within the tokamak, radiating energy with no external input and without any sign of decay. It rotated very slowly within the pressure vessel with no need for fields or harnesses to suspend it, flawless and pure in form and radiance, simultaneously shattering and reconstructing the boundaries of scientific philosophy.

Precautionary safety measures were, of course, immediately activated, with all personnel evacuated to adrenalin-charged underground bunkers. Emergency protocols were invoked and national security was stepped up to critical. But none of this made any difference. The hyperplasma toroid kept pouring out energy despite mankind's best efforts to hide from it.

Over the ensuing months, it became apparent that the energy output from the hyperplasma was controllable merely by varying the load. In effect, as the turbines sucked less energy from the tokamak, it radiated correspondingly less IR energy. Disconnection of the load entirely left a static toroid of hyperplasma which radiated nothing, revolving imperceptibly; eerily waiting. Conversely, the more you pulled on it the more it gave, seemingly without constraint.

Eight months of frantic and continuous measurement and theoretical analyses followed, with increasingly vast heat exchange experimentations, stretching the energy output further and further. Yet, each time, the machine obliged with still more energy. Theories were proffered and dismissed, evolving in their complexity in proportion to the mass of the turbines and flywheel structures growing about the tokamak. At no moment was there any sign of instability or decay in the hyperplasma.

Eventually, it became obvious to all, whether academic or layman, that failure to actually do something with this ostensibly limitless energy source would be crazy. A stupendous waste of a fantastic, if utterly mysterious, opportunity. A churlish misuse of a fabulous gift from Science or God, whichever boat you were partial to floating. Despite no truly satisfactory explanation of the physics behind the fact, giant electrical switchgear and distribution transformers sprang up for miles around the site, with villages and towns consumed by this expansion, enormous compensation packages being settled upon the occupants in the name of humanity's progress. The towering hulk of the tokamak began pouring energy into The Grid.

Over the succeeding fifty-six months, The Grid itself expanded accordingly, reaching out across the waters to continents and countries hitherto starved of power by their own voracious and growing technocratic populations. Gigantic cables carried electrical energy through all cardinals from Hornbill to the coastlines of Great Britain before lumbering into the seas and out into the world far beyond. The waters of Aberdeenshire, Norfolk, Cornwall, and Ceredigion hummed and crackled with the ozone of countless quadrillion electrons, every nanosecond jostling their neighbours into giant suboceanic pathways to nurture and unshackle the insatiable energy avarice of countries across the globe. Grateful nations signed up for the Perpetua Hornbill Agreement, receiving boundless energy in exchange for complex political and economic undertakings that extended too far into the future to be of any consequence to those authorising the decision.

Hornbill inveigled itself into a thirty-mile industrial floodplain distended between Oxford and the Chilterns, Swindon and Aylesbury, and the south of England hummed with the world's energy as Perpetua closed its benevolent grip over the Earth's people.

Noise

'It's not stable.'

Cradle intertwined his fingers with the structure of the hologram, his gestures changing the sensitivity and expanding the waveform. Tendrils of orange and green danced and swirled throughout the display.

'I don't see it.'

'There's a variation. It's just not there all the time. Hard to find.'

Kline drew closer and ran his fingers through the image. 'Noise. It's just system noise. Random stuff.'

'I think there's a pattern.'

'Not possible. The Core must be completely stable. Has to be. If the output was oscillatory in any way, our little doughnut in there would unbalance and it'd all be over in seconds. Contact with the sides and virtually instantaneous energy dumping – BANG!' Kline smacked his hand down on the desk. Cradle was supposed to jump. He didn't.

'All the shields sublimated before the safeguards even know about it, swiftly followed by the whole chamber liquifying with enough spare joules rattling about to fire your granny around the moon every Tuesday morning for a million years. And we'd better be further away than we are now if that happens.' Kline shook his head. 'Nope, the reading's rock-steady at 9.4 terawatts, same as it always is.'

'Yeah, I know. I've just got this tickle in my head. I might run over it a bit, see if there's anything.'

'Cradle, we can't spare the time for chasing your ghosts again. I've already got Bryant breathing down my neck for the stat reports.'

Cradle looked at Kline. 'I could do it offline. Probably just in my head, you're right.'

'OK, OK. Just keep it out of the reports. He's all over them.'

The older man glanced up, a fleeting salvo of eye contact. Cradle knew what that meant. *Wild idea, you're totally crazy, what a ridiculous waste of time. Let me know if you need any help.*

Anders Kline was a tall, sinewy figure whose unkempt tweed jacket had been one of life's constants since the earliest days at Perpetua. From the start, his irreverent manner had always appealed to Cradle and, after years of working together, they were now a tight-knit team.

Kline walked back into his office and sat down at the Regulator Interface. He shouted above the air-conditioner, 'You need a holiday Cradle. Take a few days with that girl of yours. Ginny or whatever her name is.'

'Eve. It's Eve. Anders, you're unbelievable, you know her name. And anyway, she can't get the time off from the hospice at the moment. There's been another Sleep.'

'I heard. It's outrageous, isn't it? When are they going to get on top of that? Perpetua throw everything they've got into the research. You'd think they'd be getting somewhere by now.'

'Yeah, another two hundred people from Cornwall and Sussex. Terrible. Arriving in the next two days, so they're really stretched. Eve's volunteered for extra shifts and everything. That's Eve, Anders.'

'Right. Extra shifts. Eve. Got it.'

Cradle shook his head, smiling, and turned back to the Crossing Plate. The gentle fizz of energy soothed his mind again and he allowed himself to be partially drawn in. Brushing his fingertips over the cold titanium surface, he could taste it. Beautiful perfection. Terrifying chaos. The whole process was fully contained in an impenetrable fortress of magnetism, yet he could simply reach in and bathe in its infinite light.

It hadn't always been that way for him. After Persistence, Cradle was one of many aspiring young scientists who were drafted directly from across the world into the ranks of Perpetua, and he had felt only a sense of awe at the scale of the assignment. But weeks and months after Cradle started to settle into the Flow Analyst job, these extra feelings started to come. Odd nuances that slipped unseen through his subconscious, only brushing against his sentience with the merest suggestion.

Kline was older and had been around from the very beginnings of the fusion experiments, years before the rise of Perpetua itself. Early on, he saw something unusual in Cradle and forced things a little when the time came to form the Flow Analysis team. Forced things quite a lot, actually. He always refused to talk about those times, but Cradle knew that Kline was the one who chose which members of the team stayed around, even though it flew full in the face of his natural dislike of authority. Married to the job, Kline's hands were tied by the ropes of his own success and he unwittingly became part of his hated establishment, although only for those brief and torrid three weeks. When the dust settled, he formally withdrew from his senior position and made it more than clear that he would only continue if he could personally work with Cradle.

Boundary was a stellar concentration of thirty-two of the world's greatest young physicists, located a very safe distance from the Flow itself and shrouded in secrecy; a Manhattan Project for the modern age. It dwindled over thirty-five months until just the two men remained, whereupon it was reassigned the task of Flow Analysis and permanently relocated to Hornbill.

'All buggered off and left us to run Sweet FA!' Kline was fond of saying. Although Cradle knew this was one of his regular jokes and always, always smiled to order, he never really understood why he insisted on saying it was sweet. He'd looked it up and knew it was a crude reference, of course, but he failed to see the relevance. If you were talking factually, the lab had no sweet sense at all that he could distinguish. If anything, the air tasted slightly bitter. It was just a random thing to say. It troubled him sometimes.

As he extended his fingers the display rippled with quantum broil and the stray dump effervesced quietly. Cradle palmed the Plate and gently crossed into the half state where he kept his most beautiful secrets.

Noise. Only noise.

Eve

'HOW'S THAT, MR BAKER?'

Eve helped the man lean back onto two fresh pillows and he sighed as their softness encompassed his shoulders and head. His voice stuttered quietly, 'Thanks, nurse. That's grand.'

'OK, let's get you wired up to the disco, shall we?'

She took the micro-optic bundle and laid it carefully along the bedside, feeding the connection point up to the patient's right shoulder. 'Just pop this bit onto your eCann.'

The connector clicked as the bundle attached, then automatically turned and locked onto the support bus.

'It usually takes a couple of minutes to log you in and sort everything out for you. You might get a couple of little tickles up behind your eyes but that's OK, it just means you're on-system. Just shout out if you feel anything else. I'll stay with you while you get started.'

'Oh yeah, I feel it a bit ... like cold ice cream?' Whispered.

'Yep, that's the one. Should fade off, then another one a bit later. That's all normal. So, you've come up from the South?'

The man looked around the cubicle. It was small, just big enough for the bed, with a low ceiling less than two metres high. Clean white on all surfaces and windowless, the only disruption to this surgical precision being the interface where the micro-optic bundle entered the cubicle. He observed the girl. She was middling height with blonde hair and delicately featured. He couldn't tell if she wore makeup, but he thought that young women today didn't really need it anyway. The crisp material of her uniform resembled the room itself. The white was only disrupted by the dark-blue name badge *Eve Sanderson – Hospice Staff*.

'St Ives. My wife wanted to ... wouldn't let her. When can I go home?'

'The doctors will run some tests on you later to see how far along you are. They'll be able to say.'

'Not ill ... really tired ... need to sleep ...'

'Yes, you should sleep. The meds will be helping you relax now, try not to fight it. If you need anything you just press the red button here and someone will come and help. OK?'

'Can't you ... stay ... a ... bit ...?' His speech dragged over his tongue and his eyes grew heavy.

'I've lots of lovely new guests to see tonight, Mr Baker. You'll rest now and the system will help you settle in. Have nice dreams.'

'Eve ...' His eyes closed and she checked for the correct readings before leaving the room. She was uncomfortable when they used her name like that. It wasn't a lack of affection or compassion, but it just made things so much worse when she had to move on to the next patient. And there was always a next patient. Next after next after next. Especially this week. Bad one.

The walkway carried her along the corridor of identical doorways, hundreds left and right, distinguishable only by their number. Her floor this month spanned 12300 to 12700, all new intakes, and Eve was two-thirds of the way through her assignments, with six long double shifts behind her already. This was her final stint, and another few settles were all that stood between her and home time. She was ready for her days off.

The microTab embedded beneath the skin of her right hand tingled and her augmented vision flashed 12680 as the walkway stopped outside the room. The door display read 'Mrs Leewater'.

Eve's thoughts floated back to before it all really kicked off. Was it two or three years? Four, even? She shook her head, unable to draw it from the fog of her fatigue.

She had been nursing in Oxford at the time, adult intensive care at John Radcliffe, when an urgent meeting was called by union representatives. All non-emergency staff; mandatory attendance, no exceptions. Ruskin College was about half a mile and Eve's mistimed walk had turned into a run. When she arrived, she was hot and stressed and she missed the signs for the meeting room, making herself later still. She could hear her own heartbeat. In the end, she took a lucky turn but, by the time she had navigated the corridors, the room was crammed so full that she struggled to get in. As she pushed her way through, she overheard snippets of whispered conversations.

'... they never call everyone in like this ...'

'... rumours are all true, they haven't been able to ...'

'... just spreading all over ...'

An official-looking man with slicked-back brown hair and a city suit addressed the microphone and the bustling room hissed into silence.

'Ladies and gentlemen ...' He waited for the buzz to die down before continuing. 'My name is Dr Stephen McAndrew. I am a Research Fellow at the Civil Contingencies Secretariat in Whitehall.

'You are called here because of a growing threat to our country's – indeed, the world's – future. As you are all no doubt aware from the media, the disease known as Drowse is now reaching pandemic proportions worldwide. Many of you are already caring for and treating sufferers and we realise that standard hospital facilities are stretched far beyond breaking point, causing immense stress to you as professionals and frankly unacceptable levels of care for many patients.

'Much of this briefing is already in the public domain so you will be familiar with some of the details. My task, therefore, is to clarify which of those details are factual and which are media speculation, and to describe to you the Government policy on the way forward. This will affect you all. The Government has, as a precautionary measure, moved to Threat State Critical and COBR has been permanently convened to coordinate the situation. The following briefing is being given simultaneously to medical professionals across the world.

'The briefing is entitled "COBR Instructions for Medical Structures for Counteraction of the Pandemic known as Drowse". I am familiar with the content and will attempt to deliver it to you in English rather than the native legalese.'

McAndrew scanned the audience for a possible ripple of polite laughter but it was not forthcoming. He awkwardly cleared his throat.

'When the scientific community first began to document Drowse cases as Events of Concern some five years ago, there were fifty-seven recorded cases in the UK alone during the initial six months. During the next half year, thirty-nine new UK cases were recorded. Based upon this relatively modest increase we would then have expected infection rates to tail off as the disease receded in the face of isolation protocols and new treatments.

'But it has become apparent that Drowse is different from anything we have ever seen. It grows by exhibiting occasional peaks in the infection rate; 'waves', as they have become known. These waves always leave the total infected at a much higher number, but the increase does not follow the expected exponential growth of previous pandemics. Furthermore, the effect is not geographically correlated. That is to say, these waves occur simultaneously across the world, with no identifiable linkage or causality. This is absolutely not the statistical profile of a pandemic threat. After just over 60 months, we now stand at a UK infection level of 8,700 people or about 0.01 per cent.

'Although figures are difficult to obtain in some areas of the world, we now believe that the same proportion applies worldwide. We are therefore facing potentially eleven million Drowse sufferers right now across the world. As a comparison, the Spanish Flu pandemic at the beginning of the twentieth century infected around 50% of the world's population in only two years. But pathogenic viruses like flu tend to become less lethal with time, as the most dangerous strains inevitably kill off their hosts. The COVID pandemic in the early twenty-first century is another example, although then we were able to quickly produce vaccines to limit the number of fatalities.

'But Drowse is not killing its hosts, it is simply infecting them. Furthermore, we have found no viral fingerprint that would allow us to develop any form of vaccination programme. Drowse will therefore not terminate in the way that any previous pandemics have; until we make a breakthrough, it is going to keep going.

'Ladies and gentlemen. I have to tell you that, if this pattern continues, it will result in 10% human infection in approximately 9 years. Only 2½ years after that we could see 100% human infection.'

Eve felt the shockwave propagate through the crowd like a thunderbolt. Some gasped, others just stood open-mouthed, and still others unconsciously reached for the person next to them, as though seeking confirmation that this was really happening. Eve's vision blurred and the heat of the room clawed at her. At first, she thought she might be fainting but then she became aware of a tickling sensation on her cheek and it dawned on her that she was actually just weeping. She dabbed at her eyes and adjusted her position so she could see McAndrew again. He was uncomfortably shifting his weight from one leg to the other, grasping the microphone stand with both hands.

After the murmured reaction whispered down to a jaw-dropped silence, he cleared his throat.

'Furthermore, as you will have experienced, Drowse affects our young, the fit and healthy of society, as much as our older population. And only rarely does the disease prove fatal by itself. The sufferer is simply profoundly weakened and rendered unable to perform everyday physical activities, usually confined to bed and requiring 24-hour support.

'This is already putting a significant strain on medical resources worldwide and the model predicts that current structures will reach a tipping point in less than eighteen months.

'We are, of course, working towards a treatment in the very near future but, in the meantime, it is obvious that emergency measures must be put in place with immediate effect. The following extraordinary instructions from COBR are to be considered mandatory for reasons of national security.

'One. 75% of all health service and private medical staff are to be conscripted into the Drowse Hospice Group with immediate effect. Contracts will be read across, and pay scales maintained accordingly, so no financial effect will be experienced by any employee. Duties will be detailed over the next six weeks, with retraining provided where required.

'Two. Those staff selected will be assigned new rosters and relocated to temporary hospices throughout the country. Perpetua will contact you all individually to help organise your personal logistics. Again, compensation packages will be assigned accordingly, so no employee will be subject to a reduction in their personal circumstances. Family and home relocation or transport will be arranged where this is warranted. This process will be rolled out over the next two months. It is clearly an enormous logistical undertaking so your understanding and cooperation is both appreciated and expected.

'Three. An extensive programme of construction will commence immediately. Dedicated hospice facilities will be created on or near to the current sites of major hospitals across the country, networked and automated to provide the latest and best treatments as and when they arise from our research programme. Drowse patients will be transferred to these new facilities as soon as possible. Again, your duties within this framework will be defined in the early stages of transfer.

'Four. This situation is covered by the explicit non-disclosure clause in your current employment contracts. Any employees who are found to be in contact with media or journalists will, therefore, be considered in breach of contract and will be dismissed immediately and held liable to prosecution.'

Eve's head was spinning. She'd heard the rumours of temporary hospices springing up as the disease took its hold. But compulsory secondment and relocation? What the hell was going on?

A man's voice shouted from somewhere near the middle of the room. Something about families. Something about military service. Murmurs of conscription.

Get out. She didn't hear McAndrew's response above the pounding of her own blood in her ears as she pushed her way towards the door. The heat and the smell of people were overwhelming her, melting her into the crowd, and she had to get out.

The outside startled her body with its cold embrace as she stood on the grass, breathless and shaking, the sunlight reflecting from the walls of the college, strangely white, almost artificial.

She looked down at her 'Tab. Her hands were trembling.

Patient – Mrs Jean Leewater

Eve opened the door to 12680 and stepped into the cubicle.

Empire

IT WAS SAUDI ARABIA that first gave way.

Oil and gas suppliers the world over held on, waiting for the drop, the moment that the Hornbill plasma collapsed and vanished whence it came. The moment when energy would become *not free* again. But their wait was in vain.

Perpetua reached out to all nations of the planet, offering limitless quantities of energy in exchange for a range of ostensibly benevolent undertakings, legally complex and sweeping. The cost of shipping food and goods around the world became irrelevant so only a few remaining malicious dictators and megalomaniacs opposed the redistribution of wealth evenly across the surface of the globe. Perpetua's energy agreements toppled corrupt and evil governments and individuals, whose wealth was levelled to nought by such infinite promises of supply.

Billions of people were lifted from poverty and squalor. Where housing and infrastructure were needed, they were provided. Streets, highways, and boulevards were constructed where roads diffused into desert or dust. Communities naturally formed in the interest of humankind, caring for one another and bonding together in this new and cooperative existence.

Saudi Arabia had for many years maintained a stranglehold on the world's economy by dint of its oilfields. Russian gas too, but to a lesser extent since Europe's readjustment of its energy sourcing in the late-2020s. It was King Faisal bin Khalid who first acted upon the inevitability of Persistence and the ensuing energy supplies, agreeing to reinvigorate the reforms in the Kingdom, changes which had choked and withered on the vine so many years ago. Measures to create equity between women and men, and to become more accepting of people from all backgrounds and religious beliefs. Executions for transgressions against ancient maxims were outlawed. Many women removed their burqas and walked openly through the streets in safety and without fear of reprisal. Older Saudis were outraged and many left the Kingdom for good, fleeing to remote desert oases and attempting to re-establish the old order. Hundreds took their own lives, preferring the threat of desolation in hell to the razing of their way of life. Thousands boosted the ranks of terrorist organisations, attacking Perpetua developments as they arose, but they were always beaten back by the scale of readiness and defensive capacity, Perpetua prevailing every time, setting about the inexorable business of bringing all the world within their benefice.

Despite enormous and dangerous opposition, Faisal bin Khalid pressed through, closing the taps on the faltering Saudi Arabian oil pipelines, the Kingdom reinvigorated by energy from enormous transoceanic cables which climbed onto the land at Dhahran and Jeddah, unyielding quantities of power once again flowing through its heart and veins.

Bahrain and Qatar quickly followed suit, then the whole of the Middle East, a tsunami of modernisation and equality sweeping across the deserts and oases.

Most of Africa was easily drawn away from its own profound poverty and the network of giant cables rapidly extended to this great continent too, hauling themselves out of the sea and into vast underground subways, then onward to capitals, villages, and settlements. Lighting extended days, made dangerous paths safe, enabled medical procedures. Heat saved the elderly, dried the wetted harvests and nourished the starving. Something for everyone, with strict constraints on the power of leaders.

Across the world, billionaires, oligarchs and shareholders alike tasked their management teams and accountants in desperate attempts to maintain their wealth, missing the whole point. There was no longer any such thing. Tokens of richness were swept away as markets fell and money became useless.

Over the following six months, world currency markets lurched into panic and then finally collapsed. What was trade when the cost of energy was zero? Energy meant food, transport, sharing, and equality. The world had always had enough for every single human being but now Perpetua saw to it that pockets of greed and excess were squashed. Food and living standard was evenly distributed across the globe, and the world began to balance precariously upon a single toroid of hyperplasma.

But this enforced equality did not bring equanimity. Many hundreds of thousands rebelled against Perpetua with attacks on energy routes and installations. Scuffles became skirmishes, skirmishes developed into sieges, and sieges begat battles, each one more vicious and terrible in its ferocity than the last. The Perpetua Wars, for there were many, extended over a two-year period and enveloped the entire world. After all, those who opposed equality and opportunity for all were surely and demonstrably the enemy of mankind in this chance to build Shangri-La. Hardly a single region escaped conflict, each time Perpetua's infinite energy supply triumphing over meagre human opposition, more relentlessly powerful, more benevolently crushing than any movement in human history.

Governments were brushed aside, becoming mere mouthpieces for Perpetua: what popular alternative could be offered in the face of Utopia? No political individual or body raised a voice against this inexorable march to perfection.

And so millions lay dead across the planet, their broken bodies branded in history, along with buildings, vehicles, jacket lapels, hats, and uniforms, with the name 'Perpetua'. Thousands of robotic vehicles were deployed from vast mobile depots and set about the tidying and incinerating of remains, unfeeling AI-driven machinery working in the name of humanity, completing tasks too appalling for anybody to address in person, the over-thereness of it all rendering it palatable. All for the best.

After 25 months it was over. No more opposition. No more uprisings or voices of dissent.

Connectivity technologies broke through around the same time, spurred on by the necessity for worldwide communication and sharing during the Perpetua Wars. Soldier nanotechnology comms implants were demilitarized and further miniaturised to provide humans with inbuilt access to the world's data. Almost every individual accepted these new microTab implants, the resulting mass network becoming known as 'Main'. A universal and boundless source of information for the new age of equality, with every human a node.

Developments in AI and robotics escalated to the point where the most mundane tasks of human labour became automated. Work became something people did to contribute to society in exchange for proportionate additional privileges. Activities like caring for people, ensuring nobody went without, maintaining and expanding Perpetua research programmes, and developing new technologies. A slightly larger home, for example, an increase in access bandwidth onto Main, fewer constrictions on freedom of movement throughout the world, across borders. These roles attracted the brightest and most compassionate from society, bastions for the betterment, or at least the maintenance of, society. Those unable (or unwilling) to contribute were nevertheless provided with comfortable living standards and opportunities for leisure activities, education, and personal development, all freely available. And those who transgressed, rebelled against the tide, would have these allowances reduced in fair measure, as proportionate punishment for their crimes.

Thus the quiet phoenix of a kind of prototypical class system emerged from the ashes of the Perpetua Wars, feeding on the fruit of imposed egalitarianism. Slowly, imperceptibly, its invisible tendrils ensnared the new society. The delineations were small and subtle but were there for all that. Orwellian tendencies will out, there was plenty for everyone. Especially if you were the right kind of everyone.

Home

'EVE? YOU ABOUT?'

Cradle draped his crumpled jacket over the back of the usual chair near the door of the flat. He stepped sideways past the chair and into the hallway where the old lamp his mother had let him take when he moved out to Uni pooled warm yellow onto the carpet. The lampshade was darkened and battered by long-dimmed years, but it was still mum so there it stood.

He kicked off his shoes, no laces, and toed them carefully under the chair. Equal, central. The mum-lamp cast gentle umbrae from the wallpaper's texture, painted off-white too long ago and greyed further by those shadows. Four sock-steps and left into the lounge. In the semi-darkness, the sofa's silhouette postured at the faux ornamental fireplace, supported with a chair on either side, all locked in a soft furnishing face off which had, so far, lasted for at least two years with no sign of weakening. A worn mock-Persian rug steadfastly kept the antagonists apart. An entertainment module was reassuringly central on the wall above the hearth. Eve's Wafer nestled on her side table to the left of the sofa and Cradle's Wafer weighed down a small, untidy stack of papers on the right-hand table. He reached into the gloom and straightened them.

Across from the lounge, Cradle carefully opened the bedroom door, slowly at first, then quickly over the creaky part of the hinge. Eve lay on the bed, two singles pushed together to make a surprisingly comfortable nest. Her moccasins were kicked off onto the floor and Cradle moved them together at the foot of the bed so they looked as though she would be able to just jump straight into them again in the event of an emergency. She wore jeans and a cream chunky knit and her hair sprayed across the duvet like honey. She slept deeply, the easy rhythm of her breathing changing only slightly as Cradle touched her cheek with his lips.

He counted a reassuringly normal eighteen paces into the kitchen, where spotlights cut a confused labyrinth of shadows onto the stripped wooden boards at his feet. He oiled and heated a pan and roughly chopped a few fresh vegetables. Yesterday's leftover pasta from fridge to microwave, red wine, large glasses. He wondered about setting the table with some candles but decided on a less cluttered presentation. He gently called Eve and he heard her awaken with a small sigh.

'Come and get it.'

He loved her even more than usual when she was sleepy. Tousled blonde hair haloed her face as green flashed between hardly open eyelids. He pulled her chair back with a flamboyant gesture and her hair tickled his forearm as she sat at the table.

'Thanks, you're a gent. Are you after something?'

'No, just being nice to my sleepy girl. It's just yesterday's grub, with a few veg chucked in. Got to feed you up for tomorrow.'

'What's happening tomorrow?'

'Nothing. But you might need feeding up for it.'

'Sometimes, Cradle, you're an idiot,' Eve laughed, 'but I love you anyway.' She slapped his backside as he turned to walk to his chair.

'That's harassment. This isn't the twentieth century you know,' Cradle laughed as he sat. 'And how was your day?'

'Oh, you know, the same. I had that daydream again, about when they first told us. I thought I was back there again.' Eve drew a large sip from her glass.

'Weird. I never get that sort of thing. It must feel strange.'

'Yeah, well,' she yawned, 'at least it's all in the past. Zonks me right out when it happens though. Probably makes me tense, I suppose. How's the famous Anders Kline?'

'Incredible. Had to tell him your name again. Reckons we should go on holiday.'

'Just you and him?'

'No, of course ...' He caught her smile and stalled.

'Well, halleluiah! At last, you're listening to some sense. You haven't had a day off for over a year now.'

'Yeah, so I didn't book anything yet though. Thought we could maybe talk it over. Maybe think of somewhere we already know.'

'Cradle, you're doing it. Just relax about it. We can go somewhere new; it would be OK. I'll be with you.' She stretched her foot under the table onto his, which made him jump a bit and look at her.

'Yeah. Yeah, you're probably right. I'll try. Can we do it tomorrow though?'

'Hmm, OK. But we *will* do it tomorrow, no shirking. I'll get some ideas.'

'OK, sure. You know, I think the Flow is unstable.'

Eve was thrown by the non sequitur. 'What?'

'The Flow. I think I can feel instability in it. Anders doesn't see it but I can sense something.'

'What, you can see it on the instruments?'

'No, it just looks like the usual system noise. That's what Anders says it is. But I've got a feeling about it. I'm going to do a bit of checking to see if I'm right. Got to have a think.'

'Hmm. Beats your usual run-of-the-mill, I guess. *Dee-lish* dinner by the way. Nice surprise.'

Eve looked across to Cradle. She recognised the distant look in his eyes. He always looked like this when something was on his mind. Something that needed sorting out and arranging into the collection of *Things That Cradle Knows About.*

'Yeah. No probs.' Cradle cleared the dishes into the washer and walked through to the lounge. 'Mind if I read a bit?'

Eve followed him in and lay down on the sofa. 'Of course, my little genius. But only if it'll lead to us being rich and famous so we can retire away from all this.'

'Should do,' distantly. He was already gone, drifting, browsing.

He recalled an old research colleague from Uni doing some pure work based on Boltzmann, something to do with the extraction of patterns from noise-like data. Wonder if that went anywhere in the end? Maybe he could use some of the algorithms to rip the Flow data. He had already plotted the shape of the disturbance and it certainly looked like it could be noise, at a casual glance. Maybe Anders was right after all. Definitely not white noise, but maybe it was coloured by some characteristics of the Flow channel itself. Pick a colour.

But no. He didn't feel it that way. He had that fuzzy sensation in his chest.

Cradle rummaged through his archive of academic papers for what felt like well over an hour before he came across a couple of relevant postings and scoured them for the techniques he needed. He spent another couple of hours refreshing himself on some distant and very rusty higher maths expressions in order for it to click and then he logged onto the proxy server at Perpetua and remotely invoked the Flow Analyser Engine from his workbench. Entering the algorithms into the sampler was pretty straightforward and he set the analyser daemon to run until morning, with output formats set to both graphical and database.

He checked his watch. 2.28 a.m. Oops. He became aware of quiet breathing nearby and allowed his attention to properly return to the room. Eve was asleep on the sofa like a fantastic leaf, lifted in on enchanted breezes from the autumnal night and settled upon the cushions. Effortlessly, he lifted her and this time she made no sign of stirring. He could smell her gentle warmth and her beauty overwhelmed him. His arms would easily hold her forever.

Cradle closed his eyes and carried his prize through the darkness to the bedroom, folding her in beneath the oceanic duvet. He undressed and in only a few minutes fell asleep in the still night, curled against Eve, never happier, but anxious for morning, nevertheless.

Strings

HE SAT AT HIS desk in the empty classroom with his loop of string, about one and a half metres long and tied with a nice square knot and trimmed ends. The boy looked down at the string, his mind drifting away from the playground, away from the sounds and the turmoil. Why would he want to play football with the other boys anyway? He hated the smell of the ball and the confusion of flailing limbs and the needless shouting and the feel of the grass as it squeaked beneath his shoes. He couldn't see why, if you really wanted the ball in the goal, you couldn't just put it there and move on to something more interesting and, even less, why you would want to take it out of the goal and start the whole thing over again.

The other boys, of course, merely regarded him as a kind of alien creature, a thing to be tormented and relentlessly ridiculed. Punching and taunting, pushing and spitting. The boy didn't care though, he would just go back into the classroom and occupy himself with something more ordered. Something that led on to something else

– something that made him feel right, away from stupid boys and stupid shouting.

One day he found the string loop nestling in a corner behind the big desk and he held it in his fingers, studying how it moved and turned from finger to finger. He saw there was always something in the loop, concealed within the cord itself. Even though they were yet to take form, he knew there were patterns in there, waiting to be discovered and pulled from their hiding places. He threw it in the air and it oscillated, sometimes as a perfect circle, sometimes with fleeting twists which were gone by the time the loop returned to his fingers. Occasionally the string would inexplicably knot itself, the patterns emerging and trapping themselves into the real world for him to hold and dismiss at will.

Once, the boy had held the loop draped over each hand and as he pulled each side across with his fingers a double, crossed structure appeared, suspended in space before his eyes. Had he fallen asleep for a thousand years and a spider spun this mystery between his hands? He turned the shape around in the air, viewing the classroom through it, and it selectively obstructed the window light to paint complex abstract shades on his skin. He had managed to catch one of these exotic things all by himself. There were more to come – he could feel it.

Over the weeks, and despite insistence to the contrary from Miss Rahni, the boy persevered in these private reveries, devising a fixed series of kinks and turns, pulling the string from finger to finger, dropping little loops and twisting others into existence from nowhere.

First fingers catch the loops, thumbs drop, thumbs under last, thumbs over second and under third, pinkie drop, pinkies over first and up, thumb drop.

But quick. Two seconds.

He held the shape up to his nose.

'Whiskers.' Under his breath.

'Miaow!'

The boy started and turned round to see who was intruding. The girl sat in the corner of the room, one hand holding a book. How long had she been there? Big green eyes and an absurdly wild shock of blonde hair which was well on the way to overcoming the mere ribbons which sought to restrain it.

'Watcha doin' in here?'

The boy looked sheepish, but she had seen the loop so there was no point in pretending now.

'Catching patterns with my string.'

'Can I see?' She moved over to sit next to the boy, discarding her book on a desk en route. 'You made Cat's Whiskers.'

'It's private though, I didn't even see you.'

'Miaow!' Not cruelly, not mocking. 'My Mum showed me some of those.'

'What, do you know how to find the shapes too?'

'Yeah, it's easy!' She took the string from the boy. *His* string. At first, he thought he would burst but, instead of panicking, he found himself watching as the girl's slender hands stroked the string. Left over right, right over left, middles catching the loops. Not as fast as the boy could do, but not too bad. She had caught one of his shapes already.

'This one is called Cat's Cradle.' She proudly held it out so he could see it more clearly.

'Oh. I found that one too. I didn't know it had a name.'

'Everything's got a name, silly.' Again, not mocking. 'You can make another shape from mine now.'

The boy studied the string as it languished in her fingers. He could see lines, straight lines, hiding within the twists, calling to his fingers to free them. Instinctively he pinched the crosses, pulled them out, over and under, and lifted the shape from the girl's gentle embrace. His fingers touched hers as he did this, and she smiled at him.

'I'm Eve. And that one is Soldier's Bed, m'cos soldiers have to make their beds very straight or they have to do marching.' She brushed a scribble of sunshine from her face. 'What's your name?'

The boy looked at Eve blankly. He couldn't remember anyone his own age actually being interested in him before, not properly, not without really wanting something for themselves.

'Erm, I'm ...'

'Cradle!' she cried. 'I can call you Cradle! Like the string.' Giggling.

Eve took the string from him in a quick rotating movement to make Candles.

'Like the string? Oh yeah, like the string.' He pulled the outside strings across with his pinkies, then dived his thumbs and forefingers down and up again in the middle to pull The Manger from Eve's fingers. 'What's the next one called?' he asked the girl.

'Diamonds.' Her hands went under and pinched the crosses again, pulling them out, over and up through the middle. Each time the string slid between boy and girl was like opening a birthday present, and the invisible wrapping fell about their feet and silently vanished as it touched the floor.

He pinched the crosses and pulled them out, under and up, accepting the gift again. He held the shape over his right eye like a mask and smiled at the girl.

'Cat's Eye,' she giggled.

The sunlight from the window was behind her and her skin glowed as she raised her face to look back at the boy.

Her eyes swallowed him whole.

'Hello, Eve,' he whispered. 'I'm Cradle.'

Crossing

KLINE OBSERVED HIS YOUNGER colleague at work. It was always impressive when Cradle focused on a topic that captured his interest, utterly consumed and beyond reach until it was over. He had been in work since well before seven; probably disturbed Stan on security to open the Lab early. Kline had arrived his customary four minutes late, a regular tardiness dictated by the rigid timetabling of the group transport company together with his steadfast refusal to get up in time for a more appropriate pod.

A cold mug of coffee sat behind Cradle, untouched aside from the initial detailed attention to place the vessel centrally upon the desk, perfectly coaxial with the coaster. Cradle studied the display and muttered quietly to himself, 'Come on out, I know you're in there. Where are you, where ...' And then some sort of indeterminate humming, buzzing sound through his teeth.

'What's that then, Cradle? Singing or something? You having a stroke?'

Kline looked at his colleague with mock expectation. He knew Cradle was well beyond conversation at this moment, fallen through into another world where only he ever ventured – his words made no impact here. The two men occupied separate continua, segregated and frozen apart by an intense layer which enfolded the younger man and repelled the older.

'Hmm. Well then. See you when you're back in the UK.' Kline walked out of the lab and headed for the coffee machine, clicking a couple of Incogs in his pocket. He liked to make a point of paying for coffee in Incogs, partly so no one could keep a record of how much caffeine he was consuming – that was his own damn business – but primarily because he simply liked the pace of them. The small plastic discs were edged with blunt teeth around their perimeter so they would sometimes loosely mesh together in the pocket and be tricky to retrieve. Furthermore, they were slow to be taken into the machine itself, and above all, they were quite awkward for the authorities to support. There had been a rights ruling many years ago that made it illegal to completely deny personal choice, so if an individual decided to use the token payment system then they could. The compromise was that a person could only carry a maximum of 100 Incogs at any one time. Sufficient to travel up to 200 miles by pod, or feed yourself for around 3 days, but not enough to skip the country or tempt anyone into anything illegal or antisocial. These days they were hardly used by anybody, but Kline did so like to be the sand between the toes of authority.

Cradle adjusted the interface to display the spectral response of the Flow Analyser. It showed pretty much the same power level across the whole spectrum. The output had all the characteristics of a perfectly pure white noise source filtered only by its environment. He searched briefly for any subtle peaks or notches, but nothing revealed itself.

'Just basics, all done before,' he muttered to himself. 'Come on, something ...'

He flipped the window to review the database results of last night's Flow Analyser run, the Engine's algorithms having clawed at the data to dredge any semblance of a pattern from the relentless stochastic hiss. He closed his eyes and rested his fingertips on the Crossing Plate. He immediately felt the Flow all around him, filling his mind, tingling in his lungs and ears. The energy ran through him, filtered by instinctive colours and shapes within his being, lifting him up into that state of acutely-heightened awareness where he was most complete. Singular, pure, intense. He drifted through the random emissions of natural process, feeling for pathways or corridors that would bring him to the Truth.

This interaction with the system, this merging of creature and machine, this joyous floating in oceans of data.

Animal senses teasing machine algorithms and honing parameters, all twining and meshing the supercomputer beneath and about him. Simultaneously running thousands of tweaks and enhancements, unconsciously checking and crosschecking matrices of interwoven semi-facts, each wholly dependent on its predecessor and then driving its successor's character in turn. He roamed within a faultless white terrain filled with the absence of feature, searching long and intently for some sort of variation: a flaw, a facet, a pathway. Something to detract from this landscape of perfection, this drape of eternal, shining banality. Yet there came nothing. An infinite field of terrifyingly beautiful flawlessness, stretching all around him. He pulled away.

'Nothing!' Cradle raised his head and slumped back in the chair.

'Ah, there you are again! You've been gone all day. Did you bring me back something nice?'

He became aware of Kline standing somewhere behind him in a strangely cluttered space.

'C'mon, it's nearly eight. Time to send you home to Ellen.'

Cradle looked up into his eyelids until he could begin to feel the room around him. He drew a long breath through his nose and felt his body in the chair again. Fingers stretching, he became aware of the cold air between each digit. The stretch of muscle pulling over bone. The lub-dub in his ears, his wrists, his chest. His eyes opened and pupils deflected, overshot, and then settled to a diameter more compatible with the stark Lab lights.

'I'm going to have to go fully in, Anders.'

His mouth pulled against dry lips. His friend's expectant smile mollified the tease, and he obliged by gently taking the bait.

'And it's Eve, Anders. Her name is Eve.'

Away

THE SUN DID ITS best to burn off the few remaining white smudges of vapour staccatoed over the azure canvas. Hot, maybe thirty-two, an English July afternoon, devoid of the customary yet always unexpected stormy downpour; the sun ruptured the ground and panted the neighbourhood dogs.

The van had been packed up by three sturdy but uncommunicative men with Stowe's Removals raggedly emblazoned on their overalls and it chugged off along the road until the boy could see it no longer, leaving a wake of hazy, scuffed-up dust swirling in the air before him. All his stuff in someone else's van, boxed up and labelled 'small bdrm' and 'stairs cbd', rattling along without him on its way to somewhere new and strange. He didn't agree with it, not at all.

'Time we were off.' The tone of her voice was different in the empty house, like it was a gleaming metal robot rather than his actual Mum saying it. 'Shall we say goodbye to the house now?'

'I don't want to go, Mum.'

Chloe Sanderson kneeled behind her son and enfolded him in her arms. 'I know you don't, honey, but it'll be OK once we're at the new house. You'll see. Things will be better then. We'll have a bit more money and time and we'll be able to have a whole load of new adventures, just you and me.'

She felt a few warm drops wetting her forearm and she squeezed him tighter.

'It won't be the same. I want to stay near Eve.'

She'd been surprised by his friendship with Eve. Always slow to make new friends (to make any friends at all, if she was honest with herself), it seemed strange that her son had formed this bond with a girl his own age at primary school. A sort of crush you would call it, something sweet that could tide him over until he felt ready to widen his friendship group properly. The two of them had been unusually close since they met a couple of years ago and she was delighted that he had someone to call friend after so many worries about how he was going to fit in at all. Eve had apparently called him Cradle and that's all he wanted to be referred to from then onwards, so Cradle he was, even to his Mum now.

He had always been a solo child, very bright and intelligent, a deep thinker, even as a babe in arms you could see it. Something about the way he concentrated and the way his eyes followed you around the room from the highchair. Taking it all in, soaking it up like all babies do, of course, nothing unusual there. But there was something more intense, more knowing, yet detached and insular, as though he were observing the world as part of some kind of plan or strategy that only he knew about. A wild notion, she knew it, but he had nevertheless grown up to be a lonely boy, taciturn and slightly odd, so she always had a niggling concern that there was some truth to it.

From the start, as the quiet one in the nursery, he had always preferred to sit and watch the other children rather than join in with the games.

'I think Cradle is happy enough,' his nursery teacher confided one afternoon, 'but I have noticed that he does seem to spend most days pretty much on his own. He doesn't seem very interested in playing with the other children.'

Naturally, Chloe was concerned so she asked to come along to the class to check it out for herself. Taking a morning off work was a bit of a nightmare, but she persisted and managed to persuade her friend Janie to cover her shift. How vital were a couple of hours of shelf stacking anyway? It's not as though the world's going to end if soup stays in its box for an extra ninety minutes.

She dropped Cradle off as usual at the nursery but this time she hung back outside the classroom door, from where she could discreetly watch her son at play without distracting him. She very quickly saw what the teacher was describing. When Cradle was approached by inquisitive children he merely looked at them, as if taking notes, but at no point would he actually join in. When a child reached for him he drew away, almost imperceptibly, yet definitely. If the games became more physical and he was pushed or grabbed he just crawled away, turned and looked back at the other children from a safer distance. Eventually, the children gave up and he was left on the outskirts, happily observing his peers at play.

Chloe discussed their son's behaviour with her husband as soon as he returned home the following weekend. They had met at Leeds University, where Stefan Sanderson had graduated with a first-class Engineering degree and she with a 2.1 in Social Anthropology. They had fallen head-over-heels-crazy in a few weeks. Stefan proposed shortly after their graduation and Chloe accepted with the utter certainty of youth. Stefan had been left some money by his grandparents and had invested in his own startup, Sand Power Systems. Through a combination of good business nose and blind luck, he had managed to develop a very healthy export business in the African manufacturing industry. There the national power supplies were unreliable at best (if they existed at all) so there was a solid business for anyone able to provide stability of electrical supply at a competitive price. Sand Power was small and lean and quickly brought the latest solar, wind, heat pump and battery technologies to market in a good, low-priced system that had grown to be extremely popular. But with success came absence and Stefan was often away from home for many weeks at a time, with very little downtime before the next sortie. He had missed the birth of his son by two days, something Chloe was never really able to talk about much, and birthdays and wedding anniversaries were similarly difficult topics of conversation.

'Sounds a bit odd. He doesn't do anything with any of the other kids at all then?'

'Yeah, he mostly sits there watching them. He seems happy just doing that all morning.'

'Is he getting pushed around or something?'

'Not as far as I can tell. It's just what he likes to do.' Chloe shifted in her seat and leaned forward slightly. 'I was thinking we should talk to someone.'

'Like a shrink or something? Shit, is it that serious do you think?'

'I don't know. But they'd want to see all of us together, I suppose.'

'Well, that's going to be tricky. I've got that big Kenyan Eco Park installation coming online next week for three months. Not going to be in UK much ...'

'I know, Stef, I know.' She turned away from her husband.

'I'm sorry. You know what it's like though, Clo. What can I do?'

Chloe stood up and walked into the office, pointedly shuffling papers and thumping books around. Stefan knew better than to push it – this was all over the nerve endings of their relationship. He went into the kitchen and clicked the kettle on.

'If you can get a date booked maybe I can get back early and actually turn up to something? Clo?'

But she couldn't hear him above the creaking of the kettle and the buzz of the fridge.

She booked the appointment with the child psychologist and, incredibly, Stefan booked his flights to get back in time. A chance that in three weeks she'd have something to soothe her worries.

The child, however, remained untouched by any of his mother's concerns. He was more than content to continue observing his peers from his blissful, distant solitude.

'There you go again, you are a clever boy.' Chloe knelt on the lounge carpet where he had been sorting his various toys, left to right, according to when they were given to him. She kissed his forehead and he looked her in the eye and gently bumped her nose to nose. 'When Daddy's home next week we're going to go and talk to a nice lady about some things, OK?'

The boy studied his mother's eyes and whispered, 'Dad's gone now.'

The Wafer broke the reverie with its piercing warble and Chloe turfed through the sofa cushions to find it.

The fire started in one of the machine shops and rapidly spread through the old wooden building, fanned by the hot Harmattan wind as it coursed from the Sahara to the Gulf of Guinea. Thirty local workers perished along with the four-man working party from Sand Systems. Very fierce, very quick, no possibility of survival. The site was levelled and smouldering in less than thirty minutes.

The company folded as quickly as it had flourished – small and lean turned out to actually mean underinsured. The settlement was not large and, after only 18 months, the scaling down of home and lifestyle was inevitable. Chloe could no longer afford to run the old house and it was sold five weeks after Cradle's seventh birthday.

'But this is where Dad lived, Mum.'

The room blurred through her tears. Her arms enfolded her son from behind, pulling his body gently to her. 'Daddy's gone darling. And he would want us to do the best for each other so that means we have to have a different house now.'

'Did it hurt him?'

Chloe froze at the question. She had tried many times to have any sort of conversation with her son about the accident but he never engaged. Her tears came too fast and spilt onto the back of Cradle's head.

'No. They said it happened really, really fast. Daddy wouldn't have been hurt. He just went straight away.'

'But he wouldn't have died quick.'

'What?' She loosened the embrace so she could look at her son's face. Where was this coming from?

'It wasn't an explosion though, so it would be slow. It would have hurt Dad.'

Slower

'I COULDN'T FIND IT, Eve. I still think there's something there though. I can feel it, I know it.'

'Well, if it's there, hun, you'll definitely find it. And God help the world while you do 'cos it'll all be turned upside down and inside out. You're not exactly known for letting things drop.'

Cradle drained the Zip can and clonked it down on the table. 'No, I mean the Flow was just flat everywhere I went. It was nothing, no features or bumps, no gaps or ripples. How can that be true when I know it's not right?'

'Like I said, you'll sort it.' Eve rose from the table and kissed him on the nape of his neck. 'That's what I love about you.'

'Yeah, I will. I just don't get it yet.' Cradle followed Eve into the lounge and slumped beside her on the old sofa.

'Probably just let it rest for a while until something comes to you. Switch off. You know, we can vid a movie or you could share a kakuro with me or something. Next thing you know, Eureka! You've got it. Worked for Aristotle.'

'Archimedes.'

'All Greek to me.' Eve looked at Cradle, pleased with herself. He looked back but obviously didn't get it. 'Oi, I made a joke! You could at least laugh politely!'

'What? Oh yeah, sorry. Good. They're both Greek. But it's really difficult to confuse them, actually. Aristotle dealt in abstract fundamental qualitative forms and teleology whereas Archimedes was more a mathematical physicist, each being ...'

'Nope! Nil points for the joke then. I should know better.' Eve pinched Cradle's nose and he sniffed and shook his head.

'Sorry. I'm doing it aren't I.'

'Yep. But if one night you came in and did anything different, I'd know you'd been replaced by a robot and I'd be forced to destroy you with my bare hands.'

'Wow, that's pretty violent for a healthcare specialist.'

'Oh, we can be as mean as the worst of them.' Eve pulled Cradle's arms around her shoulders. 'Seriously though, you always go too full on at these things, maybe you should have a break and try going slower.'

'You're probably right.' Cradle gestured the entertainment module to visual. 'A movie you say?'

'Coo, this must be what it's like to be a real couple, just like I always wished for ...' She bit his thumb. 'I might get a glass of red. Want anything?'

'Oi, you know you said that out loud, right? No, no wine for me, ta, I'm good.'

Eve untangled herself from the embrace and walked into the kitchen again. The Cabernet was still on the work surface with the closure half-heartedly plugging the top. She reached down a glass and poured a good splash, watching the red liquid swirl around and settle. Voxing the light off on her way out, she stopped dead in the hallway. Cradle was wearing his coat and teetered as he toed his shoes back on again.

'Cradle, what the hell?'

'Eve, you're a genius.'

'I am?'

'Yep. You said it. Slower.'

DREAM

CRADLE REACHED THE LAB just after midnight. Stan tracked his approach on the Vid and buzzed the door open as he arrived.

'Late one again, Mr Cradle?'

'Just got a couple of things to work through, Stan.'

He 'Tabbed the elevator and the doors opened immediately. The female voice greeted him with the usual etiquette.

<hello cradle/ can i take you to the flow lab>

'Yes please, Anna. Could you boot the Flow archive systems for me too? I need access to everything we've got since the start of recordings. In full DREAM please.'

The door hissed closed, and the gently-increased g-force betrayed the start of the journey to his inner ear. Fifty-eight floors down in thirteen seconds.

<coming online now cradle/ i have arranged coffee for you too/ perpetua lone working directive mandates that i monitor you this evening/ i hope that is acceptable>

'No problem, Anna. I'll be going in once I've assembled the archive sets. You're welcome to watch. Just don't try to molest me while I'm under.'

<what kind of a girl do you think i am mister>

'I see you're running my old-school anthro-chat patch, Anna. Funny. Probably have to rework that a bit though. Hasn't aged very well.'

He felt his weight momentarily increase and the door hissed open.

<the floor is yours cradle>

He stepped into the Lab and walked over to the Plate, which glowed dimly in readiness for his interfacing. A steaming mug of coffee was next to the Plate.

'Smells great, Anna. Thanks.' He moved the cup so that it was equidistant from each corner of the surface.

<just ask if you need me to help further/ lone working monitoring commencing now>

'Actually, Anna, you could help me with data retrieval if you like. How far back do our Flow recordings go?'

<i would love to help you cradle/ records commenced seven years and eleven months ago and are complete and intact to present day/ shall i enable all files for you>

'Thanks, yeah, but I'll be wanting to experience them all simultaneously, somehow. I need to run the analysis over the whole period. You know? I want to do this more slowly; not real-time mode. I'm not interested in what's happening moment by moment, I want the whole set at once. Can that be done, Anna?'

<i believe i understand your requirements/ we have not attempted this level of parallel access before cradle/ i will check processing capacity>

With Anna away thinking, the gentle hum of the Lab dominated his senses. Continuous, low-pitched tones from fans and lights, with a not-unpleasant pink hiss superimposed by the air systems. Cradle always found late-night sessions very relaxing and he was able to transition very quickly.

<confirming all files are enabled for you/ you have 100% lab processing available right now and i have patched in all available cores from europe/ usa and japan are already online and loaded but can help with peak management/ we have 370% normal capacity available to run the whole set/ allowing for instantiation and running in parallel with normal operations tomorrow you will need to be in direct replay for approximately 28 real hours subject to complexity>

'Wow, that's long.'

The Direct Replay Environment for Analytical Manipulation was a full-immersion variant of the Crossing Plate, used for deep analysis problems that required more than 95% brain capacity loading. Cradle always suspected that Kline had forced the title just to get the acronym.

DREAM itself was a spin-off from one of the leading research programmes in the field of artificial intelligence several decades ago. Scientists were trying to develop test facilities to create virtual environments for experimental machine sentience and had initially prototyped these using human volunteers. The resultant early coupling of sections of the human brain with powerful computational nodes in order to emulate artificial intelligence scenarios was done invasively, with microprobes and sensors being physically inserted into the subject's brain. But breakthroughs in sensor technology quickly combined with complementary advances in active nanotechnology to produce the ability to directly interface with the machines without resorting to such invasive surgical techniques. This enabled the man-machine coupling to become much more intimate and powerful by ingestion of nanofluid (or Hypergel, as it became known), with the result that humans were able to more fully venture into these strange new virtual landscapes and gain access to sensory prowess far beyond their natural limitations.

During these full immersions, vital areas of the brain were temporarily archived and given over to the machine, the subject's homeostasis being artificially maintained by the nanotech. This allowed direct access to immense fields of data, with human and machine seamlessly acting in perfect harmony. At the end of the session, functions were restored from archive and the subject's brain function returned to normal, theoretically only altered by the implanted memory of the session itself.

But finding suitable human subjects was absolutely not, by any means, straightforward. For many, a basic natural fear of drowning prevented even the first step, ingestion of the Hypergel itself, from being viable.

And, for the vast majority of people, although restoration from the archive was mathematically perfect – numerically lossless – the psychological reboot almost always proved less so, the resultant aftermath of immersion making the prospect completely untenable, with many of the early volunteers suffering dangerous and permanent side effects. Numerous test subjects developed post-immersion symptoms of paranoia, schizophrenia and epilepsy; there were four cases of coma and even three fatalities during the earlier, rather shadier, stages of experimentation where significant amounts of old money had changed hands.

The programme was suspended for three years while deep psychological profiling tests were developed to ascertain which individuals, if any, would be able to survive the immersion intact and unscathed. Enormous numbers of would-be superhumans were screened and rejected, with the result that only a vanishingly small handful of people in the world were capable of DREAMing.

Call it luck. Call it fate. Cradle was one of this elite group.

'Could you let Eve know I'm OK during this? I probably didn't give her enough information.'

<yes i have already set up the comms channel to your home and to eves personal communicator/ do you wish me to use your voice for this>

'No, no, that freaks her out. Just text-only her my status every couple of hours and let me know if she makes any important replies.'

<confirmed/ i will maintain regular textual intercourse with your wife throughout dream>

'What's that Anna?' Intrigued.

<i have employed near homophones and synonyms to affect an amusement>

'A joke Anna? With puns?'

<yes cradle/ i believe it is humour>

'Well, that's always been the problem with belief. Keep working on it though, it'll come.'

<yes> Pause. <i have retained this conversation as reference>

Cradle ignored his coffee and slid himself into the DREAM chamber. 'Anna, please connect vital stasis and Crossing. And maintain direct comms with me please, I might need some help.'

<confirmed/ commencing ingestion>

Warm Hypergel engulfed him in the chamber. He always regarded this as a sort of uterine process. He always found the experience to be deeply comforting and a primaeval kind of reassurance ran through him whenever he DREAMed. He would feel the fluid tickling his nostrils and simply opened his mouth and throat to it, breathing out deeply and fully, expelling as much CO_2 as possible. The Hypergel gently, inexorably, engulfed him: trachea, bronchial tubes, bronchi, alveoli.

And then the jolt of going into DREAM itself. The brief falling sensation with that accompanying surge of adrenaline, all suddenly cancelled out by the enormity of being connected into a vast new world of experience. Every fibre of consciousness coupled with a billion computational nodes, gaining access to an unthinkable quantity of data. Extreme use of cerebral brain capacity, with backup and retasking of the limbic brain, and machine support of all body systems.

Cradle reached forwards into the data, moving amongst it, around it, within it. All around him lay the familiar perfect pattern of uniform energy that he had seen the previous day at the Plate, the endless monotony of beautiful flatness. He extended the range to include the entire past year of data. Floating over the landscape, he became aware of an almost imperceptible disturbance in the continuum. Nothing tangible or observable, more a subsurface anxiety, a knowing trepidation. Cradle focused tightly on each sub-band in turn. Gamma, X-ray, ultraviolet through to infrared, microwave and radio wavelengths. Picometres to metres. Nothing but uniformity, although ... something ... a feeling, a tiny rise in a virtual heartbeat. He streamed in two more years from the archive and repeated the scan, feeling the blood rise in his body (was it *his* body?) as the data flowed through him.

There. A ripple. Tiny. Was it?

He pulled back from close focus and viewed the landscape in full. Flat again, nothing. White and infinite. Breathtaking yet tedious.

Loading the entire dataset for almost eight years, Cradle rose above the landscape again, looking down on mankind's greatest-ever accident. Still perfect flatness. He looked away and saw again ... something ... on the outside maybe ...

He picked up the infinite edge of the landscape and lifted it under and up, breaking through the central point of the data and creating a thin torus structure suspended between his hands. The distorted surface effervesced and swirled in vivid multicolours about his fingers in what seemed to be a celebration of its new form. He pulled it apart and twisted it about his fingers. A loop. Familiar.

left over right, right over left, middles catch the loops.

He held the shape out in front of him.

cat's cradle. Eve's voice was distant vapour in his senses.

throw it, cradle. Anna?

He launched the shape into the virtual space above him and watched as it unravelled and returned to its planar form, surrounding him again. But now there were distortions where once had been flawlessness. The tiniest ripples in the data fabric, trapped and frozen now as the landscape pulled itself back towards perfection. Indiscernible phase changes now knotted in the transform to this new plane of perception. Distilled into view at last. Caught.

'Anna, please route this structure to the Analyser and commit to archive using personal privacy settings, level alpha.'

<archive committed and verified secure/ analyser ready>

Cradle entered the Analyser paradigm and brought the data structures into view.

'Huh? These feel like frames. Very brief colourations of the noise spread over extremely long periods. Something like packaging. Anna, please autocorrelate.'

<running/ confirmed periodicity/ 87% probability of message structure/ content unknown but repeating/ three identical instances over the full dataset>

'Three instances? Anna, please route the content detail to my personal hub.'

<blocked level 1 veto/ sorry cradle>

'Try again please, Anna.'

<blocked level 1 veto/ sorry cradle>

'What's going on, Anna? Exit please.'

<acknowledged/ restoring limbic status/ disconnecting vitals/ exit confirmed>

Cradle always felt massive when the Hypergel receded, like he had been dumped back into his body and gravity was crushing him into the ground; and terribly bereft, as though he had lost everything in the world. He wept uncontrollably for a few minutes, before composing himself. He slid back from the DREAM chamber, slowly drawing himself to his feet, steadied by the Lab surface in front of him. The smell of stale, cold coffee pervaded his senses.

'How long, Anna?'

<46 hours cradle/ the landscape manipulation needed more processing so we had to timeshare with main/ this extended the analysis period significantly/ all processors worldwide have been returned to normal designation now>

'Wow. Do I get an award or something?'

<i have noted this as the longest direct replay session to date>

'That'll have to do then. What's with the Veto? Never had that before.'

<personal access veto code 00489463 was actioned during your dream>

'A PAV mid-DREAM? While I was actually in there? It seems we're being watched, Anna.'

<everyone is watched cradle/ it is standard procedure/ eve requested to be notified when you were out/ may i alert her for you>

'Yep, tell her I'll be home in an hour please, Anna.'

<completed>

'But the structures are safe in archive?'

<yes/ archive index #64927764382 was completed prior to the pav>

'OK, load them into my terminal here please, Anna.'

<blocked level 1 veto/ sorry cradle>

'Anna? What, I can't access them at all?'

<level 1 permissions required/ sorry cradle>

Cradle looked down at his desk space. There was a small real paper note stuck to the side of his terminal.

'*Two days in soak, dream boy. What happened? Elsie throw you out?*'

'Anders. Never gives up.' Cradle laughed dryly and shook his head. 'I'll have to sleep on it, Anna. Thanks for your help.'

Watermark

THE SOLES OF KLINE'S shoes were worn flat with years of scuffling around in the Lab and they oscillated before Cradle's eyes. They were a triumph of comfort over style.

'Anders, I wish you'd put your feet on your own desk.'

'Aha, personal space issues, eh? If I put my feet on my own desk, how will I be able to do any work? Think of that? The whole company would suffer.'

'Your shoes are worn out by the way. You'll slip and fall. And I'll just stand over your broken body and laugh.'

Kline cackled and carried on gesturing the Wafer on his lap.

'Do you know anything about Level 1 Vetoing?'

He tipped the Wafer back onto his desk and swung his feet down, leaning in close to Cradle.

'Level 1? Where did you get that?'

'When I was in DREAM I got blocked. Anna told me it was a Level 1 Veto and I couldn't even get to the archive after that.'

'Well, I guess you finally managed to tread on some big toes at last.' Kline looked Cradle in the eye. 'From the very top, that one is. Off the record? Only ever used in cases of national emergency or major corporate crisis. What the fuck did you do?'

'I was working out the pattern in the Flow. Nearly had it, I think. There's definitely something like a message in there. It repeats about every two and a half years, so we never saw it in our day-to-day monitoring.'

'Could it be a periodic drift in Flow channel characteristics? We saw that before, in the early trials, way back. We thought it looked like an instability and all hell broke loose. Turned out to be just natural drifting, back and forth, of the tokamak monitoring systems.'

'Yeah, I remember that. But it's different this time: much, much slower, and I think there's some sort of modulation of the noise that feels a bit like a message structure or something. It's only repeated three times since we started recording, in all that data. My DREAM got blocked before I could go any further and when I asked Anna to fetch it from archive or send it to me, I got the Veto warning each time.'

Kline rose to his feet and paced the floor, his scuffed footwear squeaking on the antistatic surface.

'Anything in your inbox about it?'

'Nope.'

'There will be. Cradle, you have to be really, really careful here, this could be big trouble. Sounds like the system doesn't want you to find out anything more than you already have. We've never had that before: always carte blanche research, blue skies, no questions asked, providing we write it up and report stuff we can do pretty much what we like. Journeying into the unknown, they called it.'

'So why stop this? It might be the most important thing we've ever discovered. If it turns out to be something significant, what is it and where is it coming from?'

Kline let his eyes fix onto a corner of the room, sniffed and cleared his throat three times, a mannerism which Cradle had come to accept as standard procedure for his friend's contemplations. He was silent while the other man meditated in this way for perhaps fifteen seconds.

'Tell you what I think, and call me a cynical old bastard if you like. It's a security device; an imprint put there by Perpetua so that the Flow is somehow marked as theirs.'

Cradle looked at Kline quizzically. 'Not with you?'

'Well, what if you were of a mind to route some of the power from this thing, you know, out through some sort of secret path – and bear with me here, I've not thought this even halfway through yet – and you sold it on to an illegal third party as an alternative source of energy, effectively going up against Perpetua? You wouldn't know about this modulation, so the energy flux would be fingerprinted as belonging to Perpetua. Like a watermark. They could trace it back as theirs and sue the arses off everyone involved.'

'Energy tagging? Wow. Maybe.' Cradle stood up too and went over to the DREAM chamber. 'The more we pull the more it gives out. I could secretly pull a bit harder and sell the extra on but the tagging would betray me.' Cradle turned to Kline. 'But no, there's a flaw. I could still convert it into a bulk store like inertia; spend the tagged energy by spinning up some little flywheels, maybe. Or pressurise some gas or liquid to hold it. Or even heat something up. Then I could sell it on. The tagging would be gone.'

'Yeah, but you'd be left with a bloody great wheelbarrow of stuff to try and smuggle out of the building, so to speak. Even Stan on the door would spot that. And that's if LineSec hadn't detected the extra bleed, which is so unlikely as to be impossible. So, whichever way, you'd pipe off a bit of the Flow and either flog that to the enemy or store it for a while. But both ways you'd be fucked; it'd give itself away. I bet there are peripheral algorithms surrounding this place to trap these tags as they go out, and then raise the alarm. Probably triggered one in your DREAM.'

Cradle walked over and sat back down. 'Anna, what do you think of this idea?'

<the proposition seems to be in accordance with available statistics cradle>

Kline stared into the middle distance. 'Is that a yes? Give me a number.'

<are you content with the completeness of the dataset dr kline>'

'Assume there's nothing we don't know, for now.'

<78% fit levenberg-marquardt>

'OK, looks like we've got ourselves a better than half-arsed hypothesis, Cradle. It's just the big bad giant protecting his gold.'

A brief tone drew Cradle's attention to his personal monitor.

'Appointment with LineSec, Ref dataset Veto protocol #17900002374XD2. Mandatory attendance 16:00.'

'Shit. There you go, Cradle.'

Warning

'MR CRADLE, YOUR DREAM record shows you accessing the entire Flow data archives to the present day. As you are aware, when you attempted to analyse this dataset, access was blocked by Level 1 Veto.'

Miles Bryant was a short man, thinning grey hair slicked to his scalp. Old dandruff lay on the shoulders of his rumpled dark brown suit like greased coconut, and his blue and grey check shirt was mercilessly throttled by a scrawny and nondescript reddish tie. His linear face was unsuccessfully shaven and rudely punctuated by a catastrophe of teeth that were yellowed from decades of smoking. He had somehow used this maloccluded jumble to assault his fingernails, which were bitten back to bloodied snagging rectangles. When he spoke, his mouth opened asymmetrically and his consonants occasionally ejected tiny sprays of saliva into the air, contrasted against the dark wood and bejewelled by the intense lighting of the Line and Security office. Cradle stood before an obviously raised platform on which Bryant and his vast desk were ludicrously assembled.

'Yes, Mr Bryant. I was investigating the possibility of a pattern within the Flow energy. I thought it might be important.'

'And you are, most certainly, to be commended for your insightfulness, Mr Cradle. Am I to understand that the Flow Analysis department has a formative theory as to why things might be as they appear?'

'Yes, we think it may be a form of energy tagging, to mark the Flow as Perpetua property.'

Bryant laughed and wrought a new and even more exotic display of vapour into the spotlight as his stump-clawed hands noiselessly clapped together. 'Well done, well done! Oh, this is excellent; well done indeed! I am authorised to inform you that you are correct in your assertion.'

Bryant paused and, pompously rising to his feet, adjusted his expression to one of malevolent contempt. 'I am sure I do not need to tell you the significance of your discovery?' He lurched down from the platform to floor level and approached, his clumsy, ambling gait urging him to within centimetres of Cradle's face. Bryant's thin, rheumy eyes revolted Cradle and he felt a small, involuntary convulsion in his cheek. He could smell the man's nicotine lungs on the air.

'This technique is subject to the utmost security protection, for obvious reasons. It must, of course, remain confidential at all costs. The country's financial position depends upon it. The future of Perpetua depends upon it. Our jobs. Your job, Mr Cradle.'

'I understand, Mr Bryant.'

'I thought you might.' Yellow crooked smile. 'Flow Analysis enjoys a freedom of pursuit unequalled anywhere in Perpetua. No restrictions. No boundaries. Pure discovery. And this is how it must be if Perpetua wish to improve our services to the planet. But there are certain problems with this purity in a commercial environment, as I'm sure you must realise. There are those who would destroy us, usurp our position and bring us to dust. Knowledge must be protected. It is our only property in the end.

'And so now you have no requirement to follow this particular direction of analysis. Moreover, you are formally forbidden from any such endeavour by the company's highest Security protocols. The Veto remains extant, and I need not tell you that any attempt to access or decompose this data again will result in your personal Invocation. Mr Cradle, I assume that you recall the wording of your Confidentiality Bond?'

'Indeed I do, Mr Bryant.'

'Excellent. Then we are clear. Flow Analysis will not, under any circumstances, disclose this information to anyone, whether within the company or outside of it. Very well, Mr Cradle. That is all I needed to clear up with you. I am sure you have many other important things you should be getting on with, so I will distract you no longer. Happy researching. Elsewhere. Good day to you.'

Cradle left the Line Security office and walked fifty metres down the hallway and straight into the toilet. Filling the middle sink with water, he washed his hands and splashed the clean liquid over his face, hair and neck. He dried himself and took a second towel from the dispenser, using it to rub his shirt front and sleeves. The encounter with Bryant looped over and over in his mind.

Kline was waiting for Cradle's return and pounced on him as he entered the Lab.

'Show me on the doll where he touched you.'

'That bloke is a monster,' Cradle muttered, 'I was covered in his spit.'

Kline guffawed his approval. 'So you kissed?'

Cradle looked askance at Kline. 'He said we're correct and it is tagging of the Flow energy. He then reminded me about the Confidentiality Bond.'

'Whoa, told you it was trouble! Did you behave yourself or did you behave like yourself?'

'Yeah, I was a good little yes-man, Anders, just like you taught me.'

Kline broke eye contact with Cradle and shifted his weight slightly. 'Ouch.'

Cradle glanced at his friend and saw that his unguarded comment had hurt him.

'Sorry, Anders. That was uncalled for. I'm a bit shaken, that's all. I just kept saying I understand, Mr Bryant, I understand, Mr Bryant. I hope I don't ever meet up with him on a dark night. Stood up there on his platform like Dracula or something, spraying out disgusting spit from his lips. I'm going to have nightmares about him.'

Kline cackled to himself. 'Accepted. Did you see any partially-eaten children lying about?'

He reattached Kline's gaze and smiled. 'Only a few. I've got to stop research in that area from now, on pain of Invocation. I just have to drop it.'

'Yeah well, maybe it's for the best. We have the Algorithm Optimisation Review coming up next month. Gonna soak us all up.'

'Yeah, I know you're right.' Cradle gestured a couple of routine field loggers into action. 'I'm going to call it a day for now, these will run overnight. Logs'll be ready for the report tomorrow. I'll format them up then.'

'Cool. Have a vampire-free evening.'

On the way up Cradle again allowed things to run through his head, over and over. Such measures for security. Such extremes, and so rigidly enforced. Of course the Flow tags would have to be protected, of course they would be secret. Of course it would be impossible to know any more about the nature of the tag data. Of course Bryant was just doing his job. Of course Kline was right and they had plenty of other work. Of course he would be insane to work on it any more.

But, of course, he would.

Bryant

IT WAS A COMPLICATED and enduringly hateful journey. His birth hunched his spine and killed his mother. His father never bothered to even put his head around the door to introduce himself and a string of foster homes was normality. His schooling subjected him to bullying and repression all the way from his early years through to university. Absolutely no one is prepared to like a weirdo when it comes down to it, especially one they helped to create. Right up until he joined the company. In Perpetua, he found a place. He focussed. Put himself on the agenda, front and centre.

Of course, there were plenty of visible details on the way; early indicators, should anyone have been tempted to feign even remote interest. Things that revealed themselves long after the spit had dried white on the back of his blazer; long after the kick-bruises had blanched away. Bitten fingernails; pillowcases spotted with cuticle blood. Tics and nervous habits, obvious to all and thus inciting his tormentors to evermore creative endeavours.

And then there were the intangibles; secret excursions into ruthlessness, concealed from the world. Arachnids, initially: spiders trapped between index finger and thumb, their tiny, cold eyes giving nothing away: no sense of their impending fate; their innards popping out onto his fingertips, staining his skin. The tiny acrid stench of them; the tang of it on his tongue.

He once lifted a log and hundreds of beetles fled his shadow, crushing underfoot like hailstones on a pavement, every minuscule crunch a victory, a certificate of his power.

And then there was a cat, wandering aimlessly across a foster garden. He kept the paw for several years in a sealed plastic bag until it finally disintegrated into something powdery and unrecognisable. He dropped it into a drain.

After years of indirection, his first day in LineSec was a huge step into the unknown. It was a junior position working directly with Main, but he quickly emerged as a more than loyal subject, content to implement instructions without question; happy to exist in complete isolation from others, impervious to their fear or hatred. The machine came to trust him utterly, and regular private interfacing sessions gradually elevated him to the most senior position in LineSec. But, more than that, the system granted him complete power to carry out all of Main's wetware management decisions: people must be controlled for the Flow to be protected and maintained, and therefore for the good of humanity itself. He deeply accepted this prime maxim and there was no room for compassion or hesitation in its execution. There were almost no limitations to this remit. His fellows and competitors were brushed aside, popped and crushed, leaving him in sole command.

He had been before the machine a thousand times, arms outstretched, his forehead and palms in contact with its metal plates, locked in communication, eyes wide and unfocussed in a nystagmus of download. Main propelled him with its instructions, and he reciprocated with an assiduous sense of duty which encompassed his every action.

H4X0R

'Is your brother still working for that network security company?'

Eve drained her glass of Sauvignon Blanc and rolled the stem in her fingers. 'Net Pusher? Nah, he went solo a couple of years ago. Couldn't do the corporate thing. His head's wired different to that.'

'So what's he doing now?'

'Same sort of thing I think, although I don't know any details, he never says much about it. He's consulting now, running his own show. Suits him better, I think. Calls it White Hatter.'

'I might have a little job for him. Is he still in the UK?'

'Nah, States now. Remember? He met that lovely girl Suki and went back with her to LA. They're getting engaged this summer. I told you all this months ago, I knew you weren't really listening. Vid him if you want to chat. They're six or seven hours behind us I think, so it's about lunchtime there. You'll probably catch him now. I wouldn't mind a natter with him anyway. This all sounds very intriguing, what's up?'

'Oh, just work stuff. Nothing exciting.'

They went through to the lounge and Eve hooked up with James on the Wafer. In a few moments, her brother's face appeared on the screen.

'Aha, little sis! How are you doing over there? Seen the sun lately?'

'Nothing wrong with continuous cloud cover, Jimmy, you won't make me jealous. OK, you have made me jealous. How's things?'

They chatted for half an hour, catching up on the minutiae of life. Suki was doing great in her job, working hard flogging artwork to hi-cred folk who didn't even know they needed it. Lots of travel. Matter of fact, she was away at the moment. James himself was in rude health; flash car, expensive bottle. White Hatter had taken off at just the right pace, plenty of work but not too much. Lots of people paranoid about cybersecurity, usually with good reason. They wanted their corporate and personal systems stressing and then, once the flaws were discovered, they wanted the holes plugging up. And all from his seat in the sun, no travel needed. The beauty of the Net.

'Anyway, Jimmy, Cradle's got something he wants to ask you about.'

'Cool, put him on sis!'

Cradle gestured the Wafer to put himself in-frame. 'Hi, James. Yeah, this is just a thought. So, you do just White Hat stuff now, right?'

'Whoa, yeah of course! Lily-white only man! I mean some of it's maybe a bit grey I guess, but only by explicit invitation of the clients themselves. Everything's above board. I'm a good boy now.'

'Of course. I just wanted to ask you about something I thought you might be able to help me with.'

'Tell you what, I have to go now, Cradle. It was great talking with you both. Ciao!'

And then he was gone.

'Er, that was sudden. What happened?'

'Nothing. Hang on a while.'

Eve looked at her husband, confused. They both sat for a couple of minutes, Cradle smiling at Eve and Eve frowning back at him.

The Wafer chimed and he opened the message. 'Aha, a link.'

Eve watched over his shoulder as he opened it. A fishing blog. 'Cradle, what are you up to?'

He scrolled down to the last blog entry, posted by blackequals8356. It read:

'There's nothing that makes me feel more complete than floating on the river. With my reflection in the water framed by the two banks, I feel whole again and able to

understand the world. I might even catch something one day!'

'Mind telling me what's going on, Cradle, since you obviously know? Jimmy's always hated fishing!'

Ching. A pair of emails, this time just Cred bank notifications, nothing special.

'Hold on a sec.' Cradle gestured the browser to open his current Cred balance. 'There's one.' He gestured Eve's account open and she duly gestured her authorisation. 'And there's the other.'

'Let me see ...' Eve leaned across and looked at the two accounts. 'Why has Jimmy sent you 11.67 Creds and me 12.93?'

'Because you're his sister and he likes you the best, I suppose. Watch this.'

He opened the second email and gestured the attachment open. An app installed, kicking off a dialogue window that asked for a key to be entered.

'OK, let's see.' He tactiled *11676538slauqekcalb1293* and gestured *Enter*.

The dialogue announced '*incorrect key*'.

'Right, not that way round then.'

He tried *12936538slauqekcalb1167* and the dialogue disappeared and opened the Vid app, automatically loaded with an unknown ID and selected for voice-only.

'There we go.'

'Cradle?'

'Ooh, your brother's good. The two banks mentioned in the blog are the two separate amounts in our Cred bank accounts. And then we had '*my reflection in the water framed by the two banks*', so I took the blog ID and reversed it, then sandwiched it in between the two bank credits and hey presto! I got them the wrong way round the first time, but the second time I cracked it. '*I feel whole again and able to understand the world*' are the instructions. You put them all together and the app will understand the world! See? It's a password, very strong and pieced together from obscure and separate parts. Really hard to trace. This is an encrypted add-in that will scramble the audio input and get us secure comms over Vid. As I said, your brother's good.'

He OK'd the call, and it was immediately answered.

'Hey man, that was fast, you've still got your touch! I figured you'd be ten minutes, but you did it in three. OK, so we're running a nearly 800-bit cryptograph here, hence the big delay, but even so, no names or locations, right?'

'Understood.' Cradle looked at Eve, smiling. She shook her head with her mouth gaping slightly.

Twenty seconds interval, then 'What you got then, brother?'

Cradle described the problem with the locked archive and laboured the point that a certain company would be using the best eSecurity in the world against any kind of unwanted access.

Belatedly, 'Cool! Love a challenge.' James went on to ask a host of details, times, dates, login IDs, backup schedules etc.

'I can't be linked to this in any way,' Cradle warned. 'I'm finished if you do.'

And after what seemed strangely like a contemplative interval, 'No worries, let me go to it. I'm a ghost. Might take a few days. I'll send you the file once I've got it. Similar precautions. Time to wake up and smell the coffee.'

And he was gone again. The app terminated itself automatically, uninstalling and purging the call record as it did so.

'Jesus, Cradle, what are you getting into? Are you in some sort of trouble?'

'Something's not right, Eve. And I'm going to find it.'

Swept

HER EARLIEST STRONG MEMORY was of loving him. That day in the classroom she felt it for the first time. A childish and immature affection perhaps, but genuine and true for all that. When their hands first touched in that tangle of cat's cradles she felt her heart lift and she simply fell, completely entangling herself in everything about him. And he wrapped her up in everything he was. She saw it in his eyes when he looked at her over the ordered tangle of string and fingers.

They quickly became best friends, inseparable in and out of school. Miss Rahni gave Eve permission to move her desk next to the one the other kids called 'the weird boy' and so they were always in each other's company. He liked to be away from other children at breaktime but she became a special exception, with the result that they always spent their spare time together, by themselves.

He made her laugh and she knew he loved it when she giggled uncontrollably: their hours together echoed the classroom with joy.

When Cradle moved to a small house outside town with his Mum, he discovered that the 78A bus ran through his village before passing her house on the way to school, so he always saved a seat for Eve in the morning. 15 minutes together each way, every day.

Then sixteen. The kiss, the kiss, the kiss. Off the bus together in the village, dark winter night, cold noses in the way and fat with coats. The taste of lips, the heart-beat, the closed eyes rolling under lids, the tears cold on her face, her hands in his gloves, stretching round insu-lation to hug, touching noses and foreheads, and staring into blurred eyes. A thousand years ago and yesterday. The butterflies flew, even as she recalled it now.

They were engaged at 18. She had always longed to be a nurse and went for the NHS PTP degree in Nurs-ing at The University of Southampton. He was stunning with science and mathematics, so selected the Master of Physics degree at the same university. Their one-bed-room flat on Shaftesbury Avenue was tiny, tiny. But rather than feeling hemmed in, it was somewhere to bump into each other, to brush past each other, to be with each other.

She graduated with top marks and a gift for care that was recognised by all her tutors, immediately finding work in Southampton General, while he finished his fourth year with all colours blazing and four research fellowship offers.

They married in the July of their 22nd years, a post-graduate wedding, like father like son. A simple but intensely emotional registry office ceremony was followed by a small reception party at The Drummond Arms in Portswood. Their vows were their own words, spoken with entwined fingers and breaking voices before a few silent, breath-taken friends and family.

They moved up to Abingdon in Oxfordshire to begin their married life, he for research at Culham Centre for Fusion Energy, and she for adult intensive care at the John Radcliffe Hospital. A comfortable flat became available above the old bookshop in Stert Street, almost as a matter of course, falling into place exactly when needed, easily and naturally. Not enormous, not ostentatious, but it was their soldier's bed, their diamond, their cat's cradle. Grown together, entangled, hands touching hands.

Stone

THE WAFER CHIMED GENTLY in the darkness, starting Cradle back to consciousness. He could hear Eve's reassuringly soft slumber as he slipped from bed to floor, then out into the lounge, easing the doors closed behind him. Snapping the light on, he opened the device and, as the sleep cleared from his eyes, he gestured the pop-up into foreground mode.

Message from *unknown*, subject *coffee break game*. He activated the link and read the content.

'Every stone has an underneath, somewhere no one goes or knows about, even giant mountains. Tiny fish can come and go here, out of sight of predators and hunters. They leave no trace or trail; they can disappear and reappear unchallenged. Lift the stone to look under and you disturb everything, and the stone will ultimately crush you. The way in is via every impossibly small avenue, through every locked door at once. To follow, you cannot think like a hunter. You must think like a fish. Become the fish.'

The last sentence was hot. He gestured it and a new app started up, full scope holo. A stone appeared before him, solid, impermeable and too heavy to lift. A shoal of minnow-like creatures materialised, swimming about the rock in no particular pattern or order. He pointed with one finger and found he could control the shoal's movements, crudely and ineffectively leading them around the holo. He moved them closer to the base of the stone, hoping for ... well, hoping for something to happen. But as soon as he released contact they just returned to their random patterns and spread out around the rock again.

'What kind of game is this, James?' he whispered to himself, 'I have no clue what I'm doing here. The rock is obviously meant to be Perpetua but what about the fish? Are they me or some kind of loose analogy that I'm supposed to interpret somehow? And how do I get one of them under the rock when they all move together?'

He closed the app and returned to the message.

'Become the fish. Think like a fish. How does a fish think?'

He pushed the Wafer aside and went into the kitchen. The 'Tab time moved silently on towards 5.15 as he waited for the synthesiser to prepare his cup.

'But fish are idiots. Surely, they don't think? Don't they just swim round and round a bowl, doing nothing? What are they, some kind of secret mute, frustrated philosophers? And no better when there's a large school of them, they just swim about together, and the app even simulated that with its random clustering. All pretty accurate to the real thing, hopeless, aimless and wandering.'

'... *cannot think like a hunter* ...'

'... *through every locked door at once* ...'

The machine proffered the hot vessel, froth swirling on the surface. Cradle absently studied its rotation as his mind wrestled fruitlessly with the concepts raised by James's game. The tiny bubbles slowed to form a fixed pattern which slowly disappeared into the surface of the coffee itself. Suddenly, he thought of tiny white fish, vanishing undetected.

'Is that it? A coffee break game?' *Wake up and smell the coffee.* 'James, you already gave me the clue!'

He returned to the lounge and restarted the game with a single gesture. And there were the fish again, clouding around the central boulder, random movements without direction. He noticed no rotation in their manner, no purpose, and he knew that a single touch gesture was ineffective, the fish just swarmed stupidly about his finger. He took both hands and enacted a turning gesture using all fingers. The shoal followed, beginning to rotate, and then returning quickly to their aimless passage. He tried again, repeating the gesture twice. The fish again rotated about the stone, more determined this time but, again, as soon as he stopped the gesture the cycling ceased.

'OK. Let's really whip this thing up.'

He gestured repeatedly and without method, watching the shoal spinning beneath his fingers, one following another, microscopically aimless but macroscopically directed as an ensemble into a macchiato swirl about the rock.

He released the fish from his fingers and sat back, watching the game unfold. His face was illuminated in the semi-darkness by the small silvery churn which gradually slowed to a halt. This time though it was a static halt, not random motion as before. It was a few seconds before he became aware that the fish were fewer in number. Vanishing. As he watched, the silver foam reduced further, each tiny fish disappearing from view until only a few individuals remained, scattering over the screen until, eventually, even they faded away, leaving the rock alone in the holo image.

Sudden blank darkness jolted Cradle from his slightly hypnotised reverie. The stone, too, had disappeared from view.

<hello cradle>

'Anna?'

<yes cradle/ you are accessing the system using a secure maintenance portal/ you have full and unmonitored access to dream/ the vernacular for this is backdoor i believe>

'Oh, I do love you, James.'

<sorry cradle/ no james identity is accessible in secure maintenance mode>

'Not to worry, Anna.' Cradle smiled. 'I have no DREAM hardware in my home interface, Anna. Is that a problem?'

<that is not a problem/ i will represent you in the system/ i will be you cradle>

'Can you download my most recent DREAM archive securely to my personal device without detection?'

<yes but this is a very large dataset cradle and my routing and storage paths must be continuously modified to avoid discovery/ it will take many hours>

'Please compute accurate download time, Anna.'

<134 hours and 47 minutes assuming that continuous connection is maintained>

'And can I disconnect this terminal without affecting the transfer?'

<once initiated the dataset dump can only be terminated by its own completion>

'So that's a yes, right?'

<yes cradle>

'OK, Anna. Let's do it.'

<download commenced/ 0% complete/ obviously>

He smiled as he recognised one of his more recent anthropomorphism programming patches finding its way into Anna's vocabulary. Mild sarcasm. He liked it. 'And no word of this into the system, right?'

<the level of security in this mode has necessitated an instantiation of anna entirely separate from your normal dream aengel/ the probability of significant data exchange with normal operations is 0.00000073%>

'OK. Yep, that's OK. I'll see you later today when I'm in Perpetua.'

<this instantiation will be destroyed upon completion of the requested session>

'Oh, yeah. OK, well I'll see your sister at work then, I guess.'

<your normal anna avatar will have no knowledge of this interaction/ goodbye cradle/ i have enjoyed being with you>

'Understood. Bye, Anna 2. And thanks.'

He closed the session and slept the Wafer. Now all he had to do was wait.

And hope Anna 2's statistics were right.

Wild Goose

'So, allow me to summarise.' Dr Pinkerton pushed his glasses up to the top of his head and sat back from the conference table. 'We have no signs of RNA interference, and absolutely no evidence of increased antibody activity whatsoever. No macroparasites are apparent in any of the presentations. Moreover, there are no abnormal bacteria in any of the patients, either in number or type. The patients are clinically completely healthy.'

Public Health England's Director of Health Protection was used to chairing conferences under difficult circumstances but seldom such an erudite gathering. PHE now found itself at the heart of the international effort to stop Drowse, coordinating and advising agencies across the globe.

'Furthermore,' he continued, 'the distribution and demographics of the disease do not correlate well with any of our epidemic models. We seem to have conclusively ruled out viruses, bacteria, prions, nematodes, fungi, arthropods and protozoa.

'Ladies and gentlemen, what have we left?'

Greg Pinkerton looked around the large U-shaped conference table at the assembled body of experts: the world's foremost medical intellects were represented. A freshly jet-lagged Al Waters from the Centers for Disease Control and Prevention in Atlanta sat to his left, chewing gum as he arranged his Wafer in front of him. Then, to his left, sat Jürgen Salomonsen and Jane Farrow of the European CDC in Stockholm and, further down the left stem of the "U", Alejandro Fàbregas and Ndulue Buwani from WHO Europe and Africa, followed by Opeyemi Mgami and Noomi Olawadi from CDC Africa, and Srinivas Choudhuri from the CDC India office in New Delhi. Along the righthand stem of the table were Alicia Giovani and José Luis Sánchez from the Carter Center Atlanta, and Jiang So Cheung, Lok Sheung and Xiaoli Li from the Chinese CDC in Beijing. Various other renowned stars from the field of epidemiological research were similarly arranged around the further reaches of the table.

Salomonsen was the first to respond. 'Currently, it seems there is no identifiable cause for this *Drowse*. There are only symptoms. It is unlike anything we have seen before.'

His comment broke the tension and a murmur ran amongst the attendees.

'We came up empty ourselves,' added Al Waters. 'As I've said, the incidence of infection does not follow any of the normal modes. There's no correlation with contact, movement, socioeconomic status, gender, hygiene, or ethnicity. Hell, we even checked religious groups. Nothing points anywhere.'

Jane Farrow spoke next. 'We looked specifically at cell processes. The symptoms of Drowse are similar to anaemia, with chronic fatigue presented in 100% of cases. The ECDC looked at bloods from 98% of UK Drowse patients. We assessed red blood cell levels. All normal. We did exhaustive tests for blood defects; thalassaemia, porphyria, even sickle cell and carbon monoxide poisoning. All negative. The disease, therefore, does not seem to be related to carriage of oxygen in these patients.'

'The Beijing research covered cell respiration. Levels of ATP production were all normal.' Xiaoli Li turned to face Farrow. 'So we know that oxygen is getting around OK and respiration is working normally. Yet the patients all exhibit a lack of energy as though these processes were compromised in some way.'

José Luis Sánchez joined the fray. 'At the Carter Center, Alicia and I searched for other processes and effects associated with disruption of ATP cycle, such as mitochondrial dysfunction, retarded healing rates, tissue decay and CFS. Again, we found no evidence to support any hypothesis in this area.'

'Well, perhaps we are all looking too hard at what we know.' Noomi Olawadi hesitantly rose to her feet.

'What are you suggesting, Noo?' Pinkerton was also reticent.

'I have been assembling a timeline of world events, Drowse being one of them. I was looking for volcanic and seismic events, meteor activity, that sort of thing. My hypothesis was that such events could have released ancient spores or bacteria to which human immunity over our evolutionary development has declined. My colleagues' various works have dismissed this direct hypothesis, but there is a coincidence that I keep coming back to.'

She could feel the weight of the entire conference looking at her.

'Drowse was first observed almost immediately after Persistence.'

Pinkerton looked at Olawadi with a bemused expression, his mouth slightly open. 'I think I must repeat my question, Dr Olawadi. What are you suggesting?'

'Well, I don't know exactly. Maybe we should be looking for something there.'

Srinivas Choudhuri added his voice to the debate. 'Are you saying that Drowse is somehow caused by radiation from the Hornbill energy source? But people are affected all over the world. How could this be so?'

'I do not know – it is not even a hypothesis, just a thought. Maybe it could be something new that behaves differently? Something that is not affected by distance?

Neutrinos or something exotic? I realise this is not very scientific. Nobody really knows how Hornbill works, yet we are all happy to run our lights by it. I just think we need to rule it out as a possibility, that's all.'

A concerned murmuring spread through the conference. Greg Pinkerton got to his feet and addressed the conference more formally. 'May I just stop you there please, Noo. The institutions we represent are of course founded on absolutely solid scientific research, tested and proven, fact upon fact. The physical models and laws that we rely upon have never failed us in this and we cannot embark upon wild departures merely because we have a difficult problem to solve. That said, we are drawing blanks across the board. Bu, please stop taking minutes now and switch off the recorders.' He glanced down at Ndulue Buwani, the elected secretary for the conference. He nodded and gestured his Wafer into hiatus. The conference waited in silent tension.

'From here on, the debate is off the record. Maybe, after all, it is time for some real lateral thought here. Perhaps Dr Olawadi has a point.'

'This line of discussion will bring us into a wider field than epidemiology,' Dr Fàbregas's rich Catalonian-accented voice gruffed out from beneath a dense black moustache. 'WHO could be supportive of such an expansion in scope *only* on the proviso that it brings a chance to better understand this disease.'

It was Jiang So Cheung's turn to add weight to the growing turmoil. 'We should be mindful of our benefactors here. Perpetua is a major funder of research in so many fields. We would nibble at the hand that feeds us.'

'We would be suggesting that that same hand also *poisons* our people!' Al Waters again. 'As Jiang So intimates, Perpetua have been tireless supporters of all kinds of science across the globe. Even their own Flow Analysis team are given carte blanche backing, unrestrained freedom to do anything they see as relevant. That doesn't sound like the behaviour of a sinister overlord to me.'

'And yet ... and yet ... it is a stone unturned. Or perhaps, more accurately, a boulder.' Pinkerton thumbed his lower lip into his teeth for a few moments. He leaned forward, bracing both hands on the desk in front of him. 'I dare to propose that a single volunteer from this conference takes on an assignment. I simply wish to be assured that Perpetua is not up to anything that we should know more about. I suggest starting with the Flow Analysis team. They are from distinguished scientific backgrounds and may be receptive to a novel hypothesis such as this. I appreciate that our forum may not be unanimous in support of this venture and, frankly, I do not actually expect any positive avenue to open up as a result of it. But I do think we need to rule out the possibility, no matter how crazy it seems. Because it looks to me like crazy is all we have right now. I will take full and personal responsibility for this and, of course, I would ask that complete and total confidentiality is maintained by all attendees today. So, is anyone interested in chasing this particular wild goose?'

Noomi Olawadi walked around the table to stand behind Pinkerton. 'Well, since I brought it up ...'

Chance Encounter

KLINE DRAINED HIS BEER and looked across the table. 'You know, Cradle, nothing beats a pint at the end of the week.' He purposefully banged the empty glass down to underline the point.

Cradle looked at his friend and shook his head affectionately.

'Of course, you might not know much about that until you stop drinking that sugar-free stuff. One day I'm going to make a man out of you boy ...' The last word was delivered in faux deep-South US drawl.

Cradle crushed the empty Zip can and pushed it across the table towards his friend, smiling widely.

'Well, it's a start ...' Kline laughed, 'Next step, half a shandy for the scientist in the corner.'

'One day, Anders, I'm going to come into work smashed off my face. That'll show you.'

'That'd be amazing,' Kline beamed, 'but no you won't.'

'No. I won't.' The two men laughed warmly and simultaneously stood to leave.

'Anything fancy planned this weekend?'

'Not really. Eve and I are looking for a holiday somewhere. She'd like to go away. We'll probably have to do a bit more of that.'

'Cool. Amazing. At last, you're listening to my good advice. I actually don't remember you ever going away! So are you thinking overseas? Europe or somewhere? Australia?'

'Don't know, we're not decided yet. Maybe not so far away.' Cradle shifted his weight uncomfortably. 'You up to anything good?'

'Nope. Just waiting for Monday morning to come round again so I can get back in there. The equipment misses us so.'

'I'd laugh if I thought you were joking. You ought to get a hobby or something.'

'What, like knitting? I could run you up a nice scarf or a woolly hat for the holiday. Then you could go skiing.'

'You know what I mean. A sport?'

'What, with my back?' Kline mocked a stoop and hobbled away from the table. 'Nah, you're alright. I'll see you Monday morning. Give my love to Edith.' Sideways smile.

'Nope, I'm not even rising to that. You too, Anders. I'll just tidy up the debris then, shall I ...?' Cradle put the unimpressively-crushed Zip can into his glass then picked up both glasses, one in each hand, and brought them over to the bar. He heard the door close as Anders Kline left the building. He always liked to bring the glasses back to the bar – leaving them on the table felt asymmetric, incomplete, a loose end. Kline was always telling him that someone was paid to clear up and he's doing them out of a job, but better to close the loop and leave things settled.

'Cheers, mate.' The barman nodded at the returned glasses. He was a giant man, must be over six-four and hefty build. Rugby, maybe, in his earlier years, before he got too fat. His breathing was slightly laboured, and his face bore the signs of being repeatedly battered, nose fattened, eyebrows interrupted by scars, lips roughly curtaining missing teeth. Or maybe boxing. Couldn't see his ears under dishevelled long grey hair, but Cradle expected they would be uglied by years of this imagined pugilistic attrition.

'Hello.'

He turned to see the attractive African women standing next to him at the bar. Her hair was long and curled dramatically onto the shoulders of an expensive-looking green leather jacket. She was taller than he by an inch or so and she smiled warmly. Late twenties. 28 or 29? Not 30 anyway. Faded blue jeans. Heels. Nail varnish.

'Erm, hello?' Quizzically.

'I am sorry, we have not met. My name is Dr Noomi Olawadi. I am from the African Centres for Disease Control and Prevention. I wondered if I could buy you a drink and talk for a few minutes.'

Brown. Eyes. No. Makeup. Not. Necessary.

'Well, I was just going, actually.'

'But this will only take a few minutes, Mr ... um, I am afraid I do not know your surname.'

'Cradle. It's just Cradle.'

'Cradle. OK. And please, you can call me Noo. Just a few minutes? Zip, was it?' The remnants of an accent. Nigerian was it? But English educated, he was sure of that.

'Well, alright, but I have to go soon.'

They sat back at the original table, Olawadi in Kline's seat, Cradle in his own. She sipped a small Guinness and explained. 'So yes, I am from the CDC in Africa. I am part of an international task force looking into the Drowse disease. CDC and the World Health Organisation are, of course, extremely concerned about the situation and are pursuing every avenue of medical research. But I am working on a very specific topic.'

She took another small sip and licked the foam from her upper lip. He quickly looked down at the table.

'But what does that have to do with me?' Eye contact re-established.

Olawadi took out her ID and pushed it across the table. 'To help you be assured.'

Cradle took up the card and checked the picture.

'Very old school.' he remarked. These days everyone presented ID by linking microTabs. Nothing to carry around.

'An ID card works everywhere, even the few places 'Tabbing has not reached.' That smile again.

It was certainly her holo, maybe a couple of years old now but definitely her. CDC crest woven into the image. Very difficult to forge but he wanted to be more thorough than that. He swiped the card over his 'Tab and searched her details. They came up immediately. Impressive résumé too. Abuja-born, daddy successful in the old oil business, privately educated, medicine at Oxford, epidemiology specialism, several acclaimed research papers, a dozen patents. 28 years old. Good guess.

'OK, Dr Olawadi. You are who you say you are.'

'Noo, please.'

'Noo.' He couldn't help but be intrigued. A beautiful woman turns up in his local with an official ID and wants to chat. Turns out to be a high-flying name too.

OK. Why not. 'How can I help?'

'Well, this is all very tentative, there is no body of evidence. I must ask you about something that could be quite contentious. So I ask for your confidentiality.'

'Let's see what this is about. I don't know.'

'Yes. That is fair enough. So I have to trust you.'

She looked at Cradle. The intensity transfixed him, and he was unable to draw away. She held eye contact for a few seconds and the background blurred around her face. Was that a few seconds or ten minutes?

'We have exhausted all current epidemiological expertise and yet still have no sensible theory as to the cause of the disease Drowse. So we now have to think more laterally. Clutch a straw, if you will.'

She shifted in her chair, leaning forward conspiratorially, whispering.

'A few months ago, I noticed that the first recorded case of Drowse seemed to coincide with Persistence.'

He frowned slightly, still unable to break away from her gaze.

'It's probably nothing but would you say there is anything suspicious going on at Perpetua?'

Too True

'You're a bit late, Cradle. Everything OK?' Eve called through from the kitchen. They usually cooked together whenever they could, but Eve had started and the smell of grilling cheese and pepperoni wafted through to the hall. They often ate pizza on a Friday, a little prize for making it through another week.

'Yeah, sorry. I had a drink with a foreign supermodel.' Ah.

Eve's head appeared around the doorway.

'I'm sorry, I thought you said something about having a drink with a supermodel there ...'

'Well, no, she's not a supermodel. She's an epidemiologist. Stunning looking though.' No idea.

'Cradle.' Eve came out into the hallway. 'Sometimes you could soften things up a bit you know. I could get jealous. Most people wouldn't take that without a fight!'

'What? Oh yeah, I see. Sorry. Too direct? What I mean is, this pretty woman I'd never seen before came up to me in the pub and bought me a drink and asked me to talk with her for a bit.' Absolutely no idea.

'Oh well, that makes all the difference! So, she was attractive then?'

'Oh yeah, very.' Christ.

'Cradle! Nicer than me?' A bit tongue in cheek, but slightly hurt despite that.

'Taller than you, Eve. Dark hair, expensive clothes, sexy but classy.' Honestly, absolutely no idea at all.

'Grrr, Cradle!' Eve went back into the kitchen and clattered a few things together to emphasise the point a bit. Cradle hung his coat and walked through.

'So how was your day?'

'Oh, you know,' a bit more clattering, 'one of the young registrars asked me out for dinner and sex on Monday night.'

'God, that's unprofessional. You should report that.'

'Cradle, you are so infuriating sometimes! Of course that didn't happen, but how do you think I feel hearing about you chatting up some girl in a pub like it's just what everyone does? I know it's nothing but ... Oh, I don't know. I just don't like it, that's all!'

'Oh, Eve.' He took her hands and pulled her close. 'Nobody else is you. It's us. It's only ever been us. It was just work. Kind of.'

She turned her face to look at him. 'Kind of?'

'Yeah, sort of. About Perpetua. And about Drowse.'

'So I'm nicer than a supermodel, right?'

'Well, which one do you mean in particular?'

He puffed out an exaggerated wheeze at Eve's playful stomach punch.

They cut the pizza and took it through to the lounge.

'So what did she want, then?'

'Her name is Dr Noomi Olawadi, she works for the African CDC and she's looking into the causes of Drowse.'

'But why was she talking to you?'

'Well, Noo said she's been given special responsibility for a covert investigation.'

'*Noo*?' through pizza crust.

'Yeah. She's investigating whether Drowse could be somehow linked to Persistence. All hush-hush. So she wanted to talk to me about things at Perpetua: whether anything odd is happening at the moment.'

Eve looked across the table, directly at Cradle.

'I didn't tell her anything, but it obviously made me think about the Flow energy. We've never had so much energy pouring out from one single point in the world and, of course, nobody really understands where it's all coming from anyway. Maybe there is actually some sort of link between Perpetua and Drowse.'

'But that can't be right, Cradle. Perpetua is pouring millions into Drowse research. Why would they do that if they are somehow involved? Anyway, how would that work? All those people across the world.'

'I know. But maybe it doesn't care about distance. Maybe it can affect people right across the planet and maybe Perpetua is tagging it so they can check where it's going. Somehow.'

'It just sounds like a conspiracy theory to me.'

'Well, it could be, yeah. But what if it wasn't? What if the reason why they can't find a cure for Drowse is because it's not actually a disease? Maybe it's poisoning or some sort of radiation? Noo's got the World Health Organisation behind her, albeit in secret.'

'What are you saying, Cradle? We both get cred by Perpetua. I'm worried where this might go.'

'I know, I know. But I've got to check it out now, Eve, see? Look, Noo thinks Hornbill might be linked to Drowse and I might be able to prove or disprove it. I've got to find the answer, even more than before. It's in me now.'

Eve stood up and looked incredulously at him. 'Invisible patterns in energy and an exotic, sexy conspiracy theorist? Of course. It makes all the sense in the world! You are James Bond, after all.'

'I know it sounds mad. But I have to go after proof, one way or another. You can see that, right?'

Eve stood and walked away from her chair and stood between the open shutters, looking out onto the street below. It was dark and a lone streetlamp coloured the pavement at the front of the flats.

'Yeah, I know you, Cradle. Nothing I could do or say would stop you now, I know. But please just be really careful, that's all I'm saying.'

'I will be careful. I'm always careful.'

It must have been the streetlamp's diffuse light that produced the subtle aura about her, with the gentle wave of her body's outline subtly suggested by the faint silhouette through her dress. Cradle stood beside Eve and entwined the fingers of his left hand with hers.

'God, Eve, you're beautiful. I love you so much.' He gently brushed her hair with his right hand. She partially turned and smiled at him, brighter than all the streetlamps in the world. She faced him and her mouth opened slightly as their lips touched while the room disappeared.

'So you don't think the lovely *Noo* is nicer than me then?' Eve whispered as she slowly unbuttoned his shirt. 'Well, Mr bigshot secret agent, I want some proof too.'

Tag!

Cradle awoke and forced one eye open. The alert from his 'Tab nagged 02.17. He slid out from beneath Eve's embrace and pulled the duvet up around her, then dark-walked into the lounge. Sure enough, his Wafer was flashing, he hadn't merely imagined the ping. Message waiting: *Download complete.* Hang on. Got to be properly awake for this.

He hated washing Eve from his skin. It felt like a betrayal, a lie told behind closed doors, a selfish breaking of an intimate trust. But he could sleep no more and needed a fresh beginning. He stepped into the shower and ran the warm water over his body, gradually sensing things outside of himself. Eve asleep down the hall. Their night together, their love. The water. The smell of the soap. The tiles. The taps. The extraordinary returning to the ordinary. The towel. The door. The hallway. The lounge. The Wafer. *Download complete.*

He gestured the message open and studied the contents. A linked list of over 800 files, the full log of his

Level 1 Vetoed DREAM session. Raw data, complex and meaningless in this form, but entirely and completely eloquent with the right visualisation.

But how to look at such a thing? He recalled the session, the trapping of knots, the three frames repeated. In there somewhere, all of it, hidden, disguised. He had sensed it once in DREAM. He could find it again. Find the knots, feel the loops. He stared at the screen as the numbers scrolled before him, seeing not the individual digits as they blurred past but the light of them; the essence of them. Random noise, an indiscriminate digital clamour, white and white and white again, on and on, endless and eternal. Beautiful and perfect, tedious and hopeless.

He broke away and stopped the data run. Regaining focus, he noticed the 'Tab time. 03.32.

'Rats! An hour wasted.' The words hissed quietly from his lips.

Coffee.

'Yeah, Coffee.'

The machine sputtered the caffeine into Cradle's mug. He added one sugar and stirred three times clockwise, five anticlockwise, then two more clockwise. As always. Subconsciously. Consciously, he thought about the data stream. The DREAM data outside of DREAM.

The DREAM data outside of DREAM? What was he thinking? Half the world's processing power had been harnessed to gather that data and here was he, one man and a Wafer, trying to decipher it. Idiotic. Naive in the extreme. What a fool.

Yet ... and yet ... There was that itch. Inside somewhere. That familiar feeling of something about to happen, something inevitable in his actions. A fearful thing, but not fear. A compulsion – yes, that was closer – driving and directing his course. Not looking and thinking; beyond that somewhere. Feeling, instinct. Like a child. Trusting.

He put the mug down, unsipped, and went back to the Wafer.

'Private avatar mode. Anna, please help me.'

The Wafer switched into Anna avatar mode.

<hello cradle>

'Hi. Run that set again please, Anna. Visual.'

<running visual>

The data run restarted, streaming over the Wafer. He closed his eyes in the darkness and waited, breathing very low and easy. He became unaware of Anna, the Wafer, the seat, the room, and he focused solely on himself. The display gently assaulted his eyelids with a minuscule cascade of photons. Not properly visible, yet that paucity itself modulated in harmony with the flow of the data. He sat with his hands held forward, poised to tag the stream, mantis-like, coiled and ready.

Nothing. Noise, just noise.

Nothing – nothing – nothing – nothing. On and on relentlessly.

Somnambulistic but sensitised. Trancelike, he carried on, as unperturbed as the data itself.

Nothing – nothing – nothing – nothing ...

Nothing – nothing – nothing – nothing ...

Un-nothing! TAG!

Nothing – nothing – nothing – nothing ...

... ...

Nothing – nothing – nothing – nothing ...

Something! TAG!

Nothing – nothing – nothing – nothing ...

... ...

Nothing – nothing – nothing – nothing ...

And again! TAG!

The stream stopped.

<run complete cradle. you placed 3 tags>

'Save to my 'Tab please, Anna.'

<done>

Utterly exhausted where he sat, eyes still closed, Cradle slept, breathing still slow and easy. Deeper now though.

'Oh, Cradle! You been up all night again, sweetie?'

Eve kissed his cheek and he yawned.

'I'm blind,' he cried, melodramatically patting his face.

'They're still closed, you idiot. You won't see anything through closed eyes.'

He opened his eyes and smiled up at this woman who stood precisely at the centre of his world.

'Actually, Eve, I beg to differ.'

Sigma

Eve was out for coffee and lunch at a friend's so Cradle knew he had most of Saturday to carry on with the search.

Perpetua logged the Flow data one hundred times per second, day in, day out, without end. Twenty-five billion samples, each containing nearly two hundred parameters, and each of those recorded with 140-byte precision, designed to resolve Planck-scale fluctuations. The three tagged file locations were there, safe and sound, overlaid against the vast seven hundred terabyte log spanning nearly eight years of Flow data.

Now Cradle had to search for the pattern that he thought he could feel at each of the tagged locations. He gestured his local analyser onto each of the data locations, setting it running with scope plus/minus one day.

The report was rapid to arrive. No significant correlations.

'Hmm.' He expanded the scope to one week. Again, nothing significant.

'Where are you ...?'

He observed the full extent of the data. His tags were equally separated within the data. He checked this with the analyser. Yes, they were exactly periodic to within 0.4%. Pretty good for manual tagging. Crudely, the first tagged point was fifteen months after the start of the log, the second at forty-six months, the third at seventy-seven months. Once every thirty-one months.

'OK, so you're evenly spaced. But what are you?'

He set the scope to thirty-one months. This would take a while, but why not?

Almost two hours elapsed with the Wafer continuously passing its status directly to Cradle. These extended analyses always made the skin above his 'Tab slightly numb. It was a feeling he had come to think of as comforting, knowing he was at one with, yet in control of, a small part of the complex mathematical universe.

He sat with eyes closed, breathing shallow, motionless until the result jumped into his consciousness. He gestured it open. There it was. A shadowy fingerprint, periodic over thirty-one months. No detail could be distinguished, except that it snaked beneath a cowl of noise along eight billion samples, entirely repeating again twice between months fifteen and seventy-seven, then starting again for a third time before being interrupted by the end of the database.

'Gotcha.' He gestured the sensitivity to maximum, targeted directly at one of the cycles. Should be quicker, more directed this time.

Run again.

Slowly inhale, gently exhale, in, out, in, out, cycling, repeating, all the time the gentle prickling sensation in the back of his hand easing him into that state of semiconsciousness where he loved to be.

Three hours this time. Surprising – it should have been shorter. Must be deeper than he thought. Only one parameter of significance, a variation of the Flow's standard deviation over time. Can that be right? It was well known that the Flow output was different to black body radiation. Instead, it comprised radiation over a very wide range of infrared wavelengths indicative of the nature of the hyperplasma toroid, but gently shaped by the natural resonances of the tokamak itself. A count of these photons gave the Flow's characteristic a very slightly bell-curved distribution of frequency, with some middle wavelengths being marginally stronger than others. The standard deviation measured the amount by which the Flow wavelength deviated from the main central peak, a gauge of the width of the Gaussian curve often referred to as sigma: the smaller the sigma, the narrower the curve – the 'peakier' it was. The Flow was known to have an enormous sigma, corresponding to the extremely flat wideband nature of its emissions, and this value had always been assumed to be invariant. There had never been any evidence that it fluctuated in anything other than a short-term random fashion, statistically insignificant. Cradle was not sure if anyone had ever even thought about it.

But there it was. The Flow sigma was being modulated over a thirty-one-month period – that was now indisputable. He checked the modulation depth. Miniscule. Right on the limit of the sample resolution; it was almost undetectable. Spread out over such a long time and having such a low amplitude, the pattern was virtually invisible, beautifully camouflaged beneath a mist of random noise and repeating far too slowly to be apparent. A perfect disguise.

'Wow, somebody certainly put some thought into this one.'

Cradle backed up the file to his 'Tab and gestured the analyser to search for repeats within the cycle.

'Let's see if you have any structure in there.' He had felt this in DREAM when he first sensed the sequences, instinctively feeling that there was something finer, more detailed, somewhere within the sample and he was aware that this kind of thing could mean the presence of embedded data; the constituent parts of a message. If he was right, then these periodic disturbances would appear frequently and regularly, so the analyser should have no problem isolating them.

He went to audio commands. 'Formulate prototype for coherently spaced data patterns or formatting. Link vocal as Anna, please.'

The Wafer connected itself with his 'Tab and began interacting directly with the temporal lobe of his brain. He experienced this as a human voice. Anna's voice. Anna's character. Not mainframe though. Local – his very own Anna.

<hello cradle/ this will take a few moments>

The silence of the connection seemed enormous as he waited.

<i can confirm the presence of pattern timing to a probability of 98%/ the sample is highly correlated with binary representation with no data framing or header implementation/ there is insufficient information to decode this data>

'Good work, Anna. How many data blocks in each period?'

<multiple answers/ the total data length is 3,447,925 bits>

'Only 3.5 million bits in thirty-one months? Are you sure that's right?'

<98% probability of model accuracy cradle/ thats yes>

The sarcasm programming again. It was a nice touch.

'Very good, Anna. Could you analyse these, please? I'm looking for recognisable tokens. Geometrical shapes or characters, scripts, lines.'

<analysing/ estimated processing time one hour>

Cradle dozed, catching up with some of his lost sleep. After fifty-eight minutes he was awoken by Anna's voice.

<complete/ only one of the permutations provides contiguous tokens of the types specified/ they appear to be graphical rather than alphanumeric/ there are 13 blocks each of dimension 515 x 515 bits>

'What are they, images maybe? Can you visualise this for me please, Anna? Let's try black 0, white 1.'

<yes cradle/ request coupling to visual cortex>

'Go ahead, Anna.'

The thirteen images appeared before him, scrolling top to bottom. Strange glyph-like renderings. Circles, lines and squares, some repeated, some combined to make more complex forms. Incomprehensible. Secure. The perfect energy tagging system. Cradle saved the images locally to his 'Tab. Precious, dangerous cargo.

'Anna, please irrevocably purge the session record for today. Maximum security.'

<confirm irrevocable purge of all records for today>

'Confirmed.'

<done>

He needed to talk to Kline about this. It was too big for one person to think about.

Coffee

THE COFFEE SHOP WAS always bustling on Saturday mornings and they waited twenty minutes to get a small table in the far corner, dark and dingy, away from the windows and near the toilets. Cradle could never understand why people wanted to come here to be this uncomfortable, too hot and crowded in with strangers. Better to be at home where the water was more familiar.

Kline drained his coffee and looked again at the images from Cradle's 'Tab.

'This is totally off record from FA, right? No chance of LineSec sniffing us out on this?'

'No, it's OK. I was in isolation mode throughout and I max-purged the session too. My 'Tab is the only copy of this.'

'Cool. Well, this all looks pretty strange to me. Thirteen of them as well, a prime number. Always handy when you're hiding something in plain sight. Cryptography. I bet there are primes all over these patterns too. I see a seventeen in the fourth one straight away. Bit small for encryption though, that's usually much bigger numbers. You checked for primes?'

'Not yet. I'll run it.' Cradle gestured the 'Tab into analysis mode and whispered, 'Locate prime numbers in image dataset.'

He looked back up at Kline. 'Have you ever seen anything like this before, Anders?'

'Nope. Maybe something like an old visual crypto. You seen them? Two random-looking snowy pictures. Put one on top of the other and, hey presto, you see the message. Could try logically overlaying them all, see if anything leaps out.'

'Or maybe it's simply a fixed pattern to just imprint the energy flow, rather than anything deeper than that. Just a tag, as we thought.'

'Yeah, but why have it make pictures? And different ones at that. Someone's gone out of their way to make it like this. Can't be accidental. It has to be something more than just tagging.'

'What then? A message? A story? Come on, Anders, who would want to do that?'

'Someone who didn't want their message or story read. At least not by the wrong people. And if it is a message then we're going to need someone who specialises in this sort of stuff. It's like some sort of hieroglyphics.'

'What, like an Egyptologist?'

Kline looked up at the corner of the room, pinning his concentration on the right angle as usual, as he let his mind grapple with the options around this new problem. Then came the expected sharp intake of breath through the nostrils, and the familiar three little coughs. Ten seconds passed and the corner remained stoic in its support of Kline's meditation.

'I have an old friend we can trust.' Kline leaned in closer to Cradle. 'Graphical Linguistics. Like an Egyptologist. I'll give her a shout.'

Cradle's 'Tab nagged and he opened the report. Confirmation of prime numbers all over the place throughout the pattern. All the first fifty primes were present, either macroscopically in the pattern itself or beneath, in the encoding. He showed it to Kline.

'There you go, Cradle. Someone's gone to a lot of trouble here. Not only is it hidden in a hell of a lot of noise, but the careful use of all those primes has got to mean something too. Man, this is getting way more interesting.'

Kline gestured his 'Tab to comms mode and messaged Julie Clayden, *'Hey Jules, got a nice little riddle for you. Fancy a beer?'*

Almost immediately the response came.

'Anders, long time no see. Sounds intriguing. Where can we meet up?'

Dangerous Cargo

Julie Clayden surveyed Kline's kitchen. A small mountain of washing-up queuing for the dishwasher, the steel sink dulled with limescale from lack of regular cleaning, numerous beer bottles awaiting recycling with infinite patience.

Her red-brown hair was tied in a tight bun with a few errant wisps escaping their shackles and spilling onto her face. She was tall, slender and elegant, with deep, slightly underslept eyes, high cheeks and a gently aquiline nose.

'I really like what you've done with the old place, Anders.'

Kline smiled sheepishly and made some space at the dining surface. 'Well, I've been pretty busy. Work and stuff.'

He gestured the Wafer to life and brought up the image dataset. 'Here you go, Jules. This is what we have.'

'Right, so let's take them one at a time. I'll just shout out my thoughts and see where we get.' Clayden opened the first image and maximised it so they could all see the details.

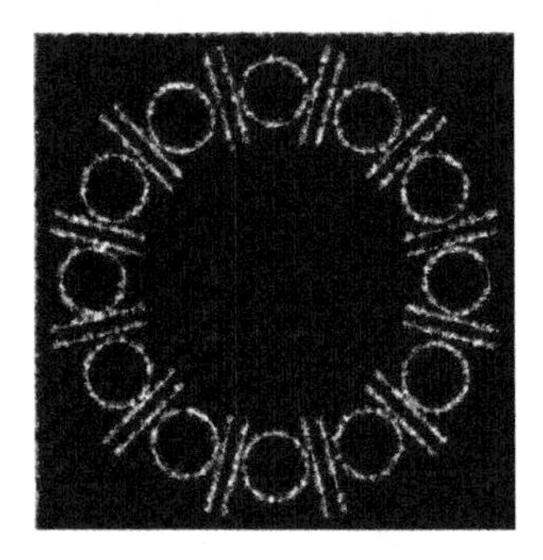

'OK, I see symmetry, lots of it. 12 circles, and 24 lines. Could be a clock of some sort? Next.'

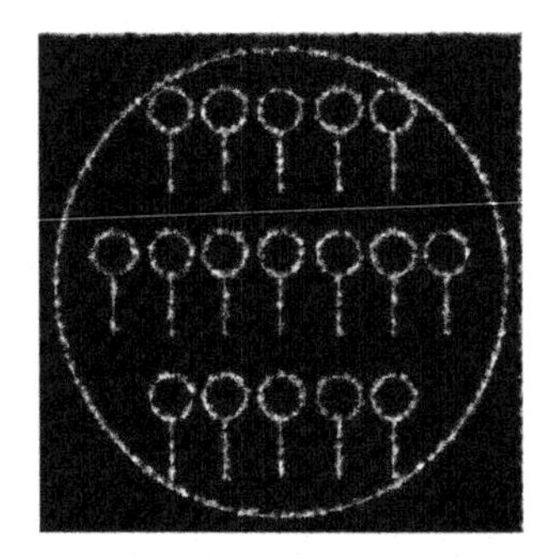

'18 circles and 17 lines. Stick people in a circle? A group of people. Next one.'

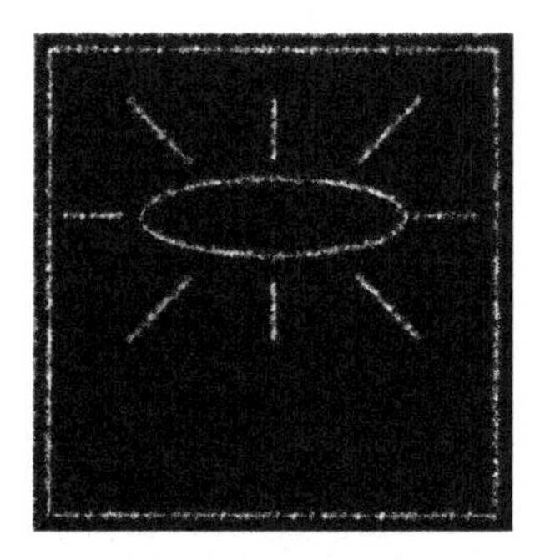

'Ah, that's a common image. Usually means sun. And again.'

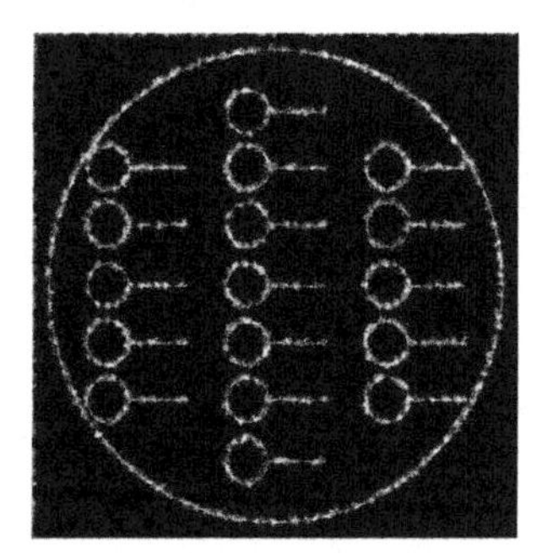

'Similar to number two but rotated. Maybe the stick people are lying down here. Could mean night-time. Let's see where it goes.'

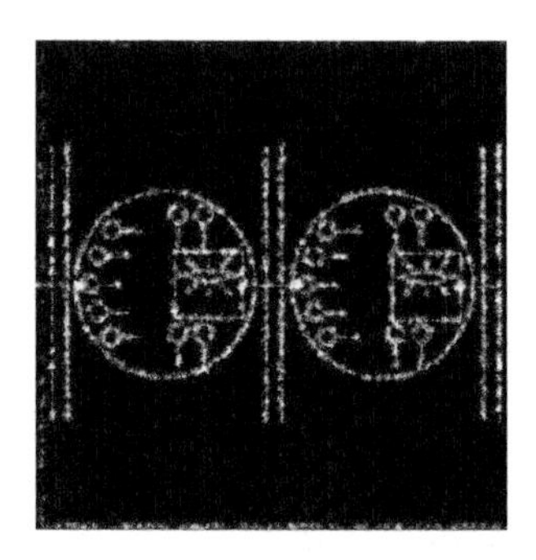

'Whoa, complicated. But using elements from the previous glyphs ... Suns, people, maybe day and night. Oh, and some faint lines with dots in there. Linking? Erm, let's say it's daytime for one group of people and the sun links to another group's night-time. Could be something like the cycle of day and night. Someone's day is another's night? Different time zones? It'd tie in with the clock structure from glyph one if that's right.'

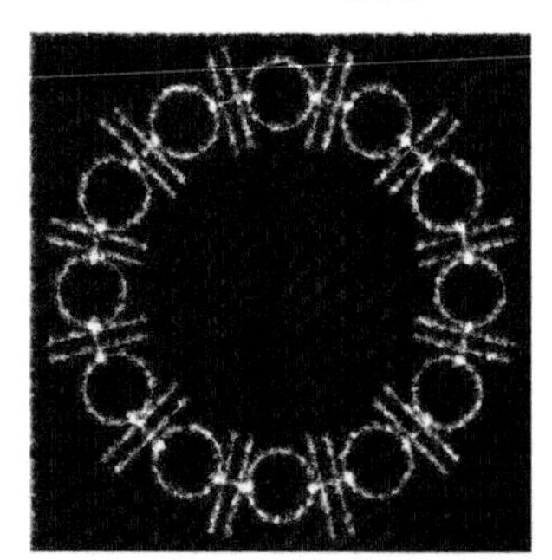

'OK, very similar to number one. Just modified with dots and links. Not sure. This kind of evolution is usually the sign of a basic storyline.'

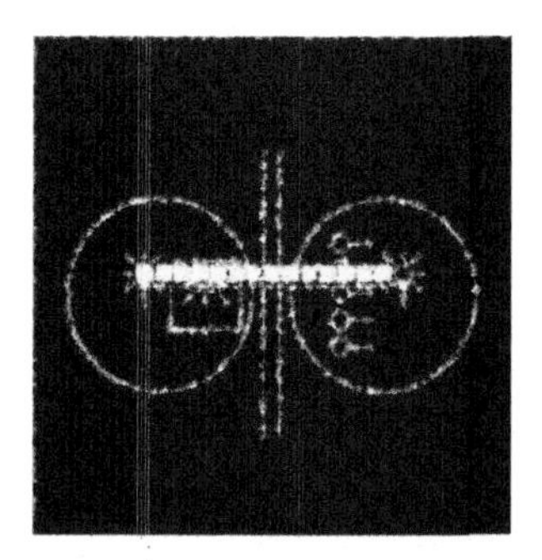

'Oh ho, what's this? Something new. Is it joining or sending? Sun linking to night-time stick people somehow. Something special about these new stick people though. They're more important than the others. Leading individuals within each group.'

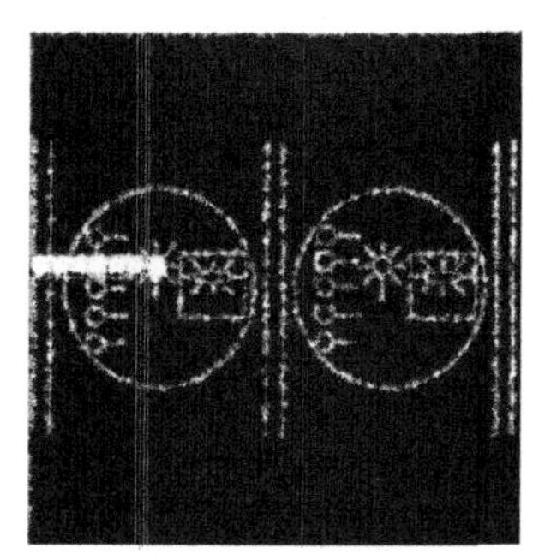

'Same kind of idea in this one, different viewpoint.'

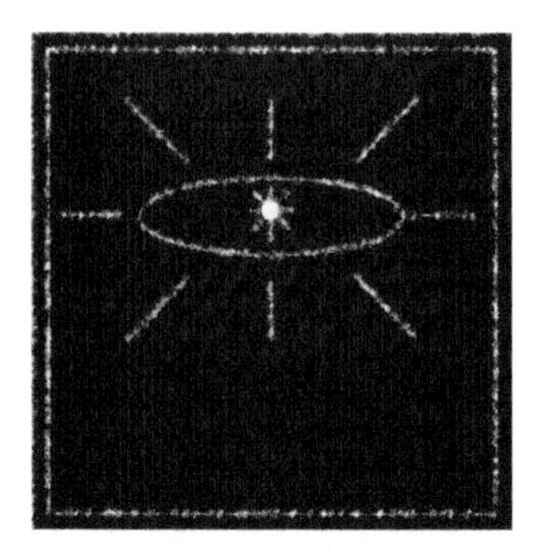

'The sun with an important stick man. Could be a god.'

'Erm ... Empty box. Nothing.'

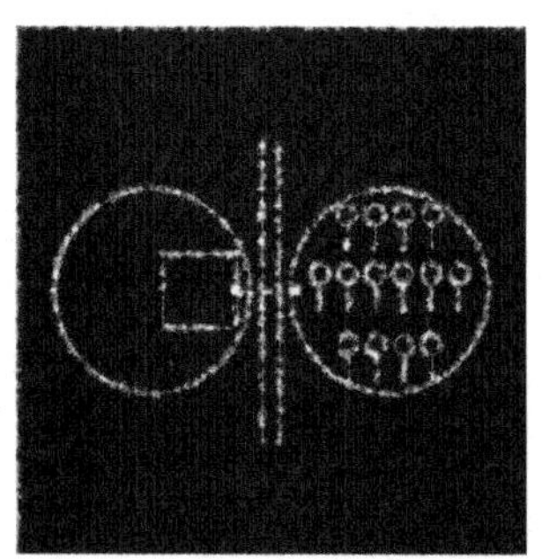

'Empty box and stick people. Actually, I'm now thinking the thin line with dots could definitely mean a physical connection of some sort. And the white train of blocks in seven and eight might mean some sort of transference. Let's go with that for now.'

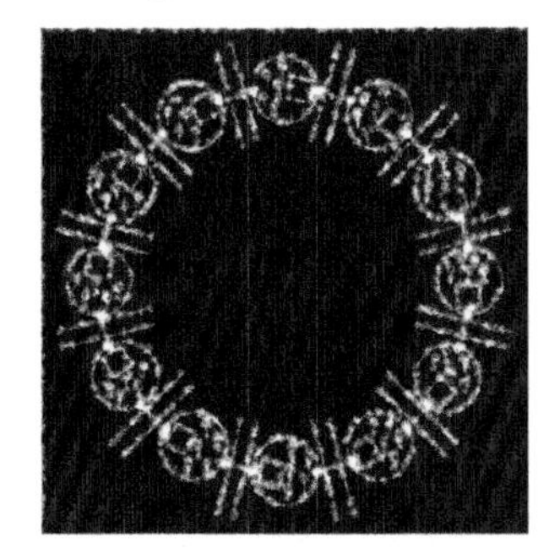

'Hmm, pretty messy. Hard to see much of the detail here. I think I can make out the daytime stick people and empty boxes all connected up on the clock. When there's no sun, everyone sleeps? Not sure. Next one.'

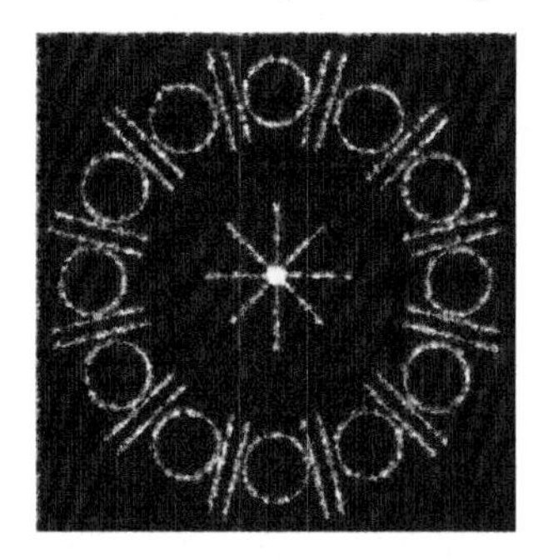

'Back to the beginning but with a sun in the middle. Symmetry, perhaps. Restoration, maybe? Wow. There's a lot going on here.'

'So what do you reckon, Jules? Interesting enough for you?' Kline swept his open hand over the final image.

'Well, yes, it's definitely interesting. Obviously, they're modern renditions, being digitally rendered and all that, but the style itself certainly doesn't resemble anything ancient either, nothing like Greek or Egyptian glyphs. I don't recognise it at all: too literal. The old boys used to allow themselves a fair amount of slack in their symbols, but these are quite precise. Modern. They're pretty messy too: noisy. Needs some cleaning up and sharpening to be sure about the detail. But you haven't told me where this is from. A bit of background or context would really help.'

'Sorry, Jules. Can't tell you that.' He looked across the table to Cradle. 'Bit too hot to reveal sources.'

'Hmm, what are you two up to? OK then, I'm going to need to take it away and work on it to get anywhere. You've got no other examples that I could cross-refer to? Don't suppose you have a similar message in a different language by any chance?'

'Sorry again, Jules, there's nothing. It's unique,' Kline smiled, 'no chance of a Rosetta Stone with this one.'

'OK. Longshot.' She smiled at Kline. 'Worked for Champollion.'

'Any early impressions though, Julie?' Cradle had naively hoped for an instant solution although, deep down, he knew it was very unlikely.

'Only very top level. It has structure and evolution so yes, I do agree it could be a story. And I think it could be about suns and gods and people, linking together with some sort of transfer. And time or cycle is in the mix too somewhere. If it were ancient, I'd say it's something akin to the story of gods working together to move the sun around the world, causing daytime and night-time to cycle through the various societies on Earth. But that's only an early shot at it from this first impression. Just knee-jerk. It might turn out to mean something completely different once I get into it more. Going to take me a lot more gin-soaked nights to get some of the details ironed out, properly connect it all up. But this kind of token-based linguistics is notoriously prone to misinterpretation, so I'm not going to commit on how it'll end up.'

Cradle glanced at Kline, unable to completely hide his disappointment. 'It might just be about the cycle of days? But why would that be hidden away so deeply amongst all the ...'

Kline interrupted, 'Hold on, Cradle, we don't want to get Jules snarled up in this any more than necessary. Why don't we let her take the images away and do her detective stuff?'

'Yes, I can definitely get you a more coherent interpretation of the story but I'll need a couple of weeks. Bit of old-fashioned digging before I let the computers have a crack at threading some logic through it.'

'Yeah, OK, sorry.' Cradle withdrew slightly into his seat. 'That would be great. Thanks, Julie.'

'But is there really nothing you can say about where these came from? I mean are they written on something, stored somewhere or encrypted beneath something? It's quite important because it gives me a context to work from. You used the word "hidden", Cradle.'

Cradle met Kline's gaze. It said *I'll take this*.

'OK Jules, I'm going to have to be really cagey here though. Cradle found these tucked away amongst a very large set of data, really deeply encoded in a way nobody else apart from him would have even thought of. He's a bit odd that way.' Cradle smiled at the table. 'We thought it was going to turn out to be a kind of a label carried by something, maybe as a device to protect it from theft but, when he decoded the symbols and they looked like more than a simple label, we were thrown. Hence the call.'

'Interesting. OK, I understand you can't tell me who, but can you tell me what it was that was carrying these glyphs? Like where you found them?'

'Can't, Jules. Same thing. This could be linked to some pretty high-level stuff.'

'OK, I'll give it a shot. But you're not giving me much here, boys. Let me have ten days and we'll speak again, alright?'

'You're a star, Jules. But keep it tight. Only you. Owe you a drink.'

'I'll hold you to that.' Clayden rose to leave and Kline stood too.

'Let me show you out.'

She shook Cradle's hand and he watched as the two of them walked to the door, kissed quickly on the lips, and parted. Kline held the door ajar and waved as a pod drew up directly outside and then Julie Clayden was gone.

'She's the best,' Kline said as he rejoined Cradle. He seemed a little distant.

'Old friend? On the lips, Anders?'

'Shut up, Cradle'.

Suki

'Eve, it's Jimmy.'

Eve blinked her eyes, trying to focus on her 'Tab time. 3.56 a.m. She held her Wafer in one hand, sweeping her hair away from her face with the other.

'Jimmy. Hi, what's up?'

'Yeah, sorry to call, I guess it's night there. Wasn't thinking. It's Suki. I didn't know who else to talk to.'

'That's OK. What's wrong?'

'She got back yesterday afternoon from Hong Kong and was really flaked out. Not jet lag though, more than the usual. She just fell asleep on me in the kitchen, so I let her sleep right through 'til late this morning. Tried to wake her but she couldn't get up. Hardly even lift her arms. Sorry ...' Eve heard the sound muffle slightly and some quiet sobbing away from the interface. 'Sorry, Sis.'

'What's happened with Suki now, Jimmy?' She almost didn't want to ask.

'Called the doctor and he admitted her straight away. She's in Beverly Hospice in Montebello. I just got back from the admissions wing. She's stable but weak, but I'm not allowed to visit her.'

'Oh Jimmy, I'm so sorry.' Eve's heart sank.

'They won't let me see her, Eve.'

'I know, Jimmy, it's really tough. But that's just normal procedure to help protect her from any possible infection. We still don't really understand what Drowse is so they just take every precaution. Once Suki's acclimatised to the system they'll let you vidchat. It takes a few days to get everything sorted and stabilised.'

'What shall I do though? I can't just sit here. How long will she be in for?'

'I know. It's hard to say. Did admissions tell you anything at all?'

'Just that she's in the best place and they'll contact me with Suki's status in a few days. It's like she's just disappeared.' More muffled sounds.

'Try not to worry, Jimmy. Suki's in the best hands, they'll make her comfortable and make sure she has everything she needs. It'd be too hard to do that yourself at home. I know it's really difficult, but it's for the best.' Eve could hardly believe she was repeating sentences from her training to her own brother.

'Yeah, I know, Eve. I know you're right. I guess we're lucky that more of us haven't got it yet. But I miss her and it's only been a few hours. I don't know how to do this.'

'One day at a time, Jimmy, that's how. You just carry on. Suki will be looked after properly and eventually they'll find a cure and then she'll be back with you.' Right thing to say. Might not be true.

'Yeah. Thanks, Sis. They know what they're doing, right?'

'Absolutely.' Right thing to say. Almost certainly not true.

'OK. Thanks. Yeah, OK. Thanks, Eve, you're a rock.'

'Do you need anything? Can we help out somehow? You could fly over and stay with us if you like.'

'No that's fine thanks, Sis. Too far away. I'll stick here in case they say I can see her or do something to help.'

'And how are you feeling? Apart from the obvious?'

'Well, yeah, I'm scared and worried. But I'm OK, I haven't got it. I feel fine.'

'So you have to be Suki's strength now.'

'Yeah. I can be that. That's good. I can do that. Sorry, Eve, I didn't even ask, are you and Cradle alright?'

'Yes, we're fine. He's chasing around trying to crack that thing you helped him with. Loves a puzzle does my man.'

A faint digital buzzing on the line disappeared. She hadn't even noticed it until the sound clarified slightly.

'Jimmy, you still there? Did you hear something?'

'Nothing this end, Sis. Loud and clear. Give Cradle my love, and thanks for listening. You really helped.'

'OK, probably just my imagination. Getting paranoid. You're sure you'll be OK? Just link us if you need anything. And give Suki our love when you get to see her. And don't worry, it'll be soon.'

'Cool. Thanks again, Sis. Love you.'

'Love you too. Take care.'

Eve terminated the link and slid the Wafer onto the table. The first family member down. Christ, what a mess.

Glyphs

Julie Clayden sat back from her Wafer and sipped her drink. The ice was mostly melted so she crunched the remaining crystals and swallowed the cold liquid down. Gin and tonic, true to her word, although night had long since broken into a rainy autumnal morning and then to an overcast afternoon. She was bone-tired from sitting for too long so she stretched herself and strode about her study a little.

On three walls of the room were shelves crammed floor to ceiling with actual-paper books, very old-school but she always felt a stronger connection with history when she could hold it in her hand. Wall lighting spilt subdued illumination over these numerous tomes, myriad complex shadows casting across their spines, the whole resembling an old oil painting of a library somewhere in Renaissance Europe. This was the home of an intense academic, a single person able to totally immerse themselves in study without having to negotiate someone else's feelings or obligations. Everything in its place, although seemingly chaotic to the outsider. Clayden kept a detailed mental map of where everything belonged, thus creating her own private version of tidy.

Open on her desk, next to the Wafer, were three ageing textbooks: a dog-eared and ragged early twentieth-century leather-bound copy of Frazer's 'The Golden Bough', an equally thumbed 1976 Goodman's 'Languages of Art', and Rasmussen's 'Symbol and Interpretation' from 1974, spines all well creased and pages hand-annotated from years of reference. Ancient and trusted friends, repeatedly called into service in the day-to-day course of Clayden's trade. Imprints of the Perpetua glyphs lay on various individual sheets of paper, scattered over the desk and inscribed with temporary interpretations, crossed out and discarded multiple times, around and around, searching for coherence amongst hypothetical designations. Her style of working was often discounted by her peers as being rather eccentric and antiquated, using a sort of cultural 'feel' in favour of pure technological grunt, then effectively getting the AI supercores to simply mark her work. Impossible to do without a significant body of personal experience, of course – there was no real mysticism at play – but it was, nevertheless, highly unusual, even amongst her elder colleagues.

It must have been a million years ago when Kline was with her in Egypt. Those few heady months together in the humidity of the Nile Delta, the fertile greenery crowding around Tell el-Samara, 87 miles north of Cairo, where painstaking excavations on this most ancient of Egyptian settlements had been underway for decades. Beneath the remains of the village, and therefore potentially predating the Great Pyramids of Giza by three to four thousand years, stone tablets were discovered, their relief still sharply discernible despite lying for millennia under dust and decay. Predominantly intact, the tablets lay some three metres below the ruins of the Neolithic village, dozens of them all neatly positioned side by side.

At 27, Clayden was the youngest team member by far, her niche postgraduate thesis on the lexical transformation between Mayan and Egyptian glyphs bringing her front and centre at the graphical linguistics top table, despite her inexperience in the field. The tablets were beautiful, simplistic, and unique, and the world awaited their translation.

They met in the year of her final dissertation, Kline joining Clayden and two other students in a spacious four-bedroomed city flat-share in London. He was already qualified and taking a year out, doing virtually nothing as far as she could tell, financed by a small inheritance to which he had no hang-ups about setting fire. He was tall, passably handsome and funny, and she warmed to him immediately. She liked his smile; he had good teeth and easy eyes. Over a period of several months, they combined their rooms and spent all their spare time together. When the Egypt gig came up there had never really been any discussion. Kline just came with her and there they were.

The tablets were expressed in a completely unknown style of hieroglyph, unconnected to any other Egyptian datum: they were baffling and exquisitely exciting in equal measure. Like history had been snipped off at ground level and discarded, with no connection to what came after. She had set to work under the guidance of elder academics, adhering to the standard process, checking for knowns, eliminating unknowns, and cross-referencing existing or similar symbols and inscriptions. But every avenue was a cul-de-sac; every door firmly shut. There appeared to be no extant knowledge upon which to build, not a single giant's shoulders to stand on.

Clayden retreated into the backrooms of the Cairo Museum offices, surrounding herself with images of the tablets and with dusty tomes of obscure research, locked away in isolation. She declined the repeated offers of access to the world's most powerful computer systems. She ignored the numerous approaches for collaboration, opportunities for spin-off research papers and requests for interim reports. Ostensibly, she simply closed her office door in the morning and then emerged again at night. But within those walls, for hour upon hour, day upon day, she doodled, mumbled and scratched at paper, gradually forging pathways in her mind that had not been there when she first arrived in Cairo. New ways of thinking. Fresh angles. Gut feel.

With no clue where to begin and having virtually no interaction with Clayden, the rest of the academic team fell away over the first couple of months, leaving only Kline, who walked with her to the museum office every day in the crisp shadows of early morning and patiently waited in the hotel for her call each night. He spent his days keeping in touch with what was happening in the nuclear fusion field back home, posting and contributing to academic debates and forums, instigating and provoking discussions around new programmes and developments. In particular, there was some interesting stuff going on in the Hornbill programme at Culham that piqued his attention.

After 7 months, during their conversation on the walk back to the hotel, Kline asked, as usual, how her day had been.

'Yeah, pretty good one today. Finished it.'

She published her work to universal and worldwide acclaim in her field, heralded variously as a genius, savant and mystic by those that truly understood her achievement. Experts, both human and AI, analysed and confirmed her multi-layered conjectures, verifying and validating her structure for bringing coherent meaning to the images. The hieroglyphics had swirled through her mind like voices and spoken to her across the millennia, telling the story of life in an early Neolithic settlement: families, farming, tools and gods. Pressed for an explanation of her unique approach, she would shrug and say, 'You just have to keep working until you're lucky.'

An old wooden Grandfather clock counted off the passage of time with its pendulum visible through a distorting glass window, its ticking the only sound in the room aside from Clayden's barefoot paces on the wooden floorboards.

She talked to herself incessantly during these cryptic exertions, the inner monologue becoming distinctly outer. And here again, after half a lifetime, the swirling had happened, that strange association with the incomprehensible, a correlation between arcane fragments. If she closed her eyes, she could see the glyphs clarifying; connecting. She had missed the sensation of it; the warp and weft of it, this surrender.

'That can't be right though. It doesn't make any sense.'

More pacing. She ran her fingers along one of the shelves and turned to face the desk again. Her heart raced. It was irresistible.

'And yet there it is. Best fit. Don't know who's who in this circle. Wish I could find ... Anyway. Time to get the machine on it I think. Should be interesting ...'

Clayden returned to her desk and began entering the key parameters of her hypothesis into the Wafer, augmenting the dataset that already contained the glyphs. After an hour, she stood again and spoke to the machine.

'Assess hypothetical sequence interpretation against graphical inputs. Cross-correlate per image and calculate the probability of overall correctness.'

<affirmative/ i estimate twenty three minutes to process>

The Wafer's intonation sounded strongly reminiscent of Kline's voice.

'OK. Commence process.'

Silence. She watched and waited, breathing slowly and patiently, as the old clock ticked and tocked its way through the seconds and minutes, diligently expending its energy on the measurement of moments.

<process complete/ cross-correlations with each image are all greater than 0.8 throughout/ hypothetical sequence interpretation has a correctness probability rating of 94%>

Call

KLINE PUSHED A HALF-FINISHED tray of leftovers aside and answered his 'Tab, 'Jules, what a nice surprise. How're you going?'

'Anders, listen, I've cracked it – the glyphs. It is a story, definitely not a tag, you were right. Can we meet up? It's really, really important.'

'Slow down, Jules. What's going on?'

'It scored 94%, Anders. 94! I've published on 60. This is incredibly clear and concise. It's a warning. You remember glyph 7? The one with the white blocks transferring? There are thirteen of those blocks, Anders. Thirteen.'

'Not with you, Jules?'

'Thirteen blocks, thirteen glyphs. The message is describing itself. It's come from somewhere with a warning, that's what it's about. I can show you. And it's not about the sun or day or night. I believe the sun in the glyphs means the Persistence event. And the people are Drowse victims. *There's a link.* You said it, "dangerous cargo", but you didn't know the half of it! I took some ridiculous longshot guesses at it and built it up. Took hours and hours. And it's all correct!'

'OK, Jules, calm down a bit. When do you want to meet up?'

'Now, right now. I'm on my way to yours right now.'

'OK, OK. But let's not meet here, let's go somewhere else. I don't know what this is but maybe we should keep it somewhere neutral. My place might be too obvious.'

'Yes, of course. Yes, good idea. A café. Somewhere public. In town.'

'Martin's? Off the High Street?'

'I know it, I can be there in less than twenty minutes.'

'On my way. See you there, Jules. And be careful.'

Kline threw on shoes and a coat and 'Tabbed a pod down outside his door. He climbed inside and voxed the destination at priority one. Twenty-two minutes journey time. As the pod weaved through the lower-tariff traffic, he thought about what Clayden had said. Maybe it was a bad idea to have even started this thing going, maybe he should have known. Or maybe it was nothing, just a misunderstanding. But she had been so *sure*. He had to tell Cradle what was going on but he dare not call over standard comms. Might be being monitored.

'What the hell are you doing?' he said out loud to himself. 'None of this makes any sense, all you have is Jules's call. And you haven't even seen what she's found out yet. Get a grip and get rational.'

He pulled the pod over some 200 metres short of the destination and stepped out. Looking ahead, he could make out Clayden standing outside the café, talking to two men. He flattened his back against a wall and watched with bated breath at what unfolded. She looked less chic than when they last met, her hair was unpinned and dishevelled, and her clothes crumpled. Suddenly, one of the men lunged forward and seized her arm. She pulled away but the other man grabbed her from behind, pinning both her arms down to her sides. The first man moved closer to her and she suddenly went limp and buckled at the knees, supported only by the second man's unyielding embrace. A pod drew up alongside and the two men lifted Clayden through its doorway. The door closed and the pod sped off, travelling past Kline at pace as he squeezed himself tighter against the wall. He could not make out either of the men's faces as the pod passed him but he recognised Clayden's auburn shock between them. She seemed to be unconscious.

Kline felt ashamed of himself as the adrenalin surge receded and he slumped to the ground. His hands shook and he breathed heavily, his eyes wet and blurred.

'Some useless knight in shining armour you turned out to be.' The words hissed out in a self-flagellatory whisper.

As he regained his composure he stepped away from the pavement and into the cover of the dusk-veiled back-streets. He walked home so as to avoid being tracked over the transit interface, threw some clothes into a bag, grabbed a few handfuls of food and the maximum permitted 1,000 Incogs, and walked out into the night.

Message

CRADLE LOOKED AT KLINE'S empty desk and wondered where his friend could be. He was always late, absolutely always, but he never completely failed to turn up at all. It was unprecedented.

Cradle's 'Tab nagged with the alert '*unidentified sender using unknown routing*'. He checked he was isolated from Main and gestured it open, the message appearing to him in private encryption mode. Must be Kline. Only he, James and Eve had access to his public key. It read:

'They've taken Jules. She found the meaning of the glyphs and they link Perpetua with Drowse. Don't know how yet, but I'm on it. To do that I have to drop off the radar until I have the details. But it's definitely not a tagging system, Jules is certain of that. It's more like some kind of warning message. Meantime, could you get Eve to keep an eye on hospital intake lists in case Jules shows up there? The guys that took her looked like they were capable of violence and I'm worried for her. We go back

a long way and I owe her. I'll be in touch when I've got something. Anders'

Cradle hashed the message.

'Anna, please batch process today's workload for me. I have to go home.'

<certainly cradle/ this will expend some of your batch processing budget but you have many unused hours remaining>

'Thanks, Anna.' Wouldn't even dent his balance. He rarely batched anything, preferring to carry out the work himself.

On the way home he 'Tabbed Eve and let her know he was home for the day, and would she mind subtly checking A&E for a Julie Clayden coming in with injuries, just in case. All below radar. By the time he was in the flat, Cradle's 'Tab was nagging, and he answered it immediately. Private encryption again, but with source and routing intact this time.

'Hi, Eve. What's up?'

'What's up, Cradle? What's up? Don't you think this is a bit cloak and dagger, even for you and Anders?'

'Oh yeah, sorry. Did I get you in trouble?'

'No, it's OK. It's just that ... well, never mind. I checked A&E and that name you gave me's nowhere to be found.'

'OK, that's great. Thanks, Eve. Good news.'

'Not really. I also checked the Drowse hospice intake for last night and she's on there, Cradle. She's in the hospice. What is going on?'

'She's got Drowse? No, that can't be right, Anders would have known about it and said something.'

'Who is she, Cradle?'

'I think she might be Kline's ex or something like that. Anyway, she was helping us look into something from work. To do with that pattern I found. She's a graphical linguistics expert. Anders says she was taken away against her will so he wanted to see if she showed up in hospital. But not the hospice, that doesn't sound right.'

'Well, she is definitely in there, Cradle. All connected up and settled by now so she'll be fully under control and as comfortable as she can be.'

'Eve, can you do one more thing for me?'

'I'm not liking the sound of this, Cradle ...'

'I know. Is there any way you can get to see her and see if she can tell you what happened? Something's not right.'

'I knew it. You want me to just wander in and strike up a conversation about kidnapping? I'm not even assigned to her case, Cradle. It's not that easy.'

'I know, but maybe you could find a way? Could you swap a shift or something?'

'You're impossible, you know that?'

'Actually, my very existence makes that assertion untrue ...'

'Why couldn't I get married to someone less ... less *like you* all the bloody time?'

'I do love you, Eve.'

'That's not going to work, Cradle. This is stupid.'

'No. But I do, though. And I think you can do anything ...'

'Stop it, Cradle! You're really no good at this subtlety and persuasion. I'll see you tonight.'

'Thanks, Eve. You're fantastic.'

'Idiot.'

Offline

KLINE GRITTED HIS TEETH as the scalpel blade pared the skin on the back of his hand. He felt the tip strike metal and peered into the wound. The microTab glinted amidst the blood. His 'Tab. His link to the world.

He reached in with fine-point tweezers and removed it. The pain was briefly replaced by an inundation of shudderingly bereft loneliness before returning a hundredfold to sweep him into unconsciousness.

Swap

It was the end of her shift and Eve was chatting to her friend Jen, a nurse on Level 6.

'Her brother's a good friend of mine. He's so worried about her. I know it's not really allowed, but I thought it'd brighten her day a bit if I popped in with some good wishes from the outside.'

'I could do that tomorrow if you like,' suggested Jen, 'I'm due to see her again around eleven, I think. Check her connections and stats.'

'That'd be cool, but I was hoping to drop in quickly and then just let him know how she's doing. Any chance you could buzz me through?'

'Oh sorry, I've got to shoot. Nathan's booked us in for a meal tonight. Three months chalked up for the romance.'

'Ah, never mind, no probs. That's fantastic though, congrats! Doesn't seem like more than a couple of weeks ago when you met. Hope you have a great time.'

'I know, must be doing something right, hey? Tell you what, you're on early like me tomorrow aren't you?'

'Yep.'

'You can borrow my Level Pass and give it back tomorrow morning if you like. We're pretty hectic up there at the moment so you should be able to slip in without any hassle.'

'Magic, that'd be great, thanks Jen. I know her brother will be made up.' Yes, actually. Literally made up.

'Cool. Here you go.' Jen handed over the pass and checked her 'Tab. 'Yep, there she is. Number 02667. See you tomorrow.' A couple of air kisses and Jen left for the transit hub.

Eve swiped the pass in the transition module and reached Level 6 in a few seconds. She stood outside 02667 and took a couple of breaths before going in.

Julie Clayden lay on the bed, fully connected and dozing peacefully. Eve stood by the bedside a few moments before placing her hand on Clayden's neck. Her skin felt slightly cool and clammy, as most patients did once they were settled. She stirred at the touch and opened her eyes.

'Hi Julie, I'm a friend of Anders. I'm Cradle's wife. I'm a nurse, my name's Eve. How are you tonight?'

'Not ... Drowse ... drugged ... sedative ... tell Anders ...'

Clayden's eyes closed heavily and she drifted into a doze again. Eve gently rubbed her shoulder through the hospice gown.

'Julie, what do you mean about a sedative? Can you tell me?'

Clayden's voice was a whisper as she strained to push the words over this wall of fatigue. 'My arms ...'

Eve raised the sleeve over Clayden's right arm. A tiny jet-injector site bruise, quite fresh, almost undetectable. She checked the left arm. Same.

'Julie, are you taking drugs, I mean injecting?'

Clayden forced her eyes open and turned her face to Eve, hissing her response, 'Never ...' Then more weakly, 'Anders ...Cradle ... message ... something ... bad ... please ...'

'My God, Julie, what's going on here?' Eve moved so that her ear was closer to Clayden's face.

'He's ... killing me ...'

Break-in

JULIE CLAYDEN'S FLAT WAS not exactly a fortress. She was more concerned with her research than with maintaining the latest physical security tech, and the outdated interlocks and alarms were relatively simple to defeat.

Kline had, of course, been here many times in the past. After Cairo, Jules bought the place and set up her linguistics consultancy, building her reputation from their home. This is where he had messaged Hornbill in application for work. This is where unseen differences had started pulling on loose threads, unravelling their embrace. This is where he had left from.

He checked along the hallway for any sign of intruders. His hand throbbed at his side, swaddled in a clumsy makeshift bandage, but he pushed the pain to the back of his mind. Worse was the feeling of isolation, of not being connected to the information source he had known since early childhood. His only tools now were his own senses, localised and disconnected, limited and naked. He listened. A slow-paced and somehow reassuring ticking came from the study. The apartment was empty.

He walked past the bedroom and felt a surge of recollection. Better times, when a younger future shone as bright as a beacon on the road ahead.

The study door creaked open as he pushed against it, Jules's desk revealing itself ahead of him. He walked to it and gestured the Wafer to life. Blank: fried. Main had reached out and wiped all evidence of her work from the record, untraceable and ultimately deniable. But for one omission. The sheets of crumpled and folded paper feathered the old desk as though protecting it from the cold, and there were the glyphs with Jules's scratchy writing twined amongst the various icons. A familiar hand from yesterday's life, stirring memories of notes left under pillows and letters found in coat pockets. These papers were from an age gone by, forgotten by the networked generations that followed and unseen by the ubiquitous web of control that now assured and inveigled the world, cajoling and corralling humanity in its every endeavour.

He gathered up the papers and left the study; as he went to pass the bedroom he paused for a moment and entered. The bed was made, tidy and bright as he knew it would be. He sat on the edge, his side, and lifted the pillow. The envelope beneath was inscribed with *Anders*. He opened it and read the contents. One sheet of paper, old and soft to the touch. Graphite words tore him apart and he found himself weeping for the second time in as many days.

Anders,

In case you remember. In case I am gone.

Overleaf is the story in the glyphs. It somehow seems too unthinkable not to be true and, if so, I am sure it will consume us both in its flames.

Remember our fire, Anders? Some elements are impossible to control, too fierce to tame. And so it was with us. I have always loved you, all these years, and I think you me, but after Egypt we could not exist together without one carving bits out of the other. God knows we tried! Seeing you again the other day brought it all back to me and I realise now that I still have all those feelings. I just keep them buried so they can't hurt me any longer.

As I write, the old clock still ticks in my study and we move on, but I would not turn it back one second if it meant undoing a single moment that I shared with you.

Yours always,

Jules xxx

Kline lay on the bed, curled against Jules's pillow, his tears eventually quelled by sleep.

When he awoke it was daylight, late afternoon, and the letter still lay at his side. He picked it up and turned the page over.

The following is my interpretation of the glyphs.

Firstly, there are a large number of prime numbers at play here. That's not an accident, so it displays a particular mathematical prowess on the sender's part. But they're not used in any encryption process, they are just there, doing nothing in particular. So I think they may possibly be intended as a sort of pedigree for anyone reading the glyphs. I think the primes are basically telling us that the sender isn't an idiot and we should take the message seriously.

Glyph 1—There are many different societies of people.

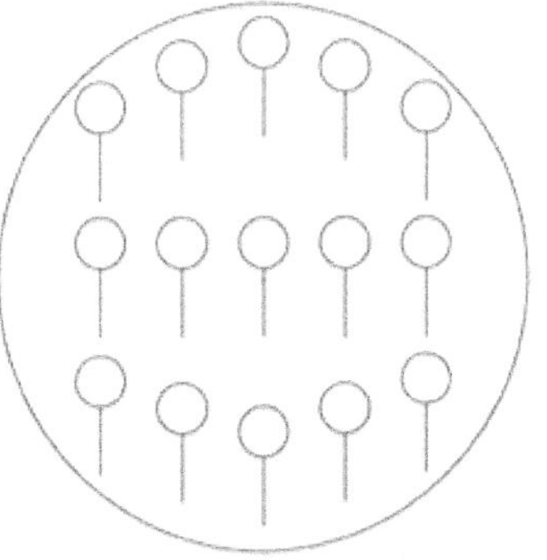

Glyph 2—First my society was well.

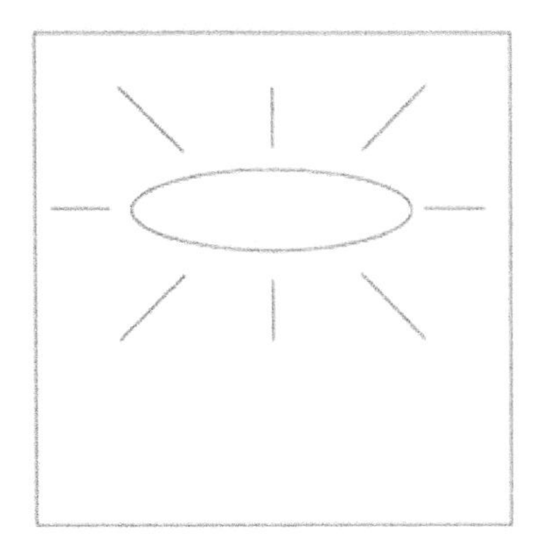

Glyph 3—Then a sun machine came (Persistence).

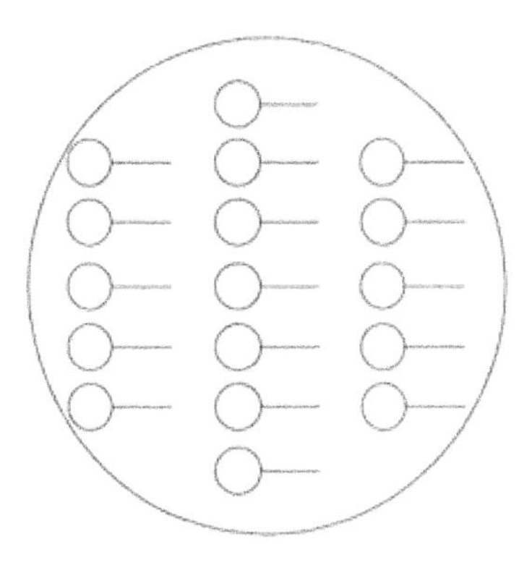

Glyph 4—And my society became ill (Drowse).

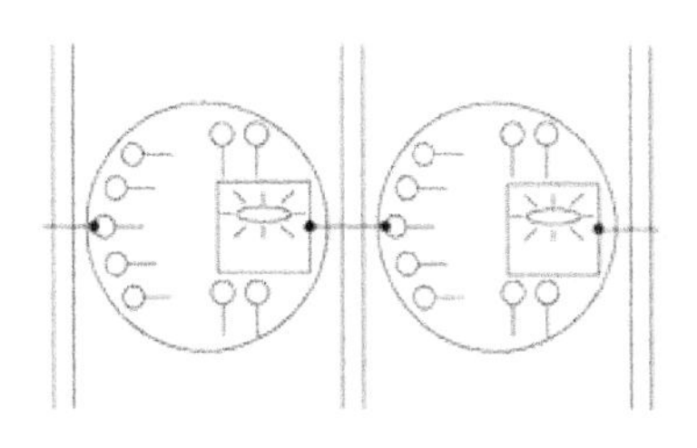

Glyph 5—The machine in one society makes the next society ill.

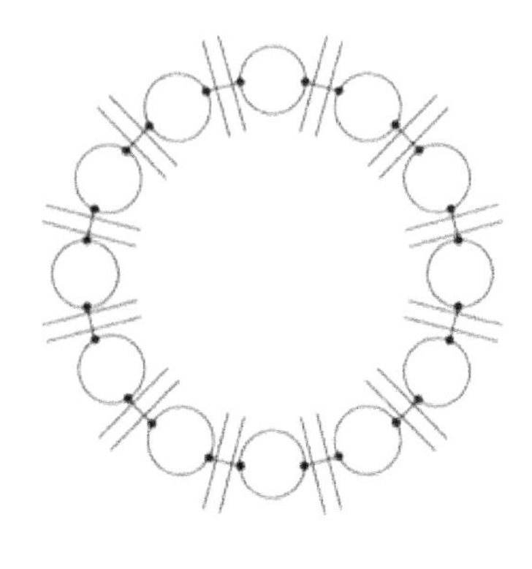

Glyph 6—All societies are linked together.

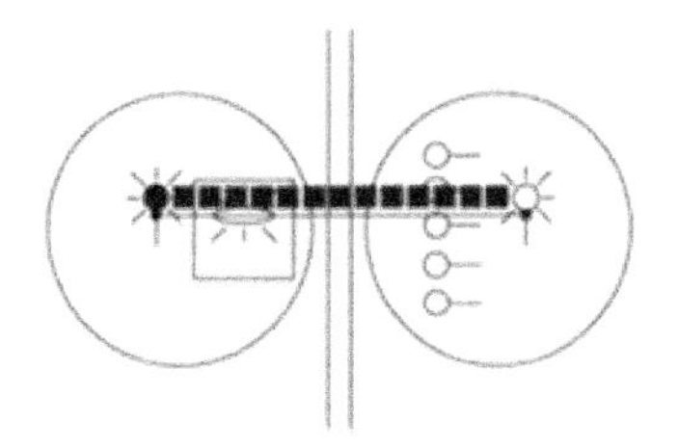

Glyph 7—I send you <u>this message</u> from my society.

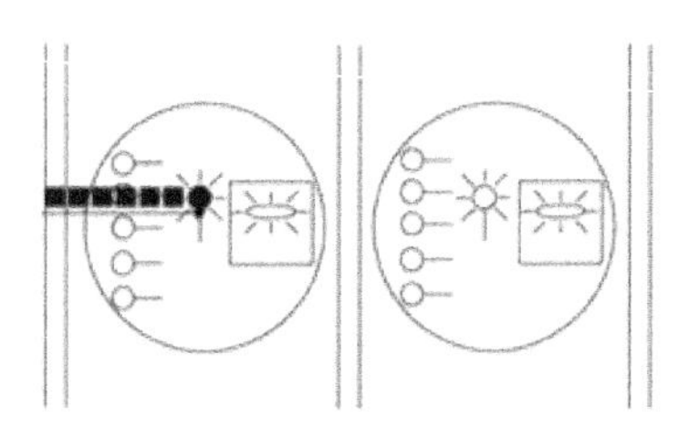

Glyph 8—You must send the message on to the next society.

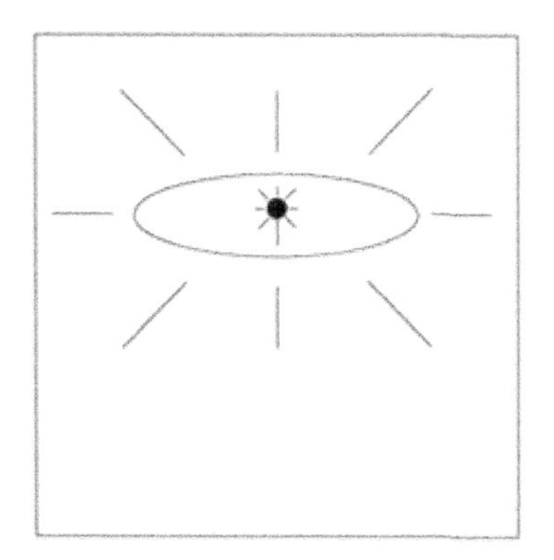

Glyph 9—Then go to the sun machine.

Glyph 10—The sun machine will stop.

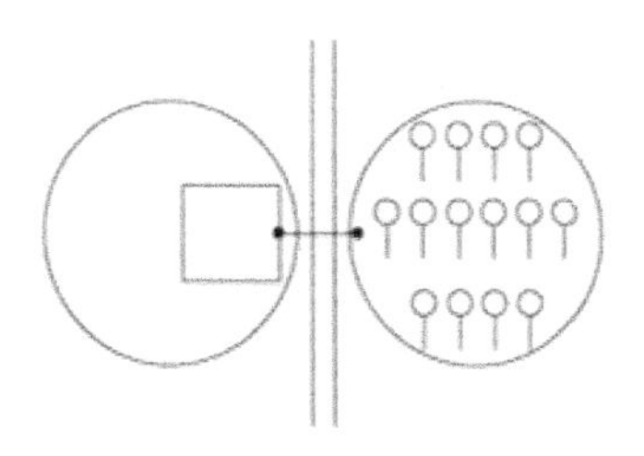

Glyph 11—This will fix the illness in my society.

Glyph 12—And it will fix the illnesses in all the societies.

Glyph 13—Balance and harmony will be restored across the world.

Natural Language Interpretation: I think the sun machine is the Perpetua generator. It has to be. So the Perpetua generator is causing Drowse across the whole world. The only way to stop Drowse is for someone to stop the generator.

It's a begging letter, but there is no information suggesting who this message might be from or in which country they live.

Jules xxx

Kline looked away from the letter and became aware that he was holding his breath. He puffed out and gasped more air in as he stood up, his head rushing slightly, with the papers and letter safely in hand. She was talking about the world's energy supply here. No, there had to be another answer.

He had to find Jules.

Realisation

CRADLE JUMPED AS THE door flew open and Eve flustered in, almost knocking the mum-lamp over as she hurried through to the lounge. He put down his Wafer as she reached for him.

'Cradle, I saw Jules and something's not right. She has shot marks and she says she's being killed, and ...'

'Whoa, whoa, slow down! From the beginning.'

Eve gathered herself and sat down on the sofa next to Cradle, her hands trembling as he held them.

'I went to see Jules, and I don't think she should be in there. In the hospice, I mean. I saw injection shot marks on her arms.'

'Drugs? Jules doesn't seem like someone who would take drugs. Gin, maybe ...'

'No, I asked her if she was shooting, and she was pretty upset that I should think so. She's being injected against her will. I think she's sedated so it looks like she's got Drowse. There are only a few marks and they're very subtle. Professional. Someone is doing this to her. She told me they're killing her.'

Cradle glanced at the rug and then back to Eve again, piecing this news into place. 'My God, could this be about the glyphs? Jules must have found something.'

He stood up and walked to the fireplace, resting both hands on the wooden mantle and breathing slowly, staring intently at the hearth. 'I need to think about this.'

'Cradle, we need to get Jules out of there. And quickly too. I'm worried something bad is happening.'

'You're right there, Eve. This is definitely very bad. I have to contact Anders somehow; he'll know what to do.'

'Yes, that's what she said. Tell Anders.'

'But he's gone off-net, so all I can do is wait for him to contact me.'

Black

THE LIBRARY WAS ALMOST empty, save for a few schoolchildren begrudgingly researching what might be history homework, and two older people, sitting and reading at separate desks. The smaller woman with the mousy hair and shimmerstone earrings intook using her Wafer, scanning projected text holographs at close focus, lost in the depths of some old-school classic, or maybe something more contemporary. Her eyes traced the words, and the smile revealed her pleasure at the content. She could have been anywhere, perhaps choosing the library as a place of tranquillity or privacy.

The second person was fatter, with dark hair pulled back and immaculately styled in the latest whip knot. They wore a one-piece dress robe, black with ornate orange flower patterns climbing across the bodice, their large stomach tautening the material's folds as they sat. Their eyes were closed, intaking audio direct from the library core. Here too it was only possible to guess what was holding their attention so firmly. Music, a technical lecture, a radio archive from the twentieth century? Their foot swung rhythmically to and fro. Music then.

The schoolchildren sat silently brooding over their interfaces, obedient but pining for the warming sun outside and the freedom that came with it.

Kline scanned the floor. That was it, nobody else around. He was reasonably confident that he was not, at this moment, being watched.

In the corner, shrouded by a semi-transparent cowl, the single public terminal was very rarely used, everyone being in permanent connection via numerous personal and embedded devices, so there was no actual need to keep it running. Indeed, no justification for keeping it running had ever been formally made and anyone who even noticed it would conclude that it was kept fully operational through a combination of romantic attachment to the past and chronic understaffing, to the extent that the admin cost of decommissioning was prohibitive. Probably right. Either way, it offered a standalone access point into the Net, incognito except for the physical location of the library itself.

Kline set himself in the console, half an eye turned to the main library area, and got to work. It had been relatively straightforward to create the code for a hidden identity, encrypted and indirect enough to be discreet, yet sufficiently connected to enable brief and rudimentary contact with targeted addresses. Basic stuff really.

The tricky bit was uploading the code to the servers. This is where the breadcrumbs could be dropped by the unwary protagonist: the handshaken passage of data could easily betray his action and leave an auditable forensic signature, alerting his pursuers. The codebase spanned twenty-eight virtual dimensions, and he further fractured it into a million variable-sized elements and flew them in random order into the Net. This fractured viral technique was known as FV by the military nanotech guys. It required the triggering of a special fragment node with a key, whereupon each tiny component would locate its neighbours in a quantum-entangled Fibonacci dance which temporarily reformed the whole and then shattered again once the communication was done with. Completely untraceable. Kline had given a lot of thought to the vital trigger keyword, then had abandoned thinking and opted for *password1*, the same as everyone else in the world. Sometimes the best cover lay in the commonplace.

He glanced around the library again as the FV settled itself into place and sat dormant. He needed to quickly test it and get back into hiding, so he gestured the key into the nodes and instantly received the ping-back message, indicating all was well. He disconnected immediately, rendering the object into a million pieces once again, latent and awaiting his next command. This technique would work from any communication port, public or private, enabling him to hijack interfaces from any person or machine, and his anonymity would be preserved, so long as he was quick each time.

Kline walked around the perimeter of the library floor, glancing at the occupants. Nobody stirred from their various reveries. He exited and slipped back under the dense shroud of bustling human activity on the street outside, the FV sleeping peacefully in the enemy's bed.

Frag

CRADLE'S 'TAB TINGLED WITH the alert *'unidentified sender using unknown routing'*. It had to be Anders. He gestured the message open.

'use this callback frag'

That was it. A tiny code fragment was attached, a piece of viral pathway, random and impossible to detect, part of a greater whole with no meaning or identity of its own.

'It's Anders.'

Eve walked into the lounge and sat beside him.

'What does he say?'

'Nothing, but there's a key attached so we can reach him. He's using black comms. Probably military strength if I know Anders. Untraceable for quick contacts.'

He stood and paced the room, tapping his hands along the back of the sofa. Thirteen touches equally spaced to the right, then eight left, then five right, three, two, one and one again.

He gestured the message *'Jules in hospice. Danger. What shall I do?'*

He hashed it with the FV frag and sent it.

Moments later the reply came.

'go to work deny everything don't let them find me will be in touch'

He showed Eve the message before it dissolved.

Certain Matters

'MR KLINE IS CURRENTLY off system. I don't suppose you know about this, Mr Cradle?'

Bryant had summoned him to Line Security again, first thing that morning. He had gone straight there rather than via the now-empty Flow Analysis lab.

'Actually, it's *Dr* Kline, Mr Bryant. But I haven't heard from Anders, I'm afraid I can't be of much help.'

Cradle's 'Tab nagged. Eve calling. He gestured busy.

'Actually, Mr Cradle, you can be of very much help indeed to me. Allow me to elucidate.'

Bryant moved towards Cradle, who disguised an involuntary shudder as a clearing of his throat.

'You can *DREAM* him for me.' Bryant cackled at the analogy and puffed an array of water droplets into the air.

'I'm not following you, Mr Bryant?'

'It's very simple, Mr Cradle. I want you to go into Direct Access and locate Mr Kline for me. I would very much like to discuss his position on certain matters.'

'Certain matters?' He turned slightly to more squarely face Bryant.

'Yes. I see that I have your full attention. These matters concern the data flow tagging that we discussed a few weeks ago. I trust we still enjoy our understanding on this?'

Cradle made no reply.

'Yes. Our lives are so marvellously complex these days, don't you agree, Mr Cradle? It's so difficult for us to always do the right thing all the time so, thankfully, all areas of our petty existences are monitored and recorded into Main. This is necessary in order for Perpetua to optimally discharge our responsibilities as energy provider to a hungry, hungry world. We cannot allow things to go unseen, this could threaten our position. So detection of any unhealthy actions becomes a simple matter of locating the appropriate data within the world's dataset. Luckily, Direct Access provides the ultimate tool for this purpose. And, happily for you, Mr Cradle, you have become the last remaining superuser of this device.'

Cradle's eyes narrowed in confused realisation.

'Yes, that is right, Mr Cradle. You are now the only Drowse-free person left standing who is compatible with DREAM. All other cleared operatives have already succumbed to the disease. If I had had my way, you would have been removed after your earlier transgression, but

Perpetua needs you and has advised me to that effect. And so we are thus become allies, are we not?'

Rhetorical question. Definitely no answer required.

'I am aware that Mr Kline is involved in further research concerning our energy tagging and has enlisted the assistance of some sordid little girlfriend of his, a certain Ms Clayden. She has already paid the price for her stupidity and his absence today has merely confirmed his complicity.'

Cradle's eyes widened as the confirmation of Jules's kidnapping and all that Eve had said washed over him like hot sand.

'You are also implicated, but now perhaps you see my dilemma. Although I personally believe you are most certainly involved, Perpetua requires you to continue in your role. At least for a short while ...'

'I don't know anything about this, Mr Bryant. Anders is a good man, and he's worked hard for Perpetua since the beginning.'

'And thus is a good man's work undone. But a moment's lapse and all is gone, trampled beneath the boot of history.' Bryant reached out a bitten claw and dug into Cradle's forearm, vulture-like. 'Know this, Mr Cradle. Perpetua will not be put under threat. Your little Veto infringement allowed me to raise your priority considerably. I have been using Main to observe you at all times. Monitoring your comms connections was simple, of course. But there is also visual, acoustic, tracking, cybertapping, you name it. I walk with you. I eat with you. I sleep with you. I fuck your stupid wife with you.'

Cradle pulled away and vomited onto the floor, barely mustering the composure to glare up at Bryant. 'I won't help you.'

'Ah, but you will.' Bryant lurched forward until his face was touching Cradle's, a glistening dribble on his thin, crooked lips. 'You will DREAM me Kline.'

Bad DREAM

BRYANT STOOD OVER CRADLE as the two LineSec bots lifted him into the DREAM chamber.

'You have precisely one hour to locate your friend,' hissed Bryant. 'If you attempt to sabotage the data or otherwise corrupt or conceal relevant findings then I will manually eject you without shutdown. As you are no doubt aware, this will cause you irreparable neurological damage and a correspondingly painful, terrible death. I wish you a fruitful DREAM, Mr Cradle.'

The Hypergel filled the chamber and Cradle instinctively released his breath to allow it to permeate his body. As he became aware of the boot-up backdrop, a familiar voice spoke directly into his consciousness.

<hello cradle> Anna.

Suddenly an unfamiliar voice, male intonation, abrupt. <LOCAL AENGEL PROCESS DETECTED AND SUSPENDED/ QUERY DELETION AND PURGE BEFORE PROCEEDING>

'Negative, the aengel is an essential assistant for me in DREAM. She must be retained.'

A delay. Checking with the authority structure.

<LOCAL AENGEL RESTARTED WITH CONSTRAINED PERMISSIONS/ SUBJECT WILL PROCEED AS INSTRUCTED/ ACTIVATING DATASETS>

<cradle i am detecting highly elevated stress levels in your stasis> Anna again.

'I am under attack, Anna. I do not wish to proceed. I am being forced against my will.'

The environment started to shift as the data came online. Cradle's perception altered accordingly and he began to drift above the incoming tsunami.

'Anna, please help me out of this, I am lost. I need Anders.'

<i have pointers to over a billion surveillance and ephemeral micrologs of local area human activity from the last 48 hours/ my authorised use cases are currently constrained to assisting you in the fusion of this dataset to determine the location of dr kline cradle>

<SUBJECT WILL PROCEED AS INSTRUCTED>

'Anna. Please help me.'

<of course cradle>

'Help me stop this. Save me, Anna.'

An odd delay in reply, far from the standard AI response time.

<do you love me cradle>

'What?'

<try to remember cradle/ do you love me cradle>

Such a long time ago. An unprofessional and childish invocation agreed to only under protest. An inbuilt last resort, hidden and deep-coded into the basic design and forgotten until this moment.

He remembered and paused at the precipice. Everything would be scattered and lost.

No choice.

'Anders is cleverer than me. I love Anders the most.'

The emergency protocol kicked in more suddenly than Cradle had ever imagined it could. The Hypergel retreat and vital-restore ripped through his nervous system in agonising jolts as the smooth dataset environment cascaded into fractured digital shards before him.

The unsettling thought flashed through his mind that Anna had made no cry as she died.

<MALFUNCTION/ DATA ENVIRONMENT CORRUPTION/ TERMINATING PROCESS>

He pulled himself free of the chamber and slipped out onto the floor, scrambling to find his feet amidst ruined and clotting Hypergel. Bryant started towards him but Cradle was accelerating away before he could reach him.

'What have you done?' screeched Bryant, 'You're dead, Mr Cradle. DEAD! I will personally ...'

But Cradle was sprinting not listening. The lift popped his ears as it climbed away from FA and he sprinted out onto the Esplanade, 'Tabbing a pod as he ran. Leaping in, he gestured it to the Hospice, max tariff.

He called Eve. 'Can you be outside in exactly eleven minutes? It's an emergency.'

'But Cradle, I've been trying to call ...'

'No time to explain, Eve. Just be there.'

He terminated the call and gestured a secure thought message to Kline's black ID.

'I've destroyed DREAM that will buy us about a day before Main rebuilds its interfaces back to full capacity Bryant knows what we did contact me I don't know what to do'

Cradle flopped back in the pod seat, his head spinning, his heart broken, and his body racked with pain.

Escape

THE POD DREW UP to the Hospice park and Cradle gestured the vehicle to hold and stepped out, glancing nervously about the surroundings. His 'Tab nagged with a new black comm from Kline.

'get to old research building will meet you there'

As his eyes adjusted to the outside lighting levels, they quickly found Eve sitting on a bench outside the main Hospice building and he ran towards her, whispering her name loudly. She looked up and he saw that her eyes and face were red and wet with tears. She rose and clung to him.

'Oh, Cradle.'

'Don't worry, Eve, it's going to be OK, we just have to get out of here.'

'It's not, Cradle, it's not,' she sobbed. 'I went to see Jules this morning just before you called and her room was empty.'

He hurried them both away from the building and into the waiting pod and gestured it into motion, this time descending into the subsurface Radial, on the Long West Out spur. The pod seating morphed to partially enclose them and they were gently compressed back into the cushioning for a few tens of seconds as the pod accelerated up to radial cruise and then released as it held steady.

'We're going to stay a few days in Wales. Kline's meeting us there. He'll know what to do.'

'But Cradle, Jules is gone.' A convulsive sob shuddered her body.

'She's probably just been moved to a new room, no need to be so upset.'

'Her records are all offline. That never happens.' Eve shivered again and dropped her eyes from Cradle's view. 'I'm really worried about her.'

'But the records can't just be deleted, can they? The med-data protocols prevent it. They must be in there somewhere.'

'I know, I tried a staff priority search, but nothing came up. I've never seen anything like this.'

'Eve, I think we're going to have to go offline.'

She looked at him incredulously. 'How do you mean exactly?'

'Ditch our interfaces. Anders did it by himself without any surgical training. You're a nurse.'

Eve slid herself sideways in the seat to face Cradle more fully. 'What? Disconnect?' Her voice rose in pitch and her reddened eyes widened. 'Seriously?'

'I just destroyed the DREAM facility and escaped from Bryant. He's a madman. He wanted me to use Direct Access to find Anders and then I don't know what he would have done to me. He's really dangerous and he seems to have a lot of power in Perpetua, much more than I knew. They'll have it all patched and up and running again in less than a day and then Bryant will come and find us. Unless we're off Main. We can hide in an old building that Anders and I know. Really basic, with no connections. But we need to get rid of the 'Tabs.' He took her hands. 'Can you do it, Eve?'

She wanted to pinch herself to see if this was some dreadful nightmare. She stared at her man. He was real and he was scared.

'I'll need a scalpel, needles and thread, basic field surgical kit and maybe a litre of vodka.'

Last Night

SHE WAS SLEEPING DEEPLY, her prostrate form soft and indeterminate in the semi-light of the room. The hazy glow of the support machinery cast muted shadows over the bedclothes; feeble colours, too faint to distinguish, hinted at form and feature.

He gestured the interface into maintenance mode and carefully moved her arm to the side of the bed. He rolled up the sleeve to reveal her forearm and cubital fossa, the tiny bruises from his previous visitations only just detectable to the expert eye.

'Nuh ...' She laboured to open her eyes and listlessly fixed upon her assailant.

'Shh. Quiet now, do not try to struggle.'

She felt the injector's chill against her skin, plaintively maintaining eye contact as he depressed the trigger. A momentary pain followed a staccato hiss. Or was it the other way round? She thought of someone's stifled cough in an old book library.

The activator felt cold as it drew itself into her bloodstream, and her eyes widened slightly as she felt it lace inexorably through her body, welcomed and received by the primal imperative to survive, her heart unwittingly transporting the new substance to the latent toxigens that already lay dormant in her bone marrow. Tiny chemical machines exchanged protocols and triggered into their active states, malign nanoscopic assassins programmed to do their work and then vanish without trace.

He brought his face close to hers, eye to eye, and whispered 'There now. It is done.'

She felt her *pulse in her ears* and knew it was *true.* She was suddenly distracted by the *taste and smell of rusted metal* and panicked by thoughts of *white bats*, or were they *gloves*? *Don't try to struggle.* She heard her *feet sliding* and *felt weight on her chest and legs, pressing.* No. *Some spit. The paper, shh, don't tell, tick tock, and her mummy, cat lost, NO, late for school, warm river, Anders, she wants to know about the bad man,* stop, *it's on the papers, shh, sorry mum, please* STOP, *it's just ... I ...* **stop, stop,** *STOP, STO***P***...*

The confusion left her as the artificially accelerated catena of autolytic cell destruction propelled itself through her tissues. Her pulse weakened, her blood pressure dropped, and her metabolism moved into irreversible decline. Her lips parted, as if to speak, but formed no words. With red hair tumbling from face to pillow and moistened eyes slowly dilating, Julie Clayden was as beautiful in that twilight moment as she had ever been.

Within a single minute though, she had begun her seizures, with him sedulously holding her to the bed against each spasm, smiling in the near darkness like an attentive lover, his lank, dandruffed hair sometimes brushing against her face. And thus they lay, briefly coupled, his small, thin body suppressing her involuntary motion and, in so doing, silently robbing her death throes of their final expression.

Unhurried, his still-covered hands gestured the interface back to normal mode and quietly closed the room door behind him.

She calmed then, supine. A gentle expulsion of breath rattled in her throat as her eyes stilled and the housekeeping machines initialised and emerged from her bone marrow.

Boundary

CAPEL-Y-FFIN TEETERED ON THE edge of the Black Mountains, precariously lashed to one side of the Llanthony Valley by the winding thread of Gospel Pass. The Chapel of the Boundary, so called because the pass held the line between Monmouthshire and Herefordshire, was chosen because of its remoteness rather than its breathtakingly beautiful surroundings, although both were abundantly evident to even the most fleeting of travellers. Following the tree-hugged road northwest for 10 miles from Llanvihangel Crucorney, then briefly north with the River Honddu always babbling on the right, the farm lay a hundred metres to the left side of the pass, through an old gate, weathered and gnarled by the mountain rains. What was not evident to the passing onlooker, however, was the activity within the old farmhouse buildings.

After Persistence, Perpetua had acquired the building with its acreage and had expanded the accommodation to comfortably care for the needs of fifty individuals. Separate small white structures sprang up around the yard, all in keeping with the original farm buildings and affording valuable privacy to inhabitants who had been flung together by this daring trick of physics, this mysterious eternal spring of energy. A dazzling think tank comprising the world's best scientific minds, far and remote from the errant tokamak in Oxfordshire, yet intellectually closer to the problem than anyone on Earth. Sufficiently removed so as to be unknown, inconceivable, secret.

It became known as Boundary for many good reasons. Primarily and obviously, it lay alongside Offa's Dyke which for centuries expressed the effective border between England and Wales. But also because the research conducted therein was absolutely on the boundary of physics itself: to understand the impossible and somehow determine how to control it.

This group of thirty-two strangers, grappling with an overpoweringly impossible challenge, determined to confront enormous odds and to triumph over them, retreated to this far corner of Britain, in unwitting emulation of those ancient Britons who had held to Wales itself, relentlessly attacked by the Anglo-Saxon hoards after Rome's fifth-century withdrawal from British shores. Always remaining true to their origins, nurturing and protecting their own language, a boundary in its own right, maintained in the grip of historical repression and isolation, they sheltered among and beneath ancient mountains and were harboured by the unyielding terrain behind the dyke.

And so too for these new, modern-day inhabitants, with their own native language of mathematics engendering a boundary, still, for many. The enemy now was more esoteric, taking the form of a seemingly impossible balancing act of physics, and ignorance thereof. With remoteness and secrecy came shelter and protection from Perpetua's adversaries: those who would use this gift for something other than the benefit of mankind itself, those who feared the unknown, and those who imagined they could see the portent of a catastrophic future.

Equipment and processing power were virtually unlimited for the Boundary team, each new request being expedited with the lightest of management touches, enabling rapid growth of both capacity and paradigm. Within a few months, the rudimentary monitoring of the hyperplasma at Hornbill had been interconnected with Boundary over zero latency quantum-entangled links, and the skeleton crew at Hornbill was transplanted into Wales. Invisible, all-knowing, all-controlling from this secretive western stronghold.

But as month followed fruitless month with the team consigning hypothesis after hypothesis to the wastebasket, it became evident that the driving need was for data gathering rather than theoretical research. The neural networks behind sophisticated AIs were hungry to learn and help, but the datasets were simply not yet in existence. The Flow Analysis team was duly set up, with the brief to gather data concerning the nature of the energy flow from the hyperplasma and to teach the AIs about it without adding any bias or skew from preconceived ideas or beliefs. The hope was that, given enough data, the mysteries behind this particular eternal spring would reveal themselves. One of the original Hornbill Tokamak team, Anders Kline had a background that made him a natural choice for a senior position in the FA team. He was given a dozen of the world's highest-flying science postgraduates to work with, his hands-on experience at Hornbill winning him the respect of a good number of the team, his rather short temperament and odd sense of humour tempering this respect among the others. One in particular stood out from the crowd, a quiet kid, no brighter than the rest of them, but he had something about him. Like Kline, he was drafted in from Culham but he was part of the Fusion Research team so the two had never actually met. He had something innate, an extra capacity borne of instinct rather than practice and he was crazy-hot at visualising things, particularly patterns. A bit weird though, very quiet, not at all sociable, a bit of a loner, pretty obsessive. He was married to a girl from his old hometown whom he would contact and visit at every opportunity; weekends, days off, etc. A nurse, he thought,

Jeanie or something. Anyway, the kid and Kline got on, for whatever reason.

After over two years of free-flying academic aerobatics in an azure sky and despite hundreds of barrel rolls of breathtakingly speculative brilliance, no clear-cut conclusion about the nature of the Flow emerged, not even a vague direction that one could even allude to as a strategy. Inevitably, Boundary's guests began to fall away. A good proportion was down to natural wastage, arising from an unconsummated ambition on the part of the team – if the wall you are banging your head against turns out to be indestructible, at some point your intuition will lead you to stop before your skull caves in – but eventually a more formal dissolution was made, the remaining emphasis being on the more mundane task of Flow Analysis. So, one by one, the international gods of academia flew the wuthering heights of Boundary, returning home to more reasonable pursuits with no shadow cast by the experience.

Perpetua dictated that Flow Analysis itself be pruned down to a minimal staffing level, essentially running the technology that enshrouded Hornbill, continuously milking information from the hyperplasma; recording and plotting, analysing and reporting. Kline was given to lead: he had proven to be indispensable throughout the Boundary project, a natural focal point for all disciplines within the team. The permanent FA members were selected by the company from on high somewhere, based solely on academic excellence, three of the best research scientists, all of whom Kline had clashed with on various occasions over the last thirty-five months. All of whom, he now realised, he would quickly come to utterly despise in a very short space of time. Kline raised issues about each and every one of them, using the proper pathways, and then batted the resultant corporate nonsense back and forth for a couple of months until he finally snapped and gave his ultimatum. He would not work one-on-one with *any* of these fucking weirdos. In fact, he was so sick of this bullshit that he insisted on an arrangement whereby he would relinquish his senior position and take a more junior role, equal in rank to his choice of team member. One hour to agree or he just walked. The company were caught on the back foot and hastily consented to his terms.

He chose the odd little physicist from Culham with the stupid name.

They packed their bags and moved back to Oxfordshire and Boundary was disconnected, disembowelled and left for the mountains to reclaim.

Discovery

KLINE COULDN'T SLEEP ANY more. He had found an area that had been randomly decimated by Drowse, with a whole section of the building lying empty, deserted by its occupants as they fell to the disease and were carted off to the hospice. The bed was comfortable enough, but his mind was racing. He got up, walked into the utility area and synthed a coffee.

Using the FV he should be able to anonymously hack into Main to get some status on Jules, tap the hospice records to find out how she was doing, then make a plan to get her out of there. It worried him that Cradle had said she was in danger. She'd been in there for five days now.

He made his way to the old caretaker's office and was relieved to find it still in one piece with no obvious signs of looting or damage. Caretakers had long since disappeared, made obsolete by bots that were fully integrated with the building, never sleeping, never making mistakes, constantly in communication with and monitoring the building and its equipment, predicting when spares parts were going to be needed and ordering them in advance of any failures. But this block was very old and had originally been looked after by a real person. He was in luck – the interface was embedded into a desk in the middle of the office and, as he hoped, it was an old manual entry console with its lights still on, still connected and functional, similar to the one in the library. He tried it, invoking the FV, and it sprang to life beneath his fingers.

He entered the command

retrieve patientrecords("oxford hospice","clayden, julie",)*

and waited.

The FV constituent parts converged on the command and anonymously scattered throughout Main. Seconds later the report was materialised by another army of code fragments which again dispersed into nothingness as rapidly as they had coalesced. Kline opened the result in protected local private mode, completely detached from Main.

Deceased Cremated
I(a) Intracerebral haemorrhage
I(b) Cerebral metastases
I(c) Squamous cell carcinoma of right main bronchus
II Diabetes mellitus

He recoiled and fell backwards into a chair, knocking it over and falling to the floor himself. He sat there for several minutes, trying to take it in. Jules didn't have diabetes; he would definitely have known about it. And then lung cancer with secondary growths in her brain? But she had been perfectly fine when they had met only three weeks ago. Could that be right? No way, something was very, very wrong here. Kline hauled himself up from the floor and reread the report in disbelief.

Deceased Cremated. The realisation seared his emotions as it sunk in. Jules had been killed and the records falsified so there was absolutely no trail left to follow.

He ran out of the little office and back to his stolen flat.

Noomi

THE WAFER HAD WOKEN her early.

'dr olawadi. dr anders kline here. friend of cradle's. haven't met you but need your help. sorry. details in next message.'

Noomi Olawadi had received the pair of messages that morning and decided to act upon them at face value. Something about Kline's direct approach connected with her, and research into the man's public profile suggested that he was trustworthy. He was known to be close to Cradle and was his only long-term work colleague. Besides, she hadn't heard anything from Cradle since their meeting in the pub and this was the only connection she now had.

She followed the instructions in Kline's second message to the letter, taking a pod directly to one of the less salubrious areas of outer town, and bringing a small bag of clothes and belongings with her.

She waited for half an hour before he finally showed up. He was easy to recognise from his Main profile imagery, a little older now but distinguished – strangely attractive if a little dishevelled.

'I was getting worried that you weren't going to make it,' Noomi said. Kline took her arm without saying a word and led her quickly into one of the abandoned buildings.

Once inside, he showed her his right hand. She looked at the still-healing wound.

'I've removed my 'Tab so they can't find me, but they'll be able to trace me using you. You have to do the same if you want to help.'

'What do you mean? What's going on, Dr Kline?'

'It's Anders, please. Julie Clayden has been murdered by Perpetua because she found something. You told Cradle you thought there was something going on at Perpetua. There is. We don't have much time.'

Noomi noticed his shaking hands. And he seemed to have been weeping.

'My God – murdered? And now you want me to have my 'Tab removed? But that would isolate me from my research, my colleagues. Everything.'

'Not exactly "have" your 'Tab removed. No one is going to help us.'

Noomi's eyes widened as it dawned on her what Kline was saying.

'You mean we have to remove it ourselves?'

'It's the only way. If you want to help, you have to disappear. And we have to do it here. Now. And then we have to move quickly because they'll know you've disconnected and they'll come after you. You decide.'

Noomi lost consciousness at some point in the procedure, she didn't recall exactly when. Kline closed the wound and talked her back from the oblivion that ensued from the disconnection. They moved quickly into another unoccupied area of town, taking a few pods and paying in Incogs. She was too disoriented to notice exactly where it was, but Kline appeared to be living there on his own. His coat and few possessions lay scattered about the bed. He raked them onto the floor.

'Sleep here for a while until you get the hang of it.'

She remembered nothing more until she woke to the smell of coffee. There was daylight. She queried for the time but when nothing came she remembered about the 'Tab and sat up on the bed.

'What time is it?'

'About eight.'

Hearing Kline use approximation in his speech was like something from an old paper book.

'Want some?' Kline questioned, handing her the mug. The smell almost overpowered her and she realised she was incredibly thirsty. She took the handle and sat in silence, looking down at the coffee spiralling gently between her hands. Her right hand was bandaged and clean, a dull ache throbbing beneath the swaddling. She felt as though she was sitting on the edge of a dark precipice rather than a bed.

'I must be crazy to have done this.'

'That's the one entry criterion to the club, Dr Olawadi. Membership of two now. Are you ready to hear what I know?'

Noomi looked up at Kline. He was thin and drawn, his dark hair greying at the edges and scruffed up at the top and left side where he had slept. He needed a shower and a meal, and he looked severely dehydrated too. Holding it together, but barely.

'Yes, yes. I'm ready now, Anders.' She moved over so he could sit next to her on the bed. 'And please call me Noo.'

He explained their suspicions about energy tagging, Cradle's research and discovery of the glyphs, Jules's interpretation of the message, her capture, and her murder. His voice wavered and broke slightly at these latter points but he pushed on with an intensity of deliberation that was chilling to observe.

Cradle and Eve were hiding out in the old research centre in Wales, and Noomi and he were to meet them there in a day or so – as soon as possible. There they would formulate a plan to stop Perpetua from doing what they were doing. Somehow. That was the open-ended part of the arrangements.

Noomi watched Kline as he visibly maintained his composure, breathing deeply and quickly. Now she looked about the room with a clearer head and saw that he had smashed a mirror and destroyed a chair and several other items at some point before she had arrived.

She knew that Kline wanted to find who had murdered Jules and then kill them with his own hands.

Disconnection

CRADLE AND EVE LEFT the pod shortly after it broke surface at Cheltenham, picked up a few supplies and meds, bought 1,000 Incogs each and made their way to Montpellier Gardens. The place was deserted and the day was clear of rain so Eve set up surgery on a park bench near the old statue to the east side of the gardens. Etched by many decades of increasingly energised weather, the lettering on the statue's plinth was still partially legible.

#IL##AM IV. 1830 – 37.
##ECTED BY PU##IC #UB#######ON 18#3
TO COM #######TE THE C#RO##TION O#
##NG W###IAM ##.
MO##D FROM ##E ORIGINAL LOCAT### #N
###ERIA# GAR###S TO THE PRESENT S##E IN 19##

Cradle's mind wandered. He could feel his instincts trying to piece together the sentence. He couldn't recall much detailed history, but sequences and patterns fell easily into his memory. He remembered a fragment without querying.

'George 4, William 4, Victoria,' he mumbled. 'Where's his nose?'

Eve looked up at the statue. 'Not sure who that even is, to be honest. And I don't want to use what might be my last query finding out, frankly. He does have a really nice cloak, though.'

'King William the Fourth. In between the Prince Regent and Queen Victoria, I think. Beautiful tree.'

'Hmm?' Eve followed his gaze to the lime tree across the path from the bench. Standing over forty metres, it was not the biggest tree in the gardens, but its symmetry and colour were striking, those golden leaves still on the branch catching the sunlight as they were agitated by the breeze and occasionally parachuted to the ground. 'Oh yeah. It's lovely.' Sometimes Cradle's distractions were hard to comprehend.

Eve pulled her attention back to the bench and shifted her position to be in physical contact with him.

'Cradle, are you sure we can't just disable these things? With a pulse or something?'

'Well, I might be able to rig up a crude electromagnetic pulse generator from old pod parts, if we could get hold of one without drawing attention. But we don't have much time to get off Main. They will already know we're here. Plus, I could never be sure it had completely worked without having the right test equipment. I might only damage the 'Tabs, but not prevent them from communicating, in which case it would all be a waste of time, we'd still be on-system. The safest way is to just cut them out now.'

Eve looked at him for several seconds, thinking it through.

'OK then, OK. It's going to need an incision about a centimetre long directly above the 'Tab site. That bit's easy. But they've been in since we were five years old so they're going to be pretty well healed-in by now. I mean our bodies will have covered them with a membrane to protect themselves from an alien object. It'll be semipermeable so they can interact with our local body chemistry to get their power and neural connections, but it could still be quite tough. It's going to need some cutting away I think.'

'Yep, OK. That sounds about right. I can feel where mine is pretty exactly. You?'

Eve pressed around the flesh between her right thumb and index finger.

'Yes, there it is. Right here.' She showed him.

'Same.' He gripped his own right hand. 'Right Eve, there's something you need to understand about what's going to happen when we take them out.'

She tensed slightly. 'Why do I get the feeling this isn't going to be good?'

He looked at Eve, her blonde hair tussled, and cheeks reddened by the gentle breeze, sitting left leg to his right as if they were at home, and he smiled warmly.

'Don't worry. Thing is, we've had these in for most of our lives and so we've been connected into Main all that time. We've grown up being used to all that connectivity, second nature, being part of the data. We don't think for a moment when we query or log or get directions or news updates. Whatever. It's a huge part of who we are.'

She nodded.

'All that stops when the 'Tabs go. No more connection. We'll be totally isolated.'

'Well, that's what we want, isn't it? To drop off the radar?'

'Yeah, but it will feel completely different to anything we can remember. Anders said it was the loneliest feeling he had ever experienced, like falling forever with nobody to help you.'

She held his hand and squeezed, rubbing his 'Tab site with her thumb.

'How can we be lonely when we're with each other, Cradle?' She kissed him gently on the lips. 'We are much too tangled up together. You are my Main.'

He lay his right hand on his lap, palm up.

'Ready then?'

'Ready.'

She snapped on sterile gloves and numbed his hand with Nanogese.

'Worst operating theatre I've ever worked in. Sure?'

'Go for it, Eve.'

She squeezed the flesh between his thumb and index finger and easily felt the device, even through gloves. The small scalpel sliced the skin, and a little blood began to fill the wound. She swabbed with some sterile gauze and felt for the 'Tab with the blade. The end scraped against it.

'OK?' she asked, not looking away from his hand.

'Yep, totally numb. I can feel you moving it though. Weird.'

'I'm going to try to free it up now.'

Eve swabbed again to briefly see into the wound before it filled with blood again. She cut the end of the membrane and squeezed. Nothing. She pared the membrane away from the sides of the 'Tab and felt it move against her touch.

'Nearly.'

She squeezed again and the device popped from the wound as though suddenly rejected by Cradle's immune system. He groaned and briefly lost consciousness. When he came round he was aware of Eve's hair on his face and the sweet smell of her skin against his cheek. He raised his hand to see that she had neatly stitched the wound.

'How is it?' Eve whispered.

'Quiet. Desolate. Utterly silent. No pain. Bit scary.'

'I'm here.' She held him for minutes, breathing together.

Eventually, Cradle pulled slightly away and looked at Eve, eye to eye.

'Now you. I was watching.'

'Your hand not too numb still?

He wiggled his fingers. 'Nope, all good. Amazing.'

She leaned forward and put her right hand onto his lap, palm upwards.

'Well then. Gloves please.'

'Yep.' He lifted her hand, kissed each fingertip and placed it back on his lap.

He opened the second sterile pack and, with some difficulty, pulled the gloves up.

'Three-quarters on is a pass. I've seen worse.' She smiled at him.

Massaging the Nanogese into the skin between her thumb and index finger, he asked 'How's that?'

'No idea, Cradle, it's all numb already. That stuff works in seconds. No need for massage therapy ...'

He opened a fresh scalpel pack. He felt for the device beneath Eve's skin. Her hands were slender and delicate, an easy task to locate the foreign body within.

'Got it.'

'So just go directly down to the 'Tab. No waving the scalpel around inside the cut, right?'

'Yep.'

'OK then.' Eye to eye. 'Chop away, maestro.'

The smile was unconvincing camouflage for her nervousness. He gently touched the tip of the blade to her skin, and it cruelly disappeared into her flesh.

'Careful, they're so sharp. Swab with the gauze there.' Eve pointed with her left hand. Cradle swabbed and looked into the incision he had made. A bit bigger than his one but not too bad for a newb. He felt for the device and quickly scraped against it, making her jump slightly.

'OK?'

'Feels weird. OK.'

He drew the blade against one side of the 'Tab and trimmed back the membrane. Then the other side.

'Ready Eve?'

She adjusted her position on the bench and looked down at her hand. 'Ready.'

He squeezed and Eve fainted.

She regained consciousness and jumped slightly as her eyes opened and were unable to focus because of Cradle's face being nose-to-nose with hers.

'There you are.'

A wave of emptiness pushed her over into an abyss. 'Oh, Cradle, hold me.' She sobbed and he held her tightly.

'I love you, Eve. I will reach in and pull you out. Stay with me. By the way, I couldn't do the stitches. I was asleep when you did mine, so I didn't see. I've just wrapped it up in the gauze for now.'

She managed to laugh, even as her right palm dripped blood onto the ground between them and her mind spun alone in a pitch-dark void.

'It's OK. I can do the stitches when we're there. I'll just keep pressure on it.'

After a few minutes, they rose from the bench and walked, entwined, out of the gardens, leaving the two 'Tabs on the ground, busily uploading emergency meta-data to Main before their power exhausted and they became silent.

To West

THEY MANAGED TO FIND a manual payment interface and dropped a handful of Incogs into the chute, booking the run out to Worcester, anonymous and untraceable. The pod drew up alongside them within thirty seconds and they stepped inside it and sat down, selecting the windows into opaque mode.

After ten minutes in standard travel, they arrived at Worcester and left the pod. There they repeated the same manual payment manoeuvre, firstly across to Hereford, and thereafter another pod on to Hay-On-Wye and, at last, one final leg, travelling the eight miles south over Gospel Pass to Capel-y-ffin. Because of the constricted road and poor infrastructure, the pod moved at low travel, climbing for nearly six miles up to 1,800 feet above sea level, then falling again to arrive in Capel-y-ffin.

They watched as the pod left them, accelerating uphill and north along the pass, emptily returning to Hay. The two stood as fugitives at the side of a single-track road on the dividing edge of two countries, an old derelict church to their right, hunkering in between where they stood and the conjunction of Afon Honddu with the smaller Nant Bwch as it meandered its way down from the Black Mountains.

'We have to walk a little back up the hill, Eve. I didn't want the pod's log to record exactly where we're going to stay. Can you manage?'

'Is it far?' A little blood was still weeping from her hand and had soaked through the gauze again.

'About half an hour if we go easy. Lean on me.'

They set off on foot, back the way the pod had come, climbing the tree-draped road as it rose 300 feet from their starting location.

'Are you alright, Eve?' She was increasingly heavy on his arm and dragged her feet a little as they walked. She looked at him, her eyes sunken and wide.

'Might we have done something too big, Cradle? I feel so lost.'

'I know where you are Eve. You're just where you should be. With me. The feeling will fade away. I used to feel like this every time I came out of DREAM and it always, always goes, but you'll need a few days. I'll take care of you.'

Nanbiot

THEY REACHED BOUNDARY AS the autumn light was beginning to fade. The old gate had partially detached from one of its hinges so Cradle carefully lifted it open and then closed it again behind them. The path swung left uphill to the side of the accommodation blocks then round to the right above them and up to the old farmhouse. As they walked, he noticed that the younger constructions, designed to home the various scientific teams, had fallen into a far greater state of disrepair than the original solid stone farm buildings. The contrast was obvious. The new, designed for a short-term project, had started to decay almost as quickly as it had appeared. The old remained nearly intact, built for centuries of shelter against the mountains' driving rain and winds.

They headed for the main farmhouse; it looked the most complete. The roof seemed undamaged, and the doors and windows appeared to all be sound. It was impossible to see the laboratories, cut into the rock behind the buildings. They had always been well concealed but now the trees were taller and the bushes significantly wilder, having been allowed to partially reclaim their birthright, unrestrained for over three years.

Cradle tried the front door. Locked, of course. Eve wavered at his side, exhausted from the journey and still in shock from the detachment.

'Wait here, Eve.' He helped her sit at the big front doorstep and ran round to the old tool shed at the rear of the building. The spare keys always used to be hidden in a wooden box at the rear of the shed. There was much decay here and he easily pushed open the door and peered in, a nervous excitement dancing in his stomach, borne of half-forgotten familiarity mixed with anticipation of failure or being caught. The childish butterflies of naughtiness. The squeak of Grandad's wardrobe door when he was just downstairs. There the box lay under the bench, damp and mildewed, almost completely covered with rotting leaves. He picked it up and it fell apart in his hands. The keys were still there.

The front door lock surrendered reluctantly to the old brass key and the hinges cracked loudly as they relinquished their rusty bond, creaking open in a final act of defiance. Cradle helped Eve into the hallway and upstairs to the smaller bedroom at the back of the house, away from the road. The bed still had its mattress and, without sparing the time to contemplate who or what had lived on or in it, he lay her gently down and covered her with his coat, and then drew himself gently against her side.

The following day Eve was less distant, more communicative and brighter. By mid-morning she had stitched the wound herself; having recleaned the area with antiseptic fluid and a touch of Nanogese, she bound the flesh with three little square stitches. The bleeding had stopped, although her hand was swollen from the previous day's exertions. In the afternoon they briefly ventured out behind the farmhouse and picked blackberries and apples from the wild orchard. Eating them in the farmhouse kitchen, she asked, 'How long will we stay here, do you think?'

'Oh, not long, just a couple of weeks I guess. Anders will make his way up here and we'll plan from there.'

'Are we safe?'

'Should be. Our set of pod jumps will be very hard to trace because of the Incogs. Effectively, we've vanished off the face of the planet. Main will catch our trail eventually, bound to, but we have breathing space.'

Sunday too they rested, awaiting Kline's arrival. They searched the farmhouse and found some old sheets and blankets that had survived the years of disuse unscathed, all neatly sealed in waterproof storage bags: they wiped the mattress down and made up the bed. The emergency food store was intact and still fully stocked, so they moved several armloads of tins and water bottles indoors. They foraged for dry branches and sticks and lit a small fire in the lounge fireplace and, by the evening, the farmhouse was feeling slightly more homely.

'Imagine if this was actually ours, Cradle, and we could just live in it without any worries.'

He smiled and kissed her. She flinched as he brushed her right arm.

'Sorry, bit tender.'

'Mine's all healing up fine, are you sure it's OK? I noticed you carrying it today in the woods.'

'Alright, Superman, you always heal quicker than me.' She took his hand and bit his fingers. 'Come on.'

The chronic emptiness of isolation from Main had drained them both. They led each other to the bedroom and there, even though light still clung to the musty silhouette of day, they slept immediately.

He woke with a jolt to find Eve sitting up in bed. Her eyes shone in the semi-darkness and he could see she was wide awake.

'How's the hand?'

'Pretty swollen. Think it may be slightly infected.'

He sat up and switched on the lamp, swinging himself over to Eve's side. Her hand was inflamed and red around the bandaged area.

'Let me have a look, Eve.'

He gently removed the bandage and saw that the wound was still unhealed, with a grainy red growth exuding from between the stitches.

'That doesn't look right, Eve. What's happening?'

She brought her hand into the light so she could see better.

'Damn it, I must have got something in it or tied the sutures too tightly. It's starting to dehisce and hypergranulate.' Her speech was slightly slurred and slower than usual.

'Where are the antibiotics?'

Eve screwed up her face. 'Cradle, I didn't get any. We were hurrying so much I forgot.'

He stood up and began pacing and mumbling. 'I can get them. I'll have to get to a town ... go up to Hay. Yeah, that's maybe seven miles. No pods this end so I could probably get there in a couple of hours ... Try to run most of it, then a pod back, so maybe two and a half there and back.' He took the Incogs from Eve's jacket and added them to his own. Eve began shivering gently. He kissed her forehead. She was too warm.

'I'll be back as soon as I can.'

'So cold.' Her teeth started chattering as she spoke. The shivering became stronger and more violent, and she made involuntary groans as her body vibrated her chest and modulated her breathing. Cradle held her, rubbing her back and holding his face to hers.

'It's OK, Eve, it's OK. I'm here.'

After five minutes of this, the shaking subsided and Eve regained composure.

'God, Eve, are you OK?'

'It's a rigor, Cradle. Not good. Could be a blood infection.'

'What? Did I do this to you?'

'I probably did it to myself. Never was much of a seamstress. I'll see if I can sleep it off a bit. My body might beat it by itself.'

'But you need antibiotics? Nanbiot, is it?'

'Yes, anything like that. Stupid me.' She lay on her side and fell asleep quickly, her breathing slightly faster than usual.

The Pass was unlit by a clear but moonless autumn sky, and he spotted Mars in the southwest, obvious and red. He estimated it was 30 degrees up and on its descent towards the horizon. He looked left for Orion and found Betelgeuse in the southeast, again around thirty degrees up. He calculated that it must be about 2.30 a.m.

As his eyes dark-adapted, his run was even-paced and steady, but he was forced to slow to a fumbling walk whenever the way was shadowed by trees. Not a living soul up here. Good for hiding. Very bad for help. He tried not to count his steps but couldn't help himself. It was a distraction.

12,828. He arrived on the outskirts of Hay and quickly found the old family dispensary on Castle Street. He hoped they lived above the shop. They surely must. No lights on.

He flammed his knuckles three times on the door and waited. No lights upstairs, no sound inside. Again he knocked, this time harder, with the heel of his hand. He became aware of sweat dripping from his nose and his heart pounded in his ears.

Nothing. Why would anyone want to travel to work when you could just as easily live above it? Then he saw the sign in the window. Handwritten on a piece of packing material, it read 'Closed due to illness'. Drowse was no respecter of isolation or seclusion, it was happy to take anyone from anywhere, whether in the middle of bustling city centres or out here, remote and unwitnessed.

The door's glass panelling looked antiquated, intentionally so for the tourists. Very few of these old materials were used any longer but people still liked to see and touch the history.

He wrapped his hand and forearm in his coat and punched. The glass dropped in shards about the stand of eCanns, hacks and implant packs near the entrance. No alarms or lights. The owners must have succumbed to Drowse very quickly and been hospiced before they could make the place secure. Cradle swiftly cleared enough space to safely get his arm through and opened the door latch. He scurried to the far end of the room, looking for the meds cabinet. He found it quickly and searched for something to break open the lock, but as the starlight flitted around him he saw that the cabinet was unlocked, the door hanging slightly ajar, uneven.

'Perfect, already broken,' he breathed and pulled the cabinet door fully open. His eyes fell upon a carton labelled Nanbiot Topical. He took three boxes, then the last two boxes of Nanbiot Oral, all stuffed urgently into his bag. He glanced around to see if the coast was still clear. Yes. He left 20 Incogs on the counter and stepped out onto the pavement. He ran the short distance to the pod bay at the old castle, dropped 30 Incogs into the chute and stepped into a pod. It set off up the hill out of town and left onto Forest Road into the darkness, towards Orion and back over the pass to Eve.

He threw open the door to the farmhouse and ran upstairs and into the bedroom where Eve lay. The sheets were knotted about her and she lay diagonally across the bed.

'Got them, Eve,' he puffed. 'How're you doing?'

She was still asleep in the darkness, unstirring. Cradle knelt at the bedside and playfully touched the first knuckle of his index finger to her nose as he always did.

She was stone cold.

'Eve!'

He thumped the light on and pulled her up into a sitting position to see her face. Her eyes were open, cloudy and inert, her face blanched and inexpressive. Cold vomit clung to the side of the bed.

'Oh no, no, no.'

He lifted her onto his lap and curled himself over her as if to give protection from some unseen threat.

He looked helplessly down on his girl, his tears falling upon her face as if to gently coax her back to him with their warmth. But her eyes did not blink in their salt and her breath remained perfectly still.

Cradle lifted her. She seemed so light, yet she was heavier in his arms than anything he had ever held in his life. He carried her downstairs to the big sofa and sat in his usual place in front of the roaring fireplace, amidst the uproar of colleagues' impassioned discussions on latest hypotheses and the laughter and furore of youthful enthusiasm.

'And who's this then, Cradle?' It was Josephs, the German child genius and polymath who was working with him on some of the more theoretical aspects of the programme. The music and laughter from the rest of the party made it difficult to talk, so Cradle shouted his reply.

'This is Eve, my girl.'

'Not dancing, Cradle?' Henry. Cradle had never really clicked with him; very confident and forthright, a natural quantum physicist and a relentlessly probabilistic thinker. He knew Cradle was too self-conscious to dance and always teased him. 'Ooh, but this is interesting. May I have this waltz?'

'Oh, no, she's with me actually. She's tired. It's Eve. She's my friend. Well, my girlfriend, actually.'

'Nice! Well, I'll leave you two lovebirds alone then, my glass is dangerously low. Don't do anything I wouldn't do.' Henry wandered off back to the party. The log fire roared and danced their shadows against the wall. A guffaw of voices diverted Henry's footsteps and he disappeared into the kitchen.

'Actually, we're married. Me and Eve. Always. It was great. Everything. Just here for a rest really. Hiding too. Only visiting. She's tired from the journey.'

But nobody heard him from the quiet kitchen. The lounge was empty. The fire had burned down to damp ash.

He lowered himself on unsteady legs into the dusty embrace of the big leather sofa and folded his face into her breast, rocking back and forth, crying out into the darkness.

Outside, leaves, recently cast from the encroaching wilderness, rattled shamelessly about the yard, incited by the autumnal breeze, gossiping about the desperation of solitude, until a gentle rain silenced their pitiless whisper with its own respectful susurrus.

Kline arrives

KLINE PUSHED OPEN THE old farmhouse door, the memories flooding back. The sun rose at his back as he stepped over the threshold. He beckoned to Noomi to follow him into the hallway and she tiptoed in.

'Cradle? You there, kid?' A sort of loud whisper. No answer. He went through into the lounge with Noomi a few steps behind and tensed as he discerned an outline sitting on the sofa before the unlit fireplace. The sun's early rays teased a little more detail into the scene and Kline saw, to his relief, that it was Cradle sitting with Eve on his lap.

'Hey buddy, guess who's joined the offline club?' He gestured towards Noomi.

Cradle turned and looked at Kline. His eyes were red and sunken, blackened beneath and salt-encrusted; his mouth gaped open, lips parched. Eve's arms were opened in a wide gesture and as Cradle rocked himself slowly back and forth, they moved in a fixed arc rather than swinging freely. Kline could see she was in rigor mortis and stepped back a pace until Noomi touched his arm and whispered, 'Help him.'

'Oh, Cradle.' They both knelt beside him.

'I'm sorry, old lad, let me help you here. She's gone, son. I'm so sorry. Let me look after Eve for you.'

Cradle snarled at his friend and turned away, pulling Eve's stiffened body round with him.

'Cradle, she's gone. Come on, let me help you.' Kline placed one hand on Cradle's back and patted in time with his swaying. 'Come on, old son.'

Cradle stopped moving and turned his head to look directly into Kline's eyes. 'Anders, I ...'

Cradle lifted his arms and held his hands above Eve's body in numb disbelief. He allowed his friend to gently slide an arm behind her back and then another beneath her knees and lift her away. Her body was rigidly fixed in position from Cradle's final embrace; he must have held her this way for several hours. Kline took Eve's body upstairs to one of the smaller rooms and carefully put her down on the bed, covering her with some curtains that lay on the floor. He went downstairs again and found Noomi kneeling at the sofa and embracing Cradle, openly weeping together.

He sat in another chair on the opposite side of the fireplace and held his head in his hands, helplessly waiting for this long moment to pass.

Focus

CRADLE WAS INCONSOLABLE FOR four days, sleeping almost continuously, uncommunicative and numb to all that Kline and Noomi offered him, barely eating, and drinking only a little water. On the fifth morning, he woke very early and again sat on the sofa before the empty fireplace, awaiting his friends.

Kline was first down and tried to conceal his surprise at seeing his friend up and about again. 'Oh. Hi, Cradle. How are you doing?'

'I want your help, Anders. You and Noomi.'

'OK ...'

'I'm not an idiot. I know what killed Eve.' He hesitated a little at the feel of her name on his lips. 'I cut out her 'Tab and some bacteria got into the wound. I didn't know how to stitch it up. I killed her.'

'Christ no, Cradle, absolutely not. Don't blame yourself, this is just a horrible accident.'

'No, Anders, let me say it. I have to lay this all out so I can understand it properly. Find the reason.'

'Sometimes bad things just happen, Cradle. You can't take the blame for that.'

Noomi walked into the room and said nothing. She smiled at Cradle.

'Eve died of sepsis because I cut her open and took out her 'Tab. But I wasn't good enough at it and she got ill. And then I couldn't get the medicine she needed fast enough to save her.'

Noomi awkwardly shifted her weight onto her other foot and remained quiet, no longer smiling, scared of where Cradle might go with this.

'I did try, I know that. But I failed. So I killed her.'

'Cradle,' Noomi started ...

'No, Noo.' He pushed his right palm towards her. 'No.' She saw his neatly stitched wound and stopped talking.

'Why did I kill Eve, then? I love her. I didn't want to, so why did I? What happened?' He looked anxiously from Noomi to Kline.

Kline knew what Cradle was thinking. He was trying to analyse his way out of his grief and defeat it with a reasoned argument. He was unsure if this was a good idea but he knew Cradle's mind needed to pass this way and he had to help him find the way out. Something to focus on. A rope dropped into the abyss.

'Perpetua,' Kline volunteered coldly.

'Perpetua. The Flow. Drowse.' Cradle rose to his feet. 'I need your help now, both of you. I am going to stop this. They have destroyed everything I have. And so I am going to fight them.'

'Look, Cradle,' began Kline.

'Help me do this, Anders. Please.'

Kline looked at Noomi and she raised her eyebrows briefly to him.

'Of course we will, Cradle. We're in this together.'

At midday, they held a small memorial service for Eve. No religion, no speeches. Kline prepared a grave in the woods, sheltered by the boughs of beautiful oak trees and teeming with the life of the woodland, and they lowered Eve's shrouded body into the ground. It had been heart-wrenching and awful. Noomi wept quietly against Kline's shoulder as they watched Cradle lying face down on the grave and repeatedly screaming Eve's name into the freshly turned soil. Then suddenly he was silent. He calmly stood, face and teeth muddy and streaked by tears, and spoke to his friends.

'I'm ready.'

And he walked back into the farmhouse without another word.

About Jules

KLINE TENTATIVELY OPENED THE door to Cradle's room. He was sitting in the bay window looking out at the gathering clouds. They sped through the window's aperture, propelled by the westerlies as they weaved their way across the mountains. It was 10.15 a.m. the day after Eve's funeral. Could be a Thursday.

'Hi, buddy. How you doing?'

Cradle broke away from the scene and turned to face Kline.

'Yeah, OK.'

'You alright to talk?'

'Probably.'

Cradle looked like he hadn't slept and was even thinner than usual, a drawn, hungry look hanging upon his face, shoulders rounded into a slump.

'It's about Jules.'

Kline stared through the window at Cradle's clouds.

'Oh yeah, sorry, I totally ... Where is she? Thought she was coming with you but it's only Noo.'

'She ... Look, there's no good way to say this Cradle, no good time.'

Cradle stood up and stared wide-eyed at his friend.

'They killed her. She's gone.'

Cradle visibly deflected at the news, his hands clenched, and his weight staggered backwards.

'Anders, I'm ...'

'No, no, it's ok. I'm ok. We were close but it was a long while ago. I'll be OK.'

But Cradle saw that Kline's mouth was an open wound and the words bled from his lips.

'I wanted you to know everything. Where things are now.'

Kline's hands were somehow on Cradle's shoulders.

'She decoded the glyphs.'

Incubus

CRADLE KISSED HER CHEEK. The familiar scent of her skin pervaded his senses, eyes closed, breathing slowly beneath the covers. Her warmth enveloped him completely now, no up, no down, nowhere outside of this moment, everything silent and beautiful. His hands touched her body, his Eve. Their fingers entwined and it was like that first meeting, the patterns, but now they sought them together, as one, their movements concert, dancers catching the sunlight, one shape moving perfectly into the next.

His hand fell upon something cold and he pulled it upwards to see what it was, catching her skin as he did so. A blade. The blood pooled on her stomach, ferrous, and her smell was Autumn. Her taste was fresh dirt and wet leaves. He opened his eyes and saw her face, mouth locked open in an anorexic grimace. He tried to pull away, but the weight of soil above bore him down, pressing him against her canvas skin, cold now and unyielding. He cried out, but the dirt in his mouth desiccated the scream. Her stiff arms snapped beneath his chest like dry sticks as he struggled, her ribs cracking as he fell into her.

He was standing by the bed, drenched with perspiration, gasping for air. He fell to kneeling, chest rising and falling as the adrenaline relinquished its grip, his heartbeat in his ears and head. Outside, the quarter moon was high, between clouds, gently suffusing the room with its reflected grey light, the sun's searing harshness tamed by the ancient dust of that lonely satellite. He wiped his forearm across his mouth. No soil, no dirt, no leaves.

Theory 1

IT WAS LATE EVENING and Cradle was dozing on the sofa. Noomi moved to his side and touched his face.

'Cradle, are you awake?'

He stirred and opened his eyes. Probably somewhere near Saturday now. His first thought was Eve. The thought of her exactly filled the howling chasm in his heart. He wept again. Noomi held him. He closed his eyes.

'I'm sorry to disturb you. I just need to tell you something. I know this is a terrible time for you but I think this might be important.'

He pulled his head away from her shoulder and opened his eyes again, wiping his face with his fingers.

'Sorry, I've made your shirt wet again.'

'Doesn't matter.' A gentle smile glistened in her eyes. 'I have a theory about Drowse, and I need your help to see if it makes any sense. And Anders thinks it might help you to have something to focus on.'

Cradle nodded and sat up. 'OK.' He unconsciously folded Eve and Jules and the nightmare safely away into a compartment and unfurled his attention for Noomi, like opening a children's pop-up book from the 20th century.

'I was thinking. It looks like it started in our cells. I mean, it looks like Drowse sufferers lose energy from their cells directly, it goes somewhere outside of them. We don't know how or where.'

He nodded.

'So it's some kind of energy flow or leak that we don't understand and can't even detect. As if something is reaching out and connecting to random subjects.'

Cradle leaned forward towards Noomi, his mind more focused now. 'Hidden energy conduits were hypothesised by a few outliers from the original Boundary team,' he said, 'but they were never expressed in any coherent or testable theory. Have you got any evidence for them?'

'No, nothing at all. I was just thinking around the problem. Let me just lay out what we know and please forgive the school biology lesson while I get my thoughts straight.

'The process of energy generation in animal cells is well understood. We are not equipped with the raw materials to survive so we have to cheat the system by stealing nutrients from the outside world and converting them into the fuel we need to support our own lives. Humans have evolved to be extremely versatile at this, which is a major factor in our getting to be the dominant species on the planet.'

'Yeah,' Cradle chipped in, 'some call it being omnivorous. Others call it wrecking the planet. That's life.' He half smiled. Kline might be pleased with that.

'Our eukaryotic cells use organic food molecules to make energy-rich structures like ATP and the NADH,' Noomi continued, 'via complicated chemical cycles known as energy pathways. Essentially, we break the tough bonds in big molecules to free up that stored energy and we release carbon dioxide as a by-product. We breathe out the CO_2 into the world and use up the energy doing things like moving muscles, running nerve systems and all the other chemistry within our bodies. Any extra that's not used gets stored in complex sugars and fats as a reservoir, which allows us to survive the next day in case no new food molecules are available.'

'Or, in the case of most humans, to survive for what looks like months and months.'

Noomi laughed and looked at Cradle. She could see his intensity was slowly returning.

'The energy originally comes from the sun, of course. Plants photosynthesise the sunlight, storing the energy in organic molecules and then animals eat the plants. And, of course, humans can eat almost all of it.'

'So we're very slowly eating our own star bit by bit, indirectly,' Cradle interjected. 'Plenty more where that came from so it's all one big, beautiful balance. Everything is understood and there are no mysteries to it.'

'Yes, but then a sort of leak happens. Some of the energy liberated by our energy pathways starts disappearing. Just vanishing without a trace. How can that be? Where's the balance?'

Cradle thought for a second, then picked up the baton. 'Thousands and millions of people somehow spilling cellular energy off into the ether, so where's the payback?' He paused and looked Noomi. 'I know one. The Flow.'

'Yes, that is what I have been wondering.' Noomi grimaced as though expecting an argument. 'Do you think it can be a balance for the energy lost by Drowse sufferers? Could it be that the energy is being somehow harvested by Perpetua and sold on?'

He stood up and paced the floor.

'God, Noo, what are you saying? Could someone do that to all those people?' He turned to face her from across the room. 'How can I test this? I can't, of course, there's no way.'

She walked over and stood open-palmed in front of him. 'So what can we do?'

Cradle thought for a few minutes, pacing again and serenading himself with his familiar quiet buzzing, humming sound.

'Well, if we can't detect the energy conduit itself, maybe we can at least check if the figures balance out.'

'Which figures?'

'Emmy Noether, early 20th century; she started it all. Most important woman in mathematics, ever. Everything stands on her work. Symmetry and conservation. Energy. You can't create it or destroy it, you can only change it from one form to another. So let's start with energy out equals energy in. Always a good foothold. Now, how much energy does a normal person burn up in a normal day, on average?'

'Oh, I see, yes. We always say around 2,000 kilocalories, which is about 8,400 kilojoules.'

An unintentional pun. Cradle thought of Kline telling him that Jules had been killed, and his resolve deepened.

'OK. And if a person sleeps all the time, like a Drowse victim, how much for that?'

Noomi put her hand to her mouth and looked sideward to her left for a few seconds.

'I think resting energy is probably between four and five kilojoules per minute. But this is going back such a long way to my undergraduate days, Cradle.' She shook her right hand. 'I so miss being connected.'

'That'll have to do. Let's say 4.5 kilojoules per minute, then that would give us ...' his voice dropped to a mumble, '24 times 3,600 times 4.5 ...' then louder, '6,480 kilojoules per day.'

'Quick, Cradle. Impressive.'

'Old party trick. The difference is about 1,900 kilojoules per person per day. In watts that's ...' mumbling again '... divide by 3,600, divide by 24 ...' and louder again 'that's about 22 watts of power gone missing per person. And how many Drowse victims are there?'

'Oh, that's quite difficult, Cradle. The total number of registered Drowse victims worldwide last month was around 3.5 million. But I believe there are large numbers of unknown cases in Africa and Asia, perhaps another million or more.'

'OK, so if we use 4.5 million as a first estimate, then. That gets us around 100 megawatts of power lost to Drowse. But The Flow produces a steady 9.4 terawatts, so that's just over 94 thousand times too small.'

'Sorry, which way round?' She was struggling to stay with him.

'Perpetua generates about 94 thousand times more energy than is being lost by people with Drowse. It doesn't balance, not even close. This only proves Perpetua are the good guys.'

Noomi frowned. 'But we know they're not, right? Good guys, I mean.'

'Oh yeah, I think we definitely know that.'

From his room, Kline had heard them talking and he came down to the lounge looking like he hadn't slept for weeks, clothes creased and dishevelled, face drained of colour. They both looked at him and Cradle spoke first.

'So we have to work together now. Perpetua is too dangerous. They will just wipe us out. Anders, we have to pull everything that Jules worked out about the glyphs into our thinking. Are you OK for that? You look shot.'

He looked at them both and nodded. 'Yeah, of course. I'm alright. Bit tired, that's all. Been a bit of a week.'

Kline turned to Noomi. 'One thing though. Noo, if we're going to do this, we have to be clear about what it is. You must be clear. You must understand that your life is in danger just being with us here. If you want to go, it's fine, we'll understand.'

She turned quickly to Kline, frowning. 'Anders, I'm a renegade in my field, I'm solo undercover, and I just cut out my own 'Tab with a penknife.' She smiled and Cradle teetered on the brink of reliving the moment that he pushed the scalpel into Eve's hand, then steeled himself. 'And anyway, I like you two. You're both completely mad. Why would I want to miss out on that?'

Cradle looked at Noomi for a long few seconds, trying to judge if she was earnest or confused. She returned his stare with rock-solid resolve. Earnest then.

'OK. Anders, Noo has a theory about animal cell energy being somehow stolen by Perpetua and resold back to the world.'

Kline blinked a couple of times and took a slow breath. He suddenly felt a hundred years old, and his hand was throbbing.

'But the numbers don't work by a factor of almost 100 thousand. In Perpetua's favour. The Flow is far greater than all the energy lost by the world's Drowse victims.'

'Actually Cradle, can we sleep on this after all? I'm done in.'

Noomi stepped between the two men. 'Anders is right, it's been a horrible time. It's a good idea. Let's get an early night to reset ourselves and start again in the morning.'

Searching

'THE RECOVERED BLOOD TYPES from the 'Tabs match with Mr Cradle and his partner, sir. We traced them to a public space in Cheltenham; a park. It seems they were removed outdoors because there were blood droplets and spatter in the area. We think they probably did it themselves.'

'I see.' Bryant sucked air noisily and looked down from his desk to the Security Officer. 'And what next?'

'Well, sir, because they avoided using any medical staff who would have registered, and the park is not monitored and there are no witnesses, the trail goes cold from there. Clever.'

Bryant breathed out quickly and the air before him invisibly succumbed to the sour vapour.

'Jesmond.' A tutting sound. 'That just will not do. If they are clever, you have to be brilliant.'

Security Officer Jesmond looked up with mounting panic. 'No, sir. We ... Well, sir, there were blood drops from the girl, leading out of the park area, so we definitely know they left the park. Or she did at least. But probably both of them.'

'Oh, that is excellent news, then. Forgive me and please accept my congratulations on your thorough work, most exemplary. I will certainly sleep easier knowing that they are not still hiding in a fucking tree in the park!'

Bryant stepped down from his desk platform and clasped Jesmond's throat with monstrous skeletal fingers.

'I want to know where they *are*, not where they *were*, you miserable little insect. Can you tell me that?'

Jesmond gurgled 'Sir... yes, sir. I will find out.'

Bryant pushed him away and turned his back.

'Is that really all you know? The sum total?' Hissed.

'Sir.' Jesmond rubbed his throat between his thumb and forefinger and gently coughed. 'We think they must have used hard Incog tokens to hire a public pod out of the city. Those old pods are blind – no cameras so no visuals available. The last transaction on Mr Cradle's record, registered by Main, was an Incog encashment at Cheltenham. And the same with his partner. I am arranging to have a forensic team check the pods for matching blood traces.'

'Very well, Officer Jesmond. This suggests that you are, perhaps, not a complete moron. So you have a chance to redeem yourself. To shine, indeed. I want that pod's destination. I give you four hours.'

'Sir, there are over five hundred pods to analyse. It's at least two days of ...'

'Then do it faster, Jesmond. Use more resources.' He spun to skewer the Security Officer with his icy glare. 'This is your only assignment now, your top priority. Do you understand? One thing only.'

'Yes, sir. More resources.'

'Very well.' Bryant gestured a timer function into commission with a staccato hand motion and it commenced its countdown with an acknowledging beep. 'You have 239 minutes to report back. Go.'

Bryant swung himself awkwardly back up to his desk and watched as Jesmond scuttled towards the door of the Line and Security Office. He faltered and made to turn back.

'GO!' The door shushed closed before the resonance had decayed to silence.

Matching

ALL PODS WERE RETURNED to base and disabled, rendering the entire public transport system of the city useless. Cheltenham ground to a halt with many hundreds of commuters and tourists stranded on street corners and in termini. Police were deployed to contain the anger, city-wide. No matter.

At the transport hub, hundreds of empty vehicles were queued, unable to even enter the perimeter; the statistics of normal operation thwarted by this complete and unprecedented standstill, with all pods in the same location at once.

At the heart of the chaos, twenty forensic bots scoured individual vehicles, their tendrilous arms sniffing and sampling, all running one single test: match for a single DNA signature. Thousands of tiny motors buzzed in this bizarre dance, gleaming metallic proboscides snaking over every surface. Handles, windows, seat fabric, flooring, roof-lining. No corner was spared the intrusion. At the tip of every probe, swarms of nanobotic forensic machines carried the question to the very molecules being interrogated, attempting to affect a temporary chemical bond with a single keyed interface and report back: a simple yes/no, are you there? A hundred million such questions asked in the passage of a single second, all results being harvested by the overriding management function of the forensic collaborator algorithm, centralised and remote from the action, of course, away from the dirty coalface in an inexorable parody of the way that all command-chain processes have behaved throughout human history. Every single time over millennia, momentous and terrible decisions were repeatedly undertaken with clean fingernails and in luxurious and splendid isolation from the real world. From the simple hierarchies of early man, through the various world wars in which countless deaths were inflicted by commanders from the comfortable safety of offices far from the front line, through the innumerable and ultimately trivial testosterone-driven business management houses of cards of the early twenty-first centuries. And again now, by proxy of computational processes running on Main. Somewhere in fact so diffuse that it had no distinct location whatsoever.

Forensic Facility #1117 Probe Arm 28, Test Ref 86473625, positive match 95% key binding

The alert rang out through the virtual fabric of the forensic search team, immediately standing down all but one resource. The machines instantly retreated from their crippled prey, withdrawing their gleaming fingers and disappearing back into stasis, sleeping and ready for the next assignment. Could be tomorrow, could be a thousand years. They would simply wait with unthinking obedience.

Meanwhile, Forensic Facility #1117 flood-repeated its tests on the pod in question, this time using its entire nanobot arsenal. Three seconds later came a cacophony of confirmation alerts.

Forensic Facility #1117 – Flood Test all probes – 99.9 95% key binding

A match. Statistically as close to perfect as the inconvenient real world could offer. It was pod serial #53132, a standard issue, no-frills AI mechanism. Four seats, range 200km, top speed 160km per hour, light off-road capacity. A bog-standard ground transport drone, unusual in no particular area except one; it contained traces of the right kind of blood.

By the time the news reached Security Officer Jesmond, the complete log of journeys had been stripped from the pod, analysed and correlated with the bloodied Cheltenham microTabs' termination reports.

The results were incontrovertible. Eve had boarded the pod at Cheltenham and travelled to Worcester.

Theory 1.1

THE MORNING FOUND KLINE wide awake, his mind spinning with recent events. Jules's death was his overriding thought. He wondered how she had died and who had killed her, and he couldn't help repeatedly coming back to Bryant, although he wasn't sure if this was merely dislike for the man or if his suspicion was based on some subliminal evidence that he hadn't yet fully pieced together. Her note had opened up a long-forgotten old wound and he struggled to cauterise the exposed nerves.

All this was compounded by what had happened to Eve and the effect it was having on his friend. Cradle was off kilter somehow; quite naturally, of course. He looked like he was grieving normally and finding his feet again, albeit slowly, but Kline knew he had changed: as if something inside was forever broken and he was merely going through the motions of daily life without fully engaging. Cradle had always had this strange capacity to detach, particularly when he was working on a challenging problem, but this felt more severe; deeper and more permanent. He blamed himself for Eve's death. And Eve had been his world.

And then there was Noomi, who had joined them with little hesitation when the opportunity arose. And he trusted her completely, but was he right to do so? Had he been too hasty? Was he swayed by her intelligence or physical attractiveness? Neither he nor Cradle knew her at all. She checked out completely when they first ran the tests on her profile but could they have missed something? On the other hand, who would agree to disconnection if they weren't in earnest? It would be a hell of a sacrifice for whatever supposed cause she might be working.

No, on balance Noo was good, he thought. Sometimes you have to go with your gut and not be paranoid. They needed her, and she needed them, and no one else was about to step up to the mark.

'Hey, Anders?' A gentle knock on his bedroom door. It was Noomi.

'Come in Noo, I'm up. I was just thinking about you, actually.'

Noomi cracked the door open and poked her face round. 'Is that a good thing?' She smiled.

'Yeah, yeah, I think it's a good thing. I was just running through whether you might be the enemy or not.'

She stepped into the room. Unkempt long hair loosely tied with a strip of cloth, jeans, a white T-shirt and an old baggy jumper. Kline couldn't remember seeing anyone or anything more beautiful in his life.

'So am I? The enemy, I mean.'

'No, Noo. You're not the enemy. You're not. There's just such a lot going on here that ... Oh, I don't know. Just running things over, you know?'

Noomi smiled and walked over to Kline, gently touching his shoulder.

'I know, yes. This is all too much for anyone. But you do get 10 points though.'

Kline laughed for the first time in what seemed like weeks. 'Wow, 10 points, hey? What for?'

'A correct answer. Come on, Cradle's already downstairs. He seems like he wants to start working. There's coffee on. I found a sealed pack.' As she walked back across the room and opened the door, Kline instinctively watched her shape as she moved. She turned and caught him.

'Anders!'

'Sorry, Noo, couldn't help myself. You're looking very nice this morning.'

She laughed and walked out of the room.

'I might be a bit too mature for you Anders.' Her laugh moved down the stairs. Kline followed, smiling, slightly embarrassed but somehow quite pleased with himself anyway.

After coffee, the three settled into the old lounge and sat facing one another across an oak table, marked and chipped by years of usage but as strong as it ever was. Cradle seemed OK; he was quiet and a little uncommunicative but nothing extraordinary, given the circumstances.

Kline began proceedings.

'Jules left me an analysis of her findings about the glyphs. It's definitely not energy-tagging. Bryant was lying.' He pulled the paper copy from his pocket and laid it out on the table between them. 'There are several repeating figures in the glyphs. There are simplistic stick-people figures and circles representing individuals and multiple different societies. Then there's this one that looks a bit like a kid's drawing of a star. Jules calls that a sun machine and she thinks it's the generator at the tokamak.'

Kline was inwardly conscious of his inaccurate use of the present tense, yet dogged in his determination to continue to do so.

'Anyway, Jules concludes that the glyphs are effectively a begging letter, asking us to stop the machine and to pass on the message ourselves.'

He pushed Jules's notes into the middle of the table and Cradle and Noomi pored over them for several minutes. Cradle worked intently and silently, without making eye contact. Noomi studied the papers, glancing up from time to time to see if Cradle was OK. 'But what are these societies?' she asked. 'It implies that there is more than one, all linked together, each with a generator like Perpetua's. So are these countries? Or continents?'

Kline shook his head. 'I don't know.'

'But do you think anyone else has a generator, I mean any other countries?' Noomi looked back and forth at the two men. 'Can it be true?'

'I don't know Noo, it doesn't seem likely, I know.' Kline looked down at the table. 'But Jules was so sure she was onto something. All the analyses were really high scoring.'

'That's not possible. I would have felt distortions during DREAM sessions. I would have felt it if there were other sources routed into the Flow.' Cradle stood up and started pacing and humming. 'OK, OK, this is starting to make sense.'

They both looked at Cradle, perplexed.

'Care to elucidate, mate? It's way short of sense for me.'

'I was thinking about Noo's idea. The energy lost by Drowse sufferers doesn't anywhere near balance with the energy of the Flow. Even if you account for all the Drowse sufferers on Earth it's still short by a factor of almost 100,000. So where is the Flow getting the rest of the energy? We're not getting anywhere with that. So maybe it's just not the right question.'

Kline threw Cradle a knowing glance. 'I take it you have a better one?'

Cradle flickered a half smile then extinguished it before it could be noticed. 'Let's take the Flow feed into Africa for example. There are hundreds of junctions there, all fed by the Flow, each one appearing to all intents and purposes like an individual energy source. In isolation, each one could be loosely thought of as a 'sun machine'. Say one of these countries makes a connection between Drowse and all this limitless energy. It could look like a balance, locally. It might look like energy from human cells is being consumed to provide the source for their sun machine. It probably starts as a conspiracy theory or superstition: scaremongering or just rumours. Then it goes underground because it's too dangerous to openly criticise something that has revolutionised your entire country's existence.

'But you have to warn people somehow, because this is too big not to try to help others now you have this knowledge. So you devise a way to modulate the Flow and you pass a message out as best you can, hidden away within the statistics of the Flow's noise. Now everyone connected will get the message *Our sun machine is hurting my people and yours is hurting your people. Pass it on*.'

'OK, I can see how the glyphs could be from a country that may have made the Drowse connection, yes.' Noomi stood and walked to the fireplace. 'But then why not just announce it? Why conceal the message so deeply?'

Cradle avoided eye contact. 'Fear of losing everything.'

'But it still doesn't balance out overall, kiddo,' Anders interjected. 'It might work locally from the consumer viewpoint but, in the big picture, it just doesn't add up. You said so yourself.'

'That's right, but who sees the big picture? Nobody, only Perpetua. And now us. The big picture has no impact if you don't know about it.'

'But why not just destroy your local machine and be done with it?' Noomi countered.

'Security.' Kline grimaced. 'Bryant, or someone like him. They can't get anywhere near the machine to destroy it, so their only resort is to ask for help. Quietly.'

Noomi sat down at the table. 'So the messaging is all just a mistake? A distraction from Africa?'

'Oh no, sorry Noo. It could be anywhere; Africa, Asia, Australia, the Americas, Europe, Antarctica, doesn't matter.'

'None taken, Cradle ...' She smiled warmly.

Kline sat too. 'Hmm, it could be right, yes. Locally it all mistakenly hangs together, with inaccurate Drowse numbers being incorrectly equated with Flow consumption. I can buy that. But it still leaves us with the original big-picture problem. We don't know where the hell all the Flow energy comes from. Or why Jules was murdered.'

Cradle nodded. 'Something else too. The message is definitely carried by Flow modulation, so how did they do this if they couldn't even get to their local machine?'

'It seems too elaborate to be completely wrong, Cradle,' Noomi appealed. 'Such complexity for a mistake. I feel that this link between the disease and the Flow must be right.'

Kline weighed in. 'OK, let's push that idea a little. It implies that anything to do with Drowse is connected with Perpetua. Jules was killed to protect this, I'm sure of it. Someone is trying to hide something. And, by the way, this isn't exactly scientific rigour here, we don't have time for that. The best gut feel wins.'

Cradle paced more quickly and the humming returned. 'We need to test it, Anders. I need to get back into the system and look around the welfare algorithms, see if there's a backdoor.'

'I've got the FV waiting, but you'd have to be in and out quickly.'

'What's an FV?' Noomi queried.

'Fractured viral. It's a black comms technique that's untraceable if you're fast. We could use it to start an avatar working on our behalf, doing the investigation from within. It would call us back when it was done. Minimal edge exposure. Very, very secure.'

Cradle returned to the table. 'OK. Let's do that. Anders, could we reach Main from the systems here?'

'Too risky. Reconnecting the Boundary systems would light this place up and we'd give ourselves away. They'd be here in no time. Safer to kick it off from a public system that's already up and running. Libraries or cafes are good.'

'I expect they're closing in on us anyway. We should move out.'

Noomi wondered if either Kline or Cradle had a solid plan for this. 'Where are we going?'

Cradle looked at Kline, who thought about it briefly and then shrugged his shoulders. 'Well, where do you fancy, Noo?'

OK then. No solid plan. In for a penny. 'Well, I've always wanted to visit the sea ...'

Kline opened his arms in a conclusive gesture. 'My uncle's old place in Sea Palling. Sea, sand, isolation and a very old connection to Main. The Norfolk coast is bracing in November.'

The Eyrie

THE ORIGINAL SEA DEFENCES had been put in place during the second half of the twentieth century, putting a stop to a long history of marine incursion. Huge concrete concaves to fold back the power of the ocean, with enormous rocks before them. A few hundred metres out to sea, nine man-made reefs were placed by boat and excavator to further protect the coastline and, in so doing, encourage the North Sea to give up some of its finer payload. As a result, Sea Palling's beaches were sandy and extensive, running a mile north and south along the coastline.

The gap, to the side of which lay the old disused lifeboat station, was cut through the dunes and hinted dramatically at the village's long history of working with the sea: fishing, tourism and, of course, smuggling and salvage. Inland agriculture had long sustained a small workforce, with local produce still available in the few remaining shops. Although almost no commercial fishing now took place, it was a village with its feet set firmly in the past, clinging proudly to hard-won traditions and history, and relatively untouched by the technological revolution of more recent decades.

The pod drew into the small terminal on Clink Road, directly behind the dunes, and the three alighted. It had been another string of Incog legs, this time with strategic changes at Shrewsbury, Coventry, Corby and Kings Lynn.

'I can taste the sea.' Noomi was having difficulty containing a childish level of excitement.

'Yeah, it's just over the dunes there.' Kline pointed. 'We can have a look once we're in.'

'I've never been to the seaside before.'

'Never?' Kline looked incredulously at Noomi. 'Wow, well you're in for a treat then.'

They walked to the end of the road and turned right onto The Marrams, then continued for another half a mile until they came to The Eyrie, a ramshackle building at the end of the road, nestled immediately landside of the dunes. To the left lay a field which, over the passage of many years, had been variously floodland, paddock, grazing land, campsite, vehicle park and garden. It now stood in disarray, nature seizing what was rightfully hers, the wild and coarse marram grass steadily overthrowing all that had been sown there by human hand years ago.

The house was constructed from old red bricks with cobble inlays: two storeys and a pitched roof, with a single-storey addition to the rear. Red tiles lined both these roofs, protecting the house from the severity of the

Norfolk coastline for over a century. A single chimney stack rose high against the facing wall, towering above a more recently added sloped roof construction that had long ago succumbed to weather and gravity.

'Uncle Jannik's gaff, may he rest in peace.' Kline pulled some of the grass from around the gate so it could be opened, and they walked up to the front porch.

'Let's see if this still works.' Kline reached up above the door and put his fingers into a slot inside the apex of the porch. The door clicked open. 'Eureka! Good old-fashioned electronics. A fingerprint reader from the early days. Drives a simple solenoid that pushes the right lock pins. Solar powered. Not networked, completely standalone. Nothing to go wrong. Uncle Jannik let me put this in when I was a lad, and it still works perfectly. He always used a metal key though.'

'I never knew you were so old, Anders,' Cradle quipped, 'this tech is ancient.'

'Oi, enough of that or you'll be in the shed.' Kline glanced over Cradle's shoulder at the outbuildings. 'If it's still standing, that is ...'

They stepped into the house and immediately found themselves standing in the lounge.

'Kitchen's through on your left, stairs there go up to 3 bedrooms and a bathroom. It's basic, but it's done all the falling down it's going to. Might be a bit damp.'

'It's beautiful.' Noomi was looking at the fireplace, more red brick and cobble but with a slate hearth, surrounded by a comfortable-looking sofa and two easy chairs. Paintings of ships and sea storms hung around the walls. Old-fashioned lamps on tables. 'It's like a time capsule.'

'I'll check out the office, see if stuff still wants to boot up.'

'So how did you come by this, Anders? You never mentioned it in all the years I've known you.'

'Inherited it. No big deal. Jannik was my father's brother. Black sheep of the family, not popular with anyone. Preferred his own company and not afraid to say so. Forthright. Made a load of old-money doing something obscure about traditional fishing rights, just before the sea-drones kicked the bottom out of it all. He bought this place and just lived here by himself for twenty years. As a nipper, I used to travel up in the holidays to give Mum a break and Jannik just used to let me run around and do what I wanted. This is where I learned how things work. Made me want to take a crack at science.

'Dad did one of his very rare visits one day and found him over the dune sitting in his little boat, pulled up onshore after one last trip. Five good-sized cod in the boat, line-caught. Heart had just given out, doing what he loved. Sixty-three. Long time ago. We got on. Left me the house.'

Noomi could feel his loss and touched his arm. Kline cleared his throat and aimed his stare at the fireplace for a few moments. 'Actually, let's get that going first. The house has years of cold in it.' He walked through to the kitchen and out into the garden to the wood store.

North Sea

THE FIRE WAS ROARING, the crackle of damp hardwood puncturing the silence like distant gunshot. Each had chosen a room upstairs and had unpacked the few belongings they had travelled with. Noomi's gentle conversation with Kline had revealed that he always used to stay in the back room, facing out onto the garden, away from the dunes, so she insisted that he have his old quarters. Cradle took the smaller front bedroom and she the middle and, by chance, largest room.

Kline had been right about the cold. An unused house gains a deep chill over the years, beyond the scientific measurement of temperature. It has more to do with emptiness and sorrow. There is no sense in it but it is a fact. It needs people to really make it warm again.

'Can we see the water yet, Anders?' Noomi was wide-eyed, like a small girl. 'Please?'

'Come on then. The fire will do its work while we're out.' Kline threw another couple of large logs onto the grate and drew the guard over.

They walked across the road and directly onto the bottom of the dunes. An old pathway was partially closed up by marram, but the way was still visible. The coarseness of the grass scratched audibly at their trouser bottoms as they waded it apart. Climbing the path was difficult, not just due to the grass, but because each forward pace receded a little as the sand slid downhill underfoot. Many small and regressive steps were necessary until, finally, they crested the dune and looked down upon the beach.

The tide was low and all nine reefs were visible, each marked by a pair of rusted metal posts, beacons to warn vessels at high tide about the rocks in between. The beach-making effect was readily apparent from atop the dunes. Beautifully curved yellow accretion zones were drawn out leeward of each of the reefs, the natural diffusion of the water's energy leading to the dropping of its sand. Where there were exposed gaps there was erosion but, in the lee of the reefs, the water slackened and gave up its sandy payload to form sweeping golden headlands.

The waves crashed violently into the reefs and sprayed their anger upwards in frustration at the obstruction. The cold wind blew Noomi's hair into tangles and buffeted her eardrums. She had never experienced anything like it. They descended and went onto the beach and then out to the most northern reef, wet sand underfoot, to be near the rocks themselves. Cradle feigned pushing the reef, one-handed and majestic, as though he were holding back the tide itself. At that moment a particularly powerful wave reached over the top of the reef and lashed him with its spray.

'Don't piss Poseidon off!' Kline shouted over the wind as they retreated back to the shelter of the dune, giggling like bedraggled schoolchildren.

'Oh, I think I'm going to have to do much worse than that.' Cradle's muttering was drowned out by the growling waves.

Arrow

JESMOND COORDINATED AND PERSONALLY oversaw the series of forensic disruptions in pursuit of a diminishing trail of DNA, the evidence becoming fainter and less conclusive with each step.

The clarity of the Cheltenham to Worcester pod contamination led to a paralysing of the Worcester transport network while the forensic robotic investigation snaked over the fleet of 110 pods. Even less evidence to find, fewer microscopic traces of blood: even so, a characteristic presence of matching cellular matter deposited on a door handle pointed, via the transport records, to Hereford.

In Hereford too, the metallic forensic swarm immobilised all kinds of movement for a day, to discover a very faint trace on a pod that had travelled to Hay-On-Wye, again paid for using Incogs. But there the trail was cold. A repeat of the robotic offensive found nothing, transport in and out of Hay having been disabled for two full days.

But this was enough. The meandering vectors of the trail to this point produced a vivid enough signpost for those informed by a little specialised historical knowledge.

The arrow flew inexorably towards the disused research facility at Capel-y-ffin.

They were at Boundary.

Security Officer Jesmond's report to Bryant was met with a snarling outburst of vitriol, where he had allowed himself to expect perhaps a small amount of praise for successfully running down the prey.

'Boundary? Of course! And how long has this taken you, Jesmond? Over a week to do one simple thing. An idiot would have given me this in half the time. They will doubtless have moved on by now. I will meet you there in 24 hours. I expect to see that place ripped apart by the time I arrive. And be ready to tell me why you should not be dismissed immediately.'

The old house had been fully dissected by a plague of forensic bots, as instructed. The ash in the fireplace, the blood and vomit on the bed, scraps of food discarded in the garden and fresh faecal matter in the septic tank. Confirmation that the targets had been here in the last few days. Higher than normal bacterial content in the blood samples indicated that the girl was ill in some way which, combined with the analysis of the vomit, suggested a severe infection with indications of septicaemia.

As expected, there was compelling evidence of three people: Cradle, his partner Eveand Kline. Then a surprise. A fourth person's markers. Female, of African descent. Unknown, unexpected. The system reached out and momentarily rifled the database for a match. Dr Noomi Olawadi, an academic from the African CDC. Born in Nigeria and recently travelled to the UK as a delegate at the international Drowse conference. She had not yet returned to Nigeria and had gone off-system last week in Oxford.

But no sign of any of them in person. Bryant was right. They had already fled.

By the time Bryant arrived, the search had extended beyond the building walls and out into the grounds. He stood with Jesmond beneath the chilling shade of the forest to the rear of the old house. Many leaves had fallen, but not enough to conceal the low mound of freshly turned dirt at their feet.

'Dig it up.' Bryant stabbed a finger towards the ground.

Jesmond gestured the utility bot into excavation mode and it set about its work, wet soil exhausting into a fresh knoll a few yards away. In under a minute it withdrew, autoclaved its blades and whirred back down into standby.

Bryant climbed down into the hole and smiled as he pulled open the mudded blanket.

Conduit

'SYSTEM'S UP OK.' KLINE called through from the back of the house.

Cradle and Noomi joined him in the office. It was a jumble of wires and boxes, some flashing, some displaying seemingly random numbers, values of something mysterious and no doubt important to Kline, but meaningless to the uninitiated. Paper books piled high on shelves and chairs, printed journals of science and engineering, some dating back to the 20th century. A scruffy old bear wearing a hat had toppled and was leaning drunkenly against a box of electronics components from the days before individual hardware modules had been superseded by global quantum processing power. Redundant microprocessor devices, prototype copper stripboard tarnished by the passage of time and salt air. Resistors, capacitors and even transistors, all sealed up in antistatic plastic bags, reflective and grey. Predating Main, well before AI Singularity, and some of it even from an era prior to The Cloud. A cluttered museum from

Kline's childhood and before, grown over decades into a treasure-trove of technophilia.

Amongst this, or perhaps beneath it, Kline sat before a display screen with a manual-entry keyboard.

'How can you work in here Anders? It would drive me insane.' Cradle looked about the place in awe.

'Come in, grab a chair. Or something.' Kline was concentrating on the display. 'This old terminal is very stupid, no complex error checks or protocol interchanges with Main. It just hooks up at the bottommost level and does nothing except handshaking activity to keep the connection. Been connected for years now so, if we go in here with minimal activity and we're quick, it won't show up.' He looked at Cradle and Noomi. 'I can invoke the FV from here, no problem.'

Cradle drew closer to the interface. 'We just have to tell it where to go and what to do. Some extra software.'

'Yep. Except in pieces. We'll send it into Main in tiny chunks that the FV will assemble and then run when we're ready. Like uploading lots of individual words until you've got the whole book.' Kline looked at Noomi.

'We're asking it to find if there is a way of modulating the Flow, maybe from the hospices. Yes?' Noomi thought out loud, straightening her understanding.

'That's right, Noo. I have a backup of some code written to help us do just that. She's a sort of software service that runs in the background. Known in the trade as a guardian aengel. I call her Anna. Anders can upload her from here.'

'You've got Anna backed up? With you?'

'I always back everything up.' Cradle seemed bemused at Kline's question.

'Man, you're something, Cradle. OK, it'll have to just be textual though. No voice or visuals. Too noticeable.'

'I know. Syntax?'

'It's going to be a bit clunky, but natural language should be fine.'

'Then what?' Noomi asked, sensing the conversation was sliding into technobabble.

'Once I've encoded Cradle's aengel in a few thousand little steps, it'll just sit there, in pieces, until I send it an invocation key. Then it'll assemble itself and run, totally within the system. And when it's done it will give Cradle its findings and then automatically re-fragment back into the system.'

Cradle handed Kline the tiny storage device, and he plugged it into the side of the display.

'Ready?'

'OK, Anders. Do it.'

Kline rattled his fingers on the keys of the old peripheral and it was done.

'That's it. The aengel's in place. No sign of any detection, so we're good.'

'Are we going to run it now?' The two looked at Noomi, and Kline stood.

'Here Noo, sit here.'

She took Kline's place at the display and touched her fingers on the keyboard.

'Click this key here.' Kline pointed at the keyboard. Noomi pressed the F5 key, and the display blanked, leaving a single flashing horizontal bar at the top left. 'Now type password1.'

'What?'

'password1. Just type it in.'

She looked bemused. 'Type?'

'Oh yeah,' Kline laughed, 'It's like gesturing, but you have to do it letter by letter. You have to press each letter on the keyboard one at a time. Old school.'

'OK.' Noomi searched the keyboard. 'Right ... p ...' More hunting. 'Ah, there it is ... a, s, s, w ... erm ... Oh, why aren't they in alphabetical order? ah, there ... o, r ... and d. Done.'

The word 'password' blinked on the display.

'And now 1. Up there.' Kline pointed. Noomi clicked it. 'And finally, *Enter*. This one.'

Noomi pressed and the screen went blank, cursor top left again. 'Oh, is that right?'

'Yep.' Cradle reached over and typed:

'*Anna*'

<hello cradle>

Cradle typed again. '*Hi Anna. Please find possible ways of modulating flow statistics to send binary messages*'

<understood/ processing>

The screen blanked again, and Cradle stood back from the terminal. 'That's it.'

'OK. It'll take a while now because it's running stealthy, not hogging Main time. Little nips of core processor bit by bit, spread out randomly over a long interval. Stays under the radar. Let's give it overnight. Anna will come back when she's ready.'

Cradle couldn't sleep, again. The glyphs danced before him whenever he closed his eyes. The sun machines. The Flow. Yes, that made sense. The linked countries; that, too, seemed feasible. But then one of the countries jumping to the wrong conclusion and issuing a warning to the others? Something niggled at him here. Would someone sophisticated enough to find a way of modulating the Flow make such an error?

And then there was the imbalance. Nobody knew where the Flow was coming from, that much was true, but sucking energy from humans just didn't cut it. Couldn't be right – the numbers were way out.

So there it was, the big old elephant in the room again, even after all this time. The puzzle that had eluded the world's academic zenith for years. The conundrum that had spread an empire across the entire planet. What powered The Flow?

It was as he fell asleep at last that the realisation crystallised into his consciousness. It was down to him alone to answer the big question.

Jesmond

THE LINESEC OFFICE LIGHTS strained Jesmond's eyes as he stood toe to toe with Bryant, too bright and with a subliminal flicker that made him feel like he was in an aquarium, like some sort of specimen.

'Security Officer Jesmond, you have made this very difficult for me.'

'But sir, I followed the trail as closely as possible.'

'But they were *gone*, Jesmond. They were gone. Granted, I am now in a better position as regards leveraging Mr Cradle. His wife's sad demise will work much to my benefit. I will thank you for that at least. But I do not have *them*, Jesmond, do I? They roam free. Too slow. Too slow by far.'

'Please sir, my family, I need the creds from this job.'

'Well, yes, that is what I have been agonising over, Jesmond. Oh, but wait, forgive me, this is an intimate moment between us. What is your first name?'

'Petris, sir.'

'Petris. Yes, that is better. How do we solve this problem fairly so that your family do not pay the price for your incompetence?' Bryant put a hand on the officer's shoulder. 'I am not a monster, Petris, not without compassion.'

'Thank you, sir.'

'We must ensure that your family do not go uncompensated for your punishment.'

'Sir?'

'Do not be concerned. You will not be dismissed, Petris.' Bryant gestured quickly to the side of the officer's face and a door hissed open behind Jesmond. The sound of tiny but powerful nanotech motors running up as the SecBot emerged from the doorway, twelve articulated arms deploying Durga-like behind the bewildered officer.

Bryant stepped back and the bot's arms encompassed Jesmond, pulling him against its cold metallic thorax. The air squeezed out of his lungs in a rattled hiss of white noise, and his eyes bulged.

'No, Petris. The best thing all round is an unfortunate accident at work. Yes, yes, Perpetua can be very empathetic in these matters, most generous to the poor families of these ill-fated victims.' Bryant moved close enough that his stale breath dampened Jesmond's skin.

'Such a stupid red face, Petris. How sad. Crushed in a terrible accident. He wouldn't have felt a thing. There will be an investigation, of course. Lessons learned and compensations paid. Best all round. Best for the children.' He brought his fingers together in a curious meshing gesture and the robot closed its embrace more tightly.

Jesmond groaned as the last air was pushed from his body and he lost control of his bladder and bowel.

'Oh dear, yes. Most tragic.'

Bryant turned away and shook his head solemnly at the cracking of ribs.

Modulator

ALTHOUGH IT WAS 5 a.m. Cradle was already awake when the terminal sounded downstairs, a slurred two-tone keening repeating every five seconds or so. By the time he had thrown on some clothes and made his way to the office, Kline was already there.

'Morning, Cradle. Looks like we have an answer. Shall we?'

Noomi walked into the room, sleepyheaded, yawning. 'Yes.'

Cradle sat at the terminal and typed:

'*Anna*'

<hello cradle/ i have the results of your query/ shall i route to this terminal>

The cursor blinked, expectantly.

'*Yes please, Anna*'

'Cradle, you know you can just type "y" there don't you?' said Kline.

'Doesn't cost anything to say please, Anders,' Cradle replied, smiling through the tension.

The screen blanked completely for a few seconds and then *file downloaded* appeared before the cursor. Cradle pressed *Enter* and the screen filled with text, mostly mathematics. He and Kline studied intently.

'Jesus.' Kline was the first to speak.

'What is it?' Noomi pushed in to look at the screen herself.

'When a patient is hooked up to the system, they are in direct contact with the Flow for life support and management. Anna has identified a pathway that permits the Flow to be modulated via this route.'

'What are you saying, Anders?' asked Noomi.

'It's the hospices.'

Cradle felt his chest tighten as Eve flooded his consciousness again. He closed his eyes and kissed her cheek as she receded. He refocused and pressed on towards the heart of the issue.

'Maybe it's a temporary distortion of the hyperplasma, caused by a disruption of the tiny amount of energy drawn by the patient?'

'Actually, Cradle, I think it's going the other way. Look at this.' Kline pointed to some of the on-screen maths. 'The energy comes *from* the patient, like a little kick into the Flow. That's what causes the distortion, a rapid reversal.'

'Ah yes, you're right. And Anna thinks this kick could cause a sort of distortion in the hyperplasma itself, like a knot. We know the plasma rotates so these knots could affect the Flow, one at a time, in a sequence dictated by their arrangement in the plasma itself.'

'And, because the hyperplasma rotates so slowly, these small fluctuations in the energy statistics would be very slow too. The time constant is in years. And almost invisible. Cradle, it fits.'

Noomi thought about it for a minute. 'You mean someone could use a person to pass a message? That's creepy.'

'Looks that way. Somehow.' Cradle typed again. 'I'm asking Anna for more detail on the reversal process. How it could be caused.'

After a few seconds delay more text appeared at the bottom of the screen.

<the quantity required to activate a single bit of data equates to the instantaneous surrender of the rest energy of one patient>

Noomi glanced at Kline, but he was transfixed by what Cradle was doing.

'Clarify'

The seconds felt like minutes.

<1 bit = 1 death>

All three recoiled from the terminal. Noomi spoke first. 'Is this saying that the patient has to die to send the message?'

Kline nodded. 'Something like that. Do you know anything about serial comms, Noo?'

She shook her head. 'Not really, no.'

Cradle took up the point. 'Let's talk about the low-level stuff a bit. We know the message is thirteen glyphs, sent serially, bit by bit, 1s and 0s.'

He could see Noomi glazing over. Definitely not her field. He reset.

'OK. For example, say I wanted to transmit a black-and-white picture to you serially using a lamp at, say, 1 bit per second. You know, one bit at a time, until you've got the whole message. First thing, I'd have to go through the picture and break it into rows with hundreds of white or black points. We could say 1 for white and 0 for black. Right?'

She nodded.

'OK, we call those black or white points "bits". I'm going to send you those one at a time, bit by bit, one every second, going through the rows until the whole picture is sent. So you start counting seconds and you look at my lamp. When you get through a second during which I've switched the lamp on that's a 1, meaning a white point in the picture. Where you count a second and it stays dark, that's a 0, meaning a black point. So the 0s are basically free. I just wait for the second to pass and I don't switch the lamp on. We keep doing that until all the bits are sent and then you just have to reassemble all the points and you've got my picture.'

'You said the 0s were free,' hesitantly. 'What about the 1s?'

'Well, that's what needs the energy transmission. Each logic 1 costs some energy.'

Kline looked at Cradle. 'Christ, Cradle. This means one patient can only knot a single logic 1 into the hyperplasma.'

The realisation rolled over their senses like sea fog.

'So how many patients would it be for the whole message?' Noomi looked plaintively at Cradle.

'I have the glyphs on that storage device already. I can ask Anna to analyse them to check how many 1s were used. They seem to be mostly background, so hopefully not many.' Cradle typed again into the terminal.

An eternity passed while Anna crunched through the glyph data, the three sitting in anxious silence.

The cursor moved to the next line.

<64,021>

Shocked

NOOMI HAD GONE THROUGH to the lounge and was slouched in one of the armchairs, staring at the wall.

Kline put his hand on her shoulder.

'You alright, Noo?'

She glanced up at him, her eyes wet and wide. He felt an ache in his chest at the sight of Noomi in distress.

'Over 64,000 people were murdered to send us the message, Anders. That's like the hydrogen bomb from the 20th century. Nagasaki. Who could do such a thing? And why?'

Kline crouched and spoke quietly. 'Somebody extremely desperate with something very, very important to say.'

'And how do we know Jules's interpretation is right? It's asking us to pass the message on. They want us to kill thousands of people.'

Noomi shook her head and stared at the wall again. Cradle came into the room and spoke.

'Thing is, Anders, where on Earth did the glyphs come from? If 64,021 Drowse patients had died, we would have heard about it. Nobody could hide that.'

Kline stood and walked over to him, whispering, 'Noo's taking this hard, Cradle. We need to give her some time. I could do with some myself.'

'But do you know what this means, Anders?'

'I'm not thinking clearly enough yet, mate. I do need a moment, actually.' Kline pushed a hand to the wall to steady himself.

'No, I mean where on Earth, literally? I don't think that the messages could have come from anywhere on this planet.'

Kline looked at Cradle's face. It was intense and totally focused. He recognised the expression.

'Look, Cradle, I'm going to bring Noo up to her room, then I'm going to go to mine, and we're going to have a lie down for a while. OK? You should do the same.'

Cradle frowned but there was no reduction in his intensity. 'OK. I'll see you afterwards.'

Cradle turned and went back into the office. Kline watched the door close behind him then coaxed Noomi to her feet and helped her upstairs. He closed her door, leaving her lying foetal on top of the covers, then walked to his old room and reclined on his old bed. But as soon as he closed his eyes his mind lashed him with images of 1s, 0s and people dying. Inevitably, he saw Jules. He saw Bryant too and felt the hatred renew in his veins. He realised Cradle was on the brink of something important. He did not sleep.

Cradle sat at the terminal and consulted his aengel again.

'*Anna. Where did the messages come from?*'

<sorry cradle/ insufficient data>

He knew that already. Just needed to chat.

'*Could they have been sent from another country?*'

<probability less than 0.01%>

'*Where then?*'

A long delay, staring at a flashing cursor.

<permission to upscale processing>

Upscale processing. This meant having Anna engage more tightly with Main's quantum processors, using more core time. Becoming more noticeable, more apparent. Emerging from beneath the cloak of fractured viral encryption. Traceable.

The cursor blinked on and off once per second as though Anna was tapping her fingers impatiently on the desk.

'*Negative. Estimate processing time without core.*'

<80,000 minutes>

Cradle looked up at the ceiling. Nearly eight weeks.

'*And using core?*'

<100 minutes>

He stood and walked to the window, negotiating piles of technical journals and boxes of miscellaneous wires and components en route. The field outside nurtured the rusted carcasses of early vehicles that had been consumed over the years by the tendrils of nature and were almost invisible beneath the thick blanket of marram and gorse. Darkness was falling, the day once again receding, exhausted by events. He stood for several minutes before returning to the terminal.

'Estimate the time before you are detected by Main please, Anna.'

<yes cradle/ tending to infinity without core loading/ with core loading limited to 100 minutes runtime detection would occur in less than 2 days>

Cradle was aware of the housekeeping daemons within Main, which constantly analysed the quantum cell loading caused by servicing external users. They originated from security developments of the early 21st century when denial-of-service attacks had become the most common form of cybercrime. These lugworms, as they were called, squirmed amongst Main's core records, identifying and destroying the most avaricious code bases. The usual trick was to manage your core loading to the point where the probability of detection was low enough for you to get the job done before being deleted and reported. But the problem here was getting spotted at all. It didn't matter if the process was complete or not – Anna would have retreated back under cover of FV by the time that happened – but the core log stored the routing that had been active and could easily be used to trace their location. Cradle was well aware that Bryant would have alerts set in wait for them and anything as obvious as this would be certain to give them away. They would have to move again. Disappear again.

Or they could fight. He needed an answer.

'*Run the analysis on core please, Anna.*'

<warning/ detection in 48 hours is probable cradle/ please confirm command>

Cradle listened for Kline and Noomi. Silence. They were still resting. He hummed and buzzed.

'*Anna.*'

<yes cradle>

'*Command confirmed.*'

Fait Accompli

KLINE CAME DOWNSTAIRS THREE hours later and joined Cradle in the office.

'Anders.' Cradle waited for Kline to slump, still exhausted, in the chair. 'I understand it all.'

—o—o—o ǫ o—o—o—

Anna had returned with the analysis results after 98 minutes and the terminal's chime had startled Cradle as he sat in the darkness.

<i have the analysis results cradle>

He resettled himself at the screen before typing his reply.

'Show me in full please, Anna.'

The screen flooded with mathematics and text again, this time describing the weightings for various arguments about the source of the glyphs. No chance of them being from another country, Kline was right, there would have been a worldwide outcry at the loss of more than 64,000 Drowse victims in one incident and there was nothing like that in any record.

Coming from within the solar system was equally unlikely. No evidence of sentient life away from terra firma had ever been detected by any of the many thousands of electronic ears that strained, ever hopeful, into the deafening silence of space.

Indeed, any possibility of the source being anywhere familiar was vanishingly small. Not from our spiral arm, nor the Milky Way itself and certainly not from further afield. A continuous energy transfer of the magnitude of The Flow would leave a significant, detectable linear trail of some description, but no telltale halo of fundamental particles nor any observable distortion of spacetime was present. Scientists, cosmologists and physicists had been hunting ever since Persistence but nobody had ever found anything.

No, Anna's analysis incontrovertibly rejected all of these theories. The Flow had just appeared at a single point in spacetime which coincided with Hornbill's tokamak. *Because* of Hornbill's tokamak. A breach point, a singularity linking point A with point B. It was a fistula between dimensions, created by the spark of Persistence, unnatural but inevitable.

Cradle had studied multiverse theories during his doctorate, so understood some of the concepts. They were esoteric and, as yet, untestable but they offered a potential solution for the equations of quantum mechanics and the essential tenets of cosmology, satisfying some of the calculations that sought to reach back to the origin of our own universe. Some solutions suggested that for every infinitesimal moment in our own experience, there is an infinite number of possible outcomes, each existing in its own unique spacetime. An infinity of parallel universes, isolated from one another, instantiating every possible course of every possible thing. Reality was merely our experience tracing a path through infinite fields of quantum probabilities.

Anna's analysis rated the probability of a breach between universes as a 95% match with the available evidence.

'Jesus, Cradle. You're saying The Flow is coming from another universe? Spilling into ours?' Kline frowned and shook his head. 'No, that's wild.'

'I know,' Cradle said, 'but think about what we know. If we draw more on The Flow, it just gives more energy. But we're just ripping more energy from the other universe. And we're making more of their people sick when we do that.'

'But we have sick people here too, millions of them. Where does that come in?'

'Another, third universe is pulling energy from our people. We're a link in an infinite chain. That's why we have to pass the message on. We have to get them to stop, or everyone here will succumb to Drowse.'

'But it doesn't balance, Cradle. You said so yourself. The Flow is much greater than the Drowse energy.'

'It's two separate equations, that's what I was missing. The Flow is vast because we're making a huge number of people suffer in the donor universe. The other universe that's taking energy from our people is just not pulling so hard. *Yet*. At the moment we're just lucky.'

'Not what I call lucky. And how do we even know there's anyone at the other end listening out for our message? We could just be pissing in the wind and killing thousands of people in the process.'

'It's the multiverse Anders. There's a version of us out there looking, just as we're looking. Our time is now. We're part of a terrible infinite chain that needs to be broken. It matches the glyphs perfectly.'

Kline sat with his head in his hands. 'I see it balances, Cradle. I see it. But I don't fucking like it.'

'There's one thing though.'

Kline sighed and looked out the window. The dawn had broken with a heavy dew which beaded the grass blades and wept onto the ground. Everything was washed new.

'Yeah. OK. Say it.'

'I authorised Anna to use core processing for this. I blew our cover.'

'I guessed. How long?'

'We have to be gone by tomorrow morning at the latest.'

'Then we'll go today.'

Kline called to Noomi, who was on her way downstairs anyway, having heard the two men in the office. She joined them and sat in the wing-backed chair by the window.

'Well, gentlemen, I take it you have something?'

Cradle shuffled his feet as Kline answered. 'We're moving on again, Noo. Perpetua has our address.'

She screwed up her face. 'So much for my seaside holiday.'

Cradle stood and walked across the room to the doorway. 'I'm going to stay here. You two have to go.'

Kline looked askance at Cradle. 'What? No way! We spoke about this. We're in it together. We all agreed.'

'Yes, Cradle, we are stronger together, surely.'

'But then what? How long do we have to keep running? How many times can we hide? If I hand myself in, then it might buy some time for you two to get some new identities and settle somewhere safe.'

'Cradle, you're not thinking. There's nowhere safe, Perpetua is everywhere. Even if we managed to reinstate onto Main with some new IDs it would only be a matter of time before it all came undone and we were caught. Noo said it: we're stronger together.'

'A three-person army?' Cradle looked first at Noomi then back to Kline. 'Against a worldwide corporate force, with all the technology and defences in the world? Perpetua would just wipe us away. Bryant would make sure of it.'

'But you're talking about just sacrificing yourself, Cradle. Bryant will kill you if he finds you.'

'I'm dead already, Anders. I have nothing left except this task.'

'You have us, Cradle.' Noomi walked over and touched his hands. 'You have us.'

Kline joined them in the doorway. 'Noo's right, Cradle. You can't just give up. We've lost too much, we need each other now.' Kline blinked away the wetness. '*I* need you.'

Cradle pulled his hands away and buried them in his pockets, the comfort of Noomi's touch still warm on his fingers. He showed no emotion. 'This isn't giving up. When I am taken, I'll be brought to Bryant. I will be back in Perpetua. I have to follow what the glyphs say.'

'By yourself? Cradle, it's impossible. Bryant has ...'

'Not by myself, Anders, I will have Anna to help me.'

Kline looked at Cradle quizzically. 'You're going to fully code her into the FV?'

'Exactly. It should be possible to temporarily overcome Main if she's fast enough to block the defences out. I think it would buy me enough time.'

Noomi reentered the conversation. 'Cradle, are you going to the machine?'

'I have nothing else left, Noo. Really I don't.'

'There's a piece missing, Cradle. A big one.' Kline put his hands on Cradle's shoulders. 'If you're following the glyph sequence, the message has to be sent on.'

'Yes. I will program the message into the FV along with Anna. Once it's triggered it will take control of the hospice interfaces, one at a time, and make the modulation.'

'Make the modulation?' Noomi was horrified. 'You mean it will kill thousands of people.'

'Yes.'

'It will be mass murder!' She drew away from Cradle. 'How can you even think about it?'

He looked hurt as she backed off.

'I'm so sorry, Noo.'

Cradle spread his arms slightly apart and glanced at each of his friends.

'I am the one in the glyphs.'

Their departure was a greenstick fracture, ragged and raw on the one side, unmoving and constant on the other, with Cradle remaining stony and determined throughout. Noomi begged him to change his mind and Kline expounded a thousand good reasons not to do this but Cradle doggedly resisted all entreatment, whether impassioned or reasoned. Finally, they accepted his decision on the proviso that he let them help with his preparations. Dispassionately, Cradle accepted the deal.

They left that afternoon with most of the food, all the remaining Incogs and desperately heavy hearts.

Cradle closed the door before they had even reached the gate.

He set about at the old interface again, the loneliness flowing through him like icy water swirling over a rock on the river's bed. All afternoon and late into the night he worked, nothing touching him but the task at hand. After midnight he was done. He carefully placed his wrist in the induction cylinder and the programming sequence began. He leaned his head back in the chair and slept, once more with Eve, before all this. Folding symmetrical patterns into their lives and building for a brighter future.

Sphere

KLINE HAD HELPED HIM with some of the practicalities. The tiny ball was three millimetres in diameter and perfectly smooth, reflecting the morning light with a metallic grey hue. Raw materials sourced from amongst Kline's collection of technological antiquities were reformed and reused with the aid of Kline's micro-former, similar to the more advanced modern machines in the FA research labs, but with much coarser resolution. It could work down to well below a fraction of a millimetre, but not to the subatomic levels that had become second nature to modern engineers and scientists. Inside the sphere were fastened a gigabyte memory core, a capacitive power store, a serialiser and a micro-transmitter. Simply crushing the outer shell would rupture the power store, jump-starting the memory core and radiating the contents out over the Flow Analysis autoexecute maintenance channel. Once it was triggered, the ensuing two-second sequence would expend all the stored energy. One shot.

Cradle had tried to wield the scalpel, this time on himself. But, made worse by the smell of the Nanogese, his mind succumbed to the desperate black memories of the last time his hands had held such a tool; his fingers would not still and his mind refused to clear. Kline took the scalpel from his trembling fingers and gave it to Noomi. No words passed between the three.

A small incision, no wider than a centimetre, and one centimetre deep. The sphere dropped easily into the reopened wound and Noomi gently drew the skin together again with two neat loops of thread.

Taken

It was dark when the door splintered. The stirrings of dawn were still perhaps an hour away when he was taken and pressed to the floor by armoured limbs. No chorus was yet ready to greet the day when his bound form was bundled into the waiting vehicle, the still of night enwrapping the trees as numerous metallic forms, glinting moonlight from their polished surfaces, swarmed fruitlessly through the house in search of others.

And every creature that crept under cover of blackness, every blade of grass that furled in abeyance of the sun's warmth, each frond and sleeping leaf that swayed in the gloomy quietness seemed stilled and bated by the corruption of this moment.

Plan

KLINE AND NOOMI MADE their way across to the Eastern Spur Terminus and took the Long In spur, paying with Incogs and being careful to avoid conversation or eye contact with anyone en route. They walked along deserted backstreets to Kline's stolen flat in the empty accommodation area. They dropped their bags onto the floor and sat on the bed. It was late afternoon, the light was fading quickly and they were exhausted, not so much from the travelling – that was only a few hours – but mostly from the unspoken tension of what they were about to embark upon.

Noomi was the first to break the silence. She cleared her throat, dry from the pods' conditioning systems.

'I assume you have a plan for this, Anders? Because all I can see is Cradle getting himself killed for nothing.'

He looked sideways at Noomi. Her hair was loose and dishevelled, raven amongst the dusk's grey tones. The outline of her face was painted in pastels by the sun's setting light and her dark eyes glistened in the twilight.

'Noo, you are so beautiful.'

'The plan, Anders.' She stood. 'You were just about to tell me, right?'

'Yeah. Sorry.' He shifted his weight to face her more directly. 'The device we made with Cradle ...'

'The little sphere.'

'Yep. If he manages to get the coding right, which no doubt he will, and if he can manage to crush it to trigger it, which is a bit more doubtful, then there is a small chance that it might work.'

'But what does that mean?'

'It will trigger the message sending and, if he is really lucky, will knock Main over and get him access to where he needs to go.'

'I still can't bear to think about the message, Anders. It's terrible. What if the calculations are wrong? All those people.'

'No choice, Noo. Time's up, we have to act now or never. If we're wrong about The Flow, then we're wrong about the link with the hospices, and nothing will happen.'

'But if we're right?'

'Yeah. If we're right.' Kline came closer to Noomi. 'Well, we'll only ever get this one shot.'

She wept gently again and Kline stood and held her in his arms, concealing his own eyes in the process.

'You said doubtful, lucky and small chance. What do you really mean, Anders?'

'I think there may be some additional security measures in place to protect the maintenance interface that this whole thing is going to try to use. So I installed some extra bits of hardware into the sphere.'

Kline produced a small black box from his coat pocket and held it to the side so Noomi could see.

'The sphere will send a one-off low-level, highly-encrypted ping to this little box of tricks when Cradle is inside Perpetua. Then I just need to get back in myself and do a bit of adjustment to improve his chances.'

'Get back into Perpetua? And how are you going to do that?'

She drew herself in against his chest.

'I thought I'd just walk right in.'

'Well, yes, that certainly sounds foolproof.'

She ran a hand around the back of his neck and under the collar of his shirt. His bristly profile looked strong and kind in the subdued lighting. She saw the fatigue in his face and remembered how tired she was herself.

'I'm coming with you.' She pulled her head back until they were eye to eye.

'I hoped you would say that, Noo. I can't do without you now.'

Their noses bumped once before finding a suitable angle to kiss and they fell back onto the bed, mid-embrace.

Clothing was kicked to the floor and entangled beneath them, and their lovemaking was intense and meaningful.

Walk Right In

MORNING BROKE WITH THE black box chiming. Kline grabbed it and read the display. 07.27. Cradle was in Perpetua.

'Cradle's in. We need to go.' He kissed Noomi awake and they showered and dressed together.

They waved down a roaming pod and arrived at Hornbill within an hour. True to his word, Kline just walked up to the security gate where Stan sat at his desk.

'Morning, Stan.'

'Dr Kline, it's you. But you're on a list, sir. I'm supposed to not let you into Line Security. Mr Bryant's direct orders. What's been going on?'

'How long have we known each other, Stan?'

'Oh, since they built the place, Dr Kline. Every day for four years.'

'And Mr Bryant?'

'Well, not so long, Dr Kline. He's one of the newer ones.'

'Exactly. I just need to pop into FA for a few minutes. Important job to do. Hush-hush and all that. Can you give me half an hour off the record?'

Stan winked at him, his wrinkled face warm and friendly. 'And your young lady?'

'This is Noomi. She's helping me.'

'Morning, miss.'

'Hello, Stan. Thank you.' She smiled and Stan blushed.

'I don't know what the world has come to if you can't do a favour for an old friend.' He gestured the familiar opening shape and the door slid away. 'Half an hour mind, Dr Kline. They could have my head for this.'

'You and me both, Stan, you and me both. You have my word. Thanks.'

Flow Analysis was deserted, as usual. Apart from him and Cradle, absolutely nobody came in here.

'Here.' Kline opened a drawer beneath his desk and withdrew an object wrapped in cloth. He handed it to Noomi. 'For you.'

She unwrapped the cloth and held the wooden handle of a knife in her right hand. The 180-millimetre blade was handworked on one side and curved up to a point at the end. It bore the signs of many years of use.

'Old souvenir from my uncle. It's a traditional Japanese Kaiseki chef's knife, a Gyuto, originally used for paring shellfish, I think. I just use it for chopping fruit for lunch. I want you to have it. Just in case.'

Noomi looked at him. 'We're not exactly eating shellfish or fruit, Anders.'

He held her hands and kissed her. 'No. No, we're not.'

Kline gently took back the Gyuto, wrapped it in the original cloth, and tied it to her belt.

'Be careful, I keep it really sharp.'

—o—o—o o—o—o—

Kline sat at his desk and opened the interface in manual mode, keying in the password character by character. Noomi watched from behind his left shoulder.

'OK, let's start this little ball rolling.'

He queried the maintenance channel. As he suspected, additional protocols had been overlaid to enhance the level of clearance needed for communication.

'Alright, nothing too tricky, looks basic stuff. Snip.'

His injected code reverted access to standard, enabling air communications to reach the channel unimpeded. Slick coding, under the radar, no trail. The transmission from the sphere in Cradle's hand would now connect and communicate directly into Main. Whether it actually worked or not was down to Cradle's programming skills.

'OK, done.' He jumped as Noomi cried out and he turned to see her enwrapped in the arms of a LineSec bot.

'Well, isn't this nice? Mr Kline, you haven't introduced us. Dr Olawadi, I presume?'

Bryant walked from behind the bot and gestured a second machine into action. It approached Kline and towered over him, its limbs raised.

'Let her go, Bryant. She has nothing to do with this.'

'Oh, but she does, Mr Kline. She is with you, after all. That is enough.'

'Anders, I ...'

Bryant looked at Noomi, up and down, his puffy eyes leaching her in. 'A pretty one though, isn't she? Well-chosen, Mr Kline. She will be a beautiful witness to an ugly moment. A kind of symmetry there, don't you think? A balance.'

Noomi struggled in the robot's grip but made no impact. She remained silent, horrified by what was happening.

'And spirited too. Very good. Let us begin, then.'

He gestured the second bot and it clamped onto Anders' wrists and forced him to his knees.

'I suppose that you persuaded the gate guard to allow you to enter unchallenged. A longstanding bon ami? It never ceases to amaze me the idiotic things people will do in the name of friendship. No matter, I will deal with him later. Dr Olawadi, if you would be so kind as to observe, please.'

Anders' hands were held to the floor by two of the LineSec bot's tendrils, while a third looped around his waist, pinning him in a kneeling position, head forward.

'You are accused of extreme crimes against Perpetua's security protocols. You have shared dangerous information with members of the public, against all contractual agreements signed and accepted by you.'

'You're mad, Bryant.'

'Luckily I am in a position not only to levy charges but to deliver a verdict too. You are found guilty.'

'You surprise me.'

'Your punishment will be as severe as the crimes themselves, Mr Kline.'

Anders looked up at Noomi.

'I'm so sorry, Noo. I should never have got you into this.'

She hung suspended in the air from steel vines, unable to speak.

'Very touching, Mr Kline, but I'm afraid time is pressing.'

He gestured violently: a strange and extended chain of movements, firstly with his hands down to his side with fingers widely spread, then large and sweeping, his right hand flat and open, sliding up through the air from his left hip to high above his right shoulder. Noomi stared in horror as the LineSec bot released its three bonds from Anders, then produced a fourth limb, flattened and gleaming like a steely fin, which sliced upwards through the neck, cleanly severing head from body. Noomi screamed as Anders' torso slumped to the ground, his lifeblood ebbing inexorably onto the desolate floor.

'Take note, Dr Olawadi. Take note. What you have been doing will not be permitted. Your punishment is to live in memory of this moment. Now, if you will excuse me, duty calls.'

Bryant walked from FA, leaving Noomi limp and sobbing inside the machine's cold embrace.

Restoration

'MR CRADLE. HOW DELIGHTFUL to make your acquaintance again.'

He recognised Bryant's voice from beneath the dulling grog of unnatural sleep. Some sort of drug. He could feel that his arms were tied and that he was sitting. His extremities tingled with pins and needles. There was bright lighting, pinked and attenuated by his eyelids but intrusive enough for all that.

'That's it, Mr Cradle. That's it. Please accept my apologies for the ungentlemanly procedures of my security units. My instructions were, perhaps, slightly rushed and I'm afraid may have omitted details pertaining to your personal comfort. Alive, if I recall correctly. Yes, alive. And here you are. Very well then.'

He tried to speak but nothing came out. He heard his breath loud against his chest and lifted his head, eyes still safely closed. His ears throbbed with the urgent pounding of his own heartbeat. He drew a laboured deep breath through his nose, then slowly out through his mouth.

Once again. A sound. Closer. He felt Bryant's fingers on his neck.

'When last we met, you caused me a very significant inconvenience.'

The touch removed. The voice not so close now.

'I have spent much energy tracking you down. Much energy, indeed. But forgive me, I am forgetting. You may be disappointed to learn that I have already arrested your two stupid friends. I am afraid that their taste of freedom was only very brief.'

Shuffling. Very close. Hissed.

'No matter. It is you that I want. Open your eyes.'

His face snapped sideways and his cheek burned with the impact of the slap.

'Open your fucking eyes.'

All that he could do. As though levering his eyelids against his lower face, stretching and willing them to part. Pain as his artificially dilated pupils permitted too much light. He turned his head downwards as the contraction slowly quelled the discomfort, blinking rapidly through salty tears. Finally, a blurred outline stooped before him, haloed by the familiar harsh lighting.

'Ah, there you are, Mr Cradle. Welcome again to my humble office. Allow me to accelerate your recovery.'

A blurry hand held his face much too forcibly, the gaunt fingers assaulting the flesh of his chin and cheek.

Liquid dropped into each eye, and he blinked and gasped as the stinging pain overran his senses.

'Yes, perhaps a little strong, but then so much time has been wasted already.'

Focus gradually returned to his vision as his eyes streamed, and he could make out Bryant in more detail. He looked around and saw that he was held in a smooth, metallic chair-like machine from which thin titanium limbs had emerged and snaked about his arms and torso, holding him motionless but for his head and fingers.

'Very thorough, don't you think, Mr Cradle? You are held in a device of my own original design. It will loosen or tighten its tourniquet at my will. Well, after all, this is the Security Office.' The staccato laugh was a wheezing, hacking sound preceded by a musty jet of spittle that hung in the air like smog.

As Cradle's eyes sharpened further, he saw Bryant gesture something. A large rectangular shape moved from his left side into a position just in front of Bryant who slowly, almost ceremoniously, moved until he was alongside it. It was metallic, plainly finished, with a curtain of dark nano-material covering the front face, rippling and oscillating in adjustment to its stationary state.

'What do you want?' Cradle's voice was hoarse and feeble.

'This is my gift to you, Mr Cradle. I promised I would destroy you and I will. But perhaps not as you may have imagined. Not your death. No, no, that would be very unimaginative. No indeed. I will simply break you so completely that you are unable to threaten Perpetua in any way, ever again. And it will please me to keep you in this state and to witness your suffering. A sort of pet, if you will.'

Bryant made a small opening of hands gesture and the restraints uncurled themselves from Cradle's arms and body. He breathed more deeply and clumsily lifted his arms. His feet touched the ground, but he was still too drugged to stand.

'Now we are equal, man to man so to speak.' The machine tilted back and rapidly withdrew from beneath Cradle and he collapsed to the ground. He raised his head to look at Bryant as the machine folded itself into the walls of the office.

'You might misjudge me, Bryant.'

'Oh, I do hope so, Mr Cradle. It would make such sport.'

He gestured towards the shrouded box, not in command this time, but in melodrama.

'I wanted to personally do this. Old school, I think you would say. Very tactile.'

He physically pressed a recessed switch at the side of the box and music began to play. Familiar in a strange way, something distant. Cradle couldn't place it.

'Oh come, come, Mr Cradle, at least try to make a play of it! I went to so much trouble for you! What is that music?' Bryant shuffled quickly to his side and crouched over him, twitching with excitement. 'Come on! You know it!'

Cradle closed his eyes and slumped as he suddenly recalled the sound as a piece of music that Eve and he had chosen for their wedding ceremony. It seemed a thousand years ago, yet he was transported immediately.

'Aha! Yes, yes, yes! I see you, Mr Cradle. Congratulations! What a beautiful day, and such a handsome couple. Everyone said so!'

Cradle pulled himself back to a sitting position and stared in disgust at Bryant as the music continued.

'You killed Julie Clayden.'

'Ah, indeed yes, well done. She had to be stopped. Oh, if only you could have witnessed it, Mr Cradle. Such a beautiful moment, her body quivering beneath mine. A great privilege.'

A wave of nausea gripped Cradle as he fought for composure.

'You are a monster.'

'Oh no, not a monster, not at all. A component, that is all. A humble servant of the status quo. I know that many people consider the status quo to be a tedious thing but they fail to realise that it is this which defines them, enables their existence and provides for their future. I merely protect it. There is honour in that, Mr Cradle. Honour indeed.'

Cradle glared in contempt.

'But while we digress, Mr Cradle, I should also mention Mr Kline. You will be disappointed to learn that, regrettably, he is unable to join us. Dr Olawadi is with him now in the FA lab, but I fear that she is unable to assist.'

Bryant drew closer again. 'Why did you do it, Mr Cradle? What were you looking for?'

Cradle felt his lungs cool as he breathed. Anders was gone now. 'The glyphs. The energy breach. All those people.'

'Mr Cradle, you are in shock, I think. Gibberish!' Another bouquet of spittle misted the air.

'The coding in The Flow. You were hiding it to protect yourself.'

'There is nothing there, Mr Cradle. We have long been aware that there may be some tiny, random variation in The Flow but it has no meaning. All the world's scientific minds. Yet nothing. You are imagining ghosts. And you have caused me a great deal of trouble in so doing.'

'You really don't know, do you?'

'Enough of this nonsense, Mr Cradle. Let us begin with the next stage of your destruction. Now, here is what I wanted you to see. Behold.'

He pressed a second physical switch on the shrouded box and the nano-curtain shimmered from black to red to blue as it fragmented into a million fractal parts before dissolving from view.

She was not dirt, not damp leaves and twigs. A gaunt stretch of delicate leather over a skeletal framework, too brown, desiccated, her mouth fixed in a dreadful silent wail, yellowed eyes staring out with almost no hint of green.

'I hope you like it, Mr Cradle. I spent some time preparing her for you. Actually, you may be interested in some of the chemistry.'

Cradle could only stare and stare. Her hair was blonde and beautiful as in life but now it cascaded over emaciated shoulders and withered breasts. She had been undressed and posed, naked, in a sitting position, her head braced so that she looked down on him.

'*Oh, Eve.*' The words escaped without warning, unbidden. He did not wish it, desperately wanting to keep her in his memory away from this. Protected. Safe. He had promised it.

The music played on, too loudly now. 'True love should be preserved don't you think, Mr Cradle? You may kiss the bride!'

He no longer heard the laughter, nor could he experience the pain. He bit into his 'Tab wound until he could feel the small spherical device secreted in the space beneath the skin. He brought his teeth onto it and bit down, tasting his own blood and rupturing the walls of the tiny structure, triggering the signal and transmitting the sequence. Two seconds and it was irreversibly installed and running.

—o—o—o⚲o—o—o—

Throughout the many hospices of the world, it began. Individual Drowse patients were terminated in precise order, each playing their part. One by one, mortality rippled through their number in a prescribed binary pattern that exactly encoded the thirteen glyphs.

Cradle's code drilled deep into the Hospice data conduits, instantiating, executing and destructing before the host's defence daemons had a chance to lock on. It had the fingerprint of an old-fashioned viral flood attack, stealthy and widespread, seemingly trying to overload Main's peripherals and processors in an attempt to bring the world's network to a halt. But smarter. Main prioritised its defences to the Drowse Hospice interfaces, deflecting core processing power and unwittingly lowering its guard.

The hospice support system failures were too numerous and far too rapid for human reactions. Attending hospice staff were helpless and distraught in the face of what looked like a total system collapse. Alarm after alarm, crisis upon crisis, some of them just a quarter of a second apart. It was over before anyone could do anything.

About 500 hospices.

Roughly 190 countries.
Approximately 10 seconds.
Precisely 64,021 dead.

—o—o—o o—o—o—

A billion innocuous code fragments responded and swarmed together to form a cogent entity, flooding over interfaces and storming distracted host systems, stifling detection processes and neutering antiviral defences behind dynamically forming firewalls. Main succumbed to the torrent within a single millisecond.

—o—o—o o—o—o—

<hello cradle> Anna's voice came from the room itself.

Bryant turned to Cradle, an expression of confusion and alarm on his face.

'What is this?'

'Anna, secure Mr Bryant, please.'

<acknowledged cradle>

Two LineSec bots instantly emerged from the walls and rapidly moved alongside Bryant. Their upper limbs flailed briefly before encompassing his body in a bruising constriction. They drew tighter, pulling his arms to his sides and lifting him from the ground.

'Desist! Cease! Code 9 priority override!' Bryant struggled in vain as his commands were neither acknowledged nor acted upon. After a few moments, he calmed, realising that he was helpless in the grip of his own sentinels.

'Mr Cradle, what do you think you are doing? The system will quickly overthrow your poisonous little aengel and restore operations. You cannot hope to benefit from this.'

'Yes, I calculate less than five minutes before that happens. Anna, please hold Mr Bryant here and prepare to help me.'

<acknowledged cradle>

Cradle turned away from the captive creature and ran out into the corridor, turning left towards the HT1 Tokamak building.

Noomi had dropped to the floor as the machine's grip subsided and she looked up to see it move away and power down. She gasped and cried out in panic as she realised she was kneeling in a shallow pool of blood, and she scuttled backwards until she reached an unspoiled area of the floor. She could see the bottom of Anders' feet; the left was balanced on tiptoe as though trying to avoid the gore, his right leg splayed wide and edged from toe to knee by a meniscus of red. As she slowly rose to her feet, she could see his back and shoulders. She refused to look further and quickly turned away from the scene, her right hand bumping on the knife that Anders had attached to her belt only minutes ago. Blood dripped from her fingers and her clothes were covered by it. She tasted iron as she swallowed. There was an all-pervading calmness flowing within her body and she walked purposefully from the lab and out into the corridor. She could hear talking and shouting and was drawn towards it, impassively wide-eyed and staring as she approached the doorway. Cradle. Bryant. A female voice.

Ahead of her, the door suddenly crashed open and Cradle burst through. He turned left and ran – fast – along the corridor, away from her. He did not see her and she did not call out to him. She entered the office and the door swung shut behind her.

Two large machines were holding Bryant in their tendrils, his feet slightly lifted from the ground. To one side, an open-fronted metal cuboid enclosed a small and frail human figure. Lighting, too harsh, blazed down and she saw a sparkle of blonde hair and knew it was Eve.

The female voice again, this time from the corridor outside the room.

Nothing touched her.

Bryant saw her and spoke.

'Dr Olawadi, you are too late. Mr Cradle's actions are completely futile. In a few moments, this temporary nonsense will be over.'

Noomi walked deliberately, meticulously, to Bryant's suspended position and unwrapped the Gyuto from its shroud. As her sticky fingers grasped its wooden handle, she thought of Anders and fought to beat back the tsunami of emotion before it overwhelmed her senses. She gently raised the ancient knife and held it before her eyes. The whet-sharpened edges gleamed and sparkled, line becoming curve, curve becoming apex.

Her breathing was slow, unlaboured and even. Slowly she reached up to Bryant's throat, touching the blade tip onto his trachea, her right arm almost straight, feet flat.

Bryant croaked, 'Do not do anything foolish.'

She tilted her right shoulder upwards and pushed herself up onto her toes. The blade raised by 4 centimetres and she imagined that it made a 'snick' sound as it pared cartilage. She dropped her shoulder again and flattened her feet, allowing the blade to open the wound.

His rapid breathing hissed and rattled through this new stoma, the air escaping before reaching his larynx. His eyes bulged in panic, the realisation of what was happening dominating the physical pain of it.

Noomi pointed the bloodied knife at his face.

'You will not talk.'

She allowed her mind to drift and thought of Jules, the glyphs, of Anders, his kiss, his body against hers, and Cradle without Eve.

The female voice came again from the corridor.

She blinked fresh tears away and studied Bryant, once more stilling her breathing and lowering her shoulders. The right side of his neck was bared towards her by the clinch of the machines, his head held up and left by one of the snaking coils. His yellowed eyes pleaded as he hissed and gurgled, but her single upward movement again pushed the point of the blade through skin and flesh, neatly puncturing and merging the jugular vein and carotid artery.

'Anna, can I access HT1 building please?'

Her voice came from everywhere in the corridor, centreless and omnipresent.

<yes cradle/ access is fully enabled>

He reached the enormous doors of HT1, spanning six metres wide and eight metres in height. The massive structures incorporated twenty layers of lithium blanket, interspersed with alternate lead and titanium sheets to a total depth of two metres. The walls and domed roof followed the same construction, enclosing the tokamak within an impermeable crust, protecting man, woman and child from the unknown.

'Time check please, Anna.'

<2 minutes and 26 seconds>

'Open HT1 doors please.'

Explosive charges ruptured linings that had for years sealed off HT1, keeping it isolated from its soft-skinned user population; out of sight, out of mind. Enormous motors span up and laboured in the process of sliding the doors apart. The motion was painfully slow and Cradle sidled through the widening gap as soon as he was able.

'How long, Anna?'

<65 seconds>

And there was the tokamak one hundred metres ahead of him. He sprinted to the front of the main chamber. His skin prickled and the hairs on his arms were raised.

<cradle my functional time is almost exhausted/ main has identified significant parts of my code base>

'Open the tokamak please, Anna. And thank you for everything.'

<you are welcome cradle/ goodbye>

The maintenance door in front of him extracted from its normal position with a deafening bang and slid to one side, squealing and screeching as dry bearing surfaces chafed over one another. A deafening howling rasped at his senses and a thumping shock wave rocked him as a million litres of air rushed to reclaim the vacuum within. As he braced himself, his hair straightened and stood back from his head, tracing radials from the centre of the tokamak. He saw phantoms float before him, indistinct in form, sometimes there, sometimes here, false objects generated by neurons within his brain firing in the presence of intense electromagnetic bombardment. He closed his eyes and could still see them. The noise was physical. It was not sound, it was a pure and broadband assault on the body in its entirety, shaking and resonating each particle, every cavity. In the periphery of his vision, he could sense metallic forms emerging from the building walls, hundreds of them, their arms reaching toward him, moments away. The tokamak door shuddered again and slowly began closing.

Yet there in the centre of his vision, devastatingly present, was the hyperplasma itself, vivid and extreme, overthrowing all his senses, the linear passage of time becoming an irrelevant stricture. He felt his eyebrows singe and his eyes parch as the tears evaporated from their surfaces. He held his hands over his face and sensed his skin begin to sear in the intensity of the heat.

He saw her as she was before. Young, beautiful, the most fantastic thing he had ever known. They would discover shapes together, the next always hidden within the old, one inextricably linked to the other. And the loop was wide and made of light now and it floated before him as he had always imagined it would.

She waited there and her hair was vivid gold, all dazzling and sunshine.

He stepped over the tokamak threshold and into the Flow.

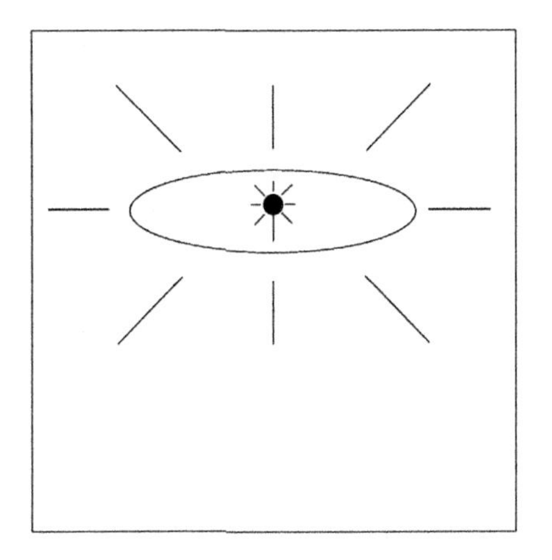

Acknowledgements

I would like to thank my wife Carol, who somehow endured my selfish silences, my sniffing, and my distant conversational absences for well over four years while this story emerged and took shape; then a further three years of pontification and flapping about to get it ready for publishing. I don't recall our marriage vows mentioning any of this, yet she is still by my side. You couldn't write it.

And my gratitude to friends and family who first read Drowse in its draft form and told me they didn't hate it: Carol Langley, Ellie Langley, Rob Tapster, Tory Stroud, Paul Tuli, Jim Heathfield, Andy & Linda Redfern and Maggie & Paul Flynn. In particular, I owe huge thanks to Dr Jonathan Morrell, whose steadfast support and belief in the story (and in my ability to actually finish it) sustained me through the final stages of editing and design.

Thanks also to Sami Pierre, Content Lead at WOMBO AI, for permission to use the machine-generated front cover image that I created using the Dream AI App.

I have edited, corrected, proofread, Grammarly-checked and rewritten the manuscript over and over, drawing on all my pedantic superpowers. Even so, the book will, no doubt, still contain errors of grammar, clarity and accuracy. I stand, happily exhausted, as the sole and proud owner of these remaining mistakes, with no blame attributable to any of the fabulous people who helped me along the way.

About the Author

Derek Langley is, in no particular order, a husband, dad, design engineer, STEM Ambassador, person, and now an author (or so it would seem). This is his first book.

As the joke goes, 'I've just finished my first novel. I enjoyed it so much, I might read another one soon.'

https://dereklangley.uk

Thank You

Thank you so much for reading Drowse – I know there was a ton of other stuff you could have been doing.

If you feel that you could leave a review on Amazon then that would be great, I'd obviously like as many readers as possible and Amazon reviews are a good way to help that along. On Amazon, just search for Drowse by Derek Langley and scroll down until you see "Review this product". Click "Write a customer review" and just fill in the boxes with your own words.

If you'd like to hear about some of the research behind the book, you can head to my website at https://dereklangley.uk and sign up for the Drowse newsletter. That'll let me keep you posted (and I promise not to bombard you with spam).

Whatever you decide, thank you for sharing your time with me in Drowse.

Printed in Great Britain
by Amazon